TERR

BY

JAMES HILTON

CHAPTER ONE

I

I FIRST met him outside the Tube Station at Hampstead; he had travelled on my train, and I had noticed him particularly because, like me, he was wearing a rather shabby overcoat over a dress-suit. At the corner of Rosslyn Hill I went into a shop for some tobacco, and when I came out he was waiting for me. He asked me in a rather shy voice if I could direct him to the End House.

I told him that I could, and that since I was going to the End House myself he had better come with me. We walked quite a long way without saying a word. Every now and then as we neared lamp-posts or brilliantly-lit shops I glanced sideways at him, and each time he was looking grimly ahead, as if life were a tremendous ordeal. He was rather good-looking, in a restrained sort of way; tall, well-proportioned, fair-haired and blue-eyed, he had all the attributes of the matinee idol except that he didn't look like one. Towards the top of Heath Street I tried to get him into conversation. "I suppose we're both guests at Severn's dinner-party to-night?" I remarked. "I suppose so," he answered rather gloomily, and then suddenly, with a sort of shy vehemence, he added: "I hate dinner-parties."

"Oh, but you won't hate this one," I assured him. "Severn's people are always interesting.... By the way, haven't you been before?"

"No. I didn't meet Severn till last week—didn't particularly want to, either. Somebody introduced us at the College—just casually, that was all—and then, a couple of days later, he sent me this invitation."

"Just what he *would* do. But you needn't worry—you won't be bored."

He answered, with heavy despair: "I shall be worse than bored."

And he was. It would have been funny if it hadn't been rather pathetic. Severn had just won Manchester South in a bye-election, and that, no doubt, gave the party a predominantly political flavour. But there was, all the same, a fair seasoning of art and music, and I noticed that my shy acquaintance had been put between Mildred Gorton, the novelist, and Mrs. Hathersage (Olga Trepine, of the Caucasian Ballet). At that time, of course, I didn't know anything at all about him—whether he were a writer, a painter, a politician, a pianist, or just plain nothing-at-all. All I could see was that both Mildred and Olga were having a dreadful time trying to get a word out of him.

It was Mrs. Severn who enlightened my ignorance. I was next to her, and during a sudden gust of chatter all about us, she whispered to me: "You see that man over there next to Mildred Gorton? ... His name's Terrington. I want you to talk to him afterwards. You'll find him very reserved."

I told her then of my previous meeting with him, and she said: "It's a shame, really, to have put him next to Mildred; she'll scare him to death.... Geoffrey got to know him somehow or other last week. He says he's fearfully clever in his own line—he's a research-lecturer in bacteriology at University College."

"That sounds tremendously impressive, anyhow," I replied, and I promised I would take him under my wing when we adjourned to the drawing-room afterwards.

End House dinners were long and good, but I always liked most of all the hour or so after, when Mrs. Severn, if she were sufficiently persuaded, would play Chopin or sing. She was really more of a *diseuse* than a singer; indeed, the thing to do was to tell her that she reminded you of Yvette Guilbert. She did, and she just loved being told it.

That evening she yielded to persuasion earlier than usual, and it was just as she sat down at the piano that I managed to squirm my way across the room to Terrington. He was standing by the French windows examining (but hardly, I should think, admiring) a recent portrait of Severn by a celebrated artist, and when I asked him how things were going he stared at me reproachfully and replied: "I oughtn't to have come here. I don't know what on earth to say to all these people. They're all terribly big guns—except me."

"And me too," I responded cheerfully. "But then, don't forget, we represent young and unknown genius—the hope of the future and all that sort of thing. Severn's idea, you know, to give us a chance of mixing with the top-dogs."

That didn't seem to console him especially, but just then Mrs. Severn began to sing. It was an old French ballad (I remember that the chorus consisted of the word "Rataplan" repeated many times), and it was exactly what suited her voice and style. I gathered, more from the way she sang it than from the words, that it was about a court intrigue, a wicked lord chamberlain, poisoned goblets, and so on—"divinely medieval," as I heard Mildred Gorton whispering to somebody.

When it was over I looked at my companion. "Not bad, eh?" I said, and he shrugged his shoulders with a gesture that might have meant anything. A few moments later, having apparently analysed himself, he remarked that it was the sort of thing that made him feel uncomfortable.

Those were the last words he spoke to anybody until he stood in the hall conventionally assuring Mr. and Mrs. Severn that he had had a most delightful time. We left the End House together about half-past ten, and walked back along the edge of the Heath. There was a frost glistening on the roadway, and a pale haze hung over the valley towards London. He was anything but talkative. I don't think we spoke a dozen words all the way down to the Tube Station. We both had return tickets, and it wasn't till we reached Mornington Crescent (my own station) that I said, feeling curiously reluctant to bid him good-bye: "Look here, I live just round the corner. Why not come in and have a drink with me before you go home? It isn't late at all, you know."

"If—if you like," he answered doubtfully.

He thawed a little when I lit the gas-fire in my room and made him sit in front of it. He said he didn't care for whisky, so I made strong coffee. Then I offered him cigarettes, but he said he didn't smoke. At last, by the simple method of not seeming to care what he did or didn't do, I got him to talk. He began abruptly: "I made a fool of myself to-night."

I replied: "I don't think you did. It's by talking a lot rather than by not talking enough, that people most often make fools of themselves."

"Severn must have thought me a complete ass."

"Nonsense. I know Severn. He'd make sure you weren't a complete ass before he invited you."

"Why *did* he invite me, anyway?"

"Probably because he liked you when he first met you, and because he had heard good things about you. He likes young men with no money and heaps of brains—like you and me, that's to say. (I presume you haven't any money—*I* haven't, anyway.) He takes us up just as he might buy a low-priced share that he fancied might treble in value if he waited long enough.... Please don't think I'm being *really* cynical about him. He's a damned good fellow, and there isn't a trace of offensive patronage in his attitude. He's too young to be a snob."

"Young, is he?"

"Well, thirty-five. That's young for a man in his line. I suppose you know what he is—K.C., and so on?"

"I don't know anything about him at all."

"But the Stapleton case—surely you remember all that in the newspapers?"

"I don't. I never read the newspapers."

"Good Lord—you must be a hermit! ... Anyhow, Severn's quite a big man, and likely as not he'll end on the Woolsack. He knows everybody worth knowing, and positively rolls in money and influence. And all that at thirty-five, mind you, and with a wife still in her twenties and one child aged ten. He did everything early."

He seemed startled, and I went on, satisfied that he was interested: "Severn married her when she was eighteen—and a shop-girl in Paris. Still, she must have been rather an exceptional shop-girl. Severn probably spotted her just as he spots all the other winners. But his people are Eton and Oxford to the teeth, and they wouldn't look at her, or him either, for a long while afterwards. He'll tell you the whole story of his early struggles if you give him half a chance—he's awfully proud of them."

We chatted on till nearly midnight, and then, since the last tube train had gone, I walked with him to his rather dingy lodgings in Swinton

Street, near King's Cross. (Evidently he *was* poor; perhaps even poorer than I.) "You must come to tea with me soon," I said, shaking hands with him at the door. I suggested the following Wednesday, but he answered: "I'm afraid I could never come for tea—I work at the College until seven."

"Even on Saturdays?" I queried, and he nodded.

"And Sundays?" He smiled then and said: "On Sundays I go out for the day. Next Sunday I'm going for a tramp across the hills from Dorking to Reigate, and if you'd care to come with me...."

II

He didn't drink, he didn't smoke, he didn't read newspapers, and he didn't ever go out to tea. Then what on earth *did* he do? I found out one thing, at any rate, on that following Sunday; he *walked*. He called it tramping, but no tramp that ever lived went at his pace. By the time we reached Reigate I longed for a corner seat in a railway compartment. All he said was: "Ten miles isn't really enough. I usually do twelve or fifteen."

We didn't talk much during the walk. I was far too breathless most of the time to gasp more than a few words consecutively, but I thought a good deal. I thought, for instance: Why am I running myself out of breath on these confounded hills with a man who, so far, has shown himself to be no more than a conglomeration of abstinences? And the only answer I could arrive at was: You want to get to know him, and this, apparently, is the only way.

I believe it *was* the only way. I believe that nobody—no man, at any rate—could have become his friend without those long preliminary periods of silence. He was a locked box, and you had to believe, rather than know, that there was something in it. I believed, and later on I knew; but the revelation was very slow. Within a couple of months, perhaps, I knew the ordinary obvious things about his life that most people would have let me know within a couple of hours. Even then he didn't exactly tell me anything. I deduced, or picked up information by accident, or else asked a deliberate question and received a rather embarrassed or grudging answer. The first time I went up to his room at the College, for example, I saw "Dr. M. Terrington" painted on the outside of the door. Till then I hadn't had the least idea that he was a doctor, and nor had Severn, for at the dinner-party he had introduced him as plain "mister." Anyhow, the information on the door seemed clear enough to me, though it wasn't till a week after that I really learned the truth, and then only by chance. I had cut my hand, and he bandaged it for me very skilfully, which led me to make some complimentary remark about his "doctor's skill." He told me then that he wasn't a medical doctor at all, but a "mere Ph.D." He spoke of it as if it were quite a minor distinction instead of being (as I afterwards found out) almost unique for a man of his age.

Gradually, in such ways as this, I got to know the truth about him. It wasn't at all exciting. He had sprung from poor parents (both of them now dead), and had worked his way up to the university by a series of scholarships and exhibitions which, though distinguished enough in themselves, would be tedious to record. He had no relatives who ever troubled about him, and I think I can say that until he came into contact with me and the Severns he had no friends either. He worked hard, knew nobody, went nowhere, and cared for nothing but his microscopes and slides. Twice a week he lectured to a very small class, and the fees from this, along with certain scholarship monies, made his existence just financially possible.

He had so little to do with anybody that I can recall only three remarks made about him by people who knew him before I did. The first was made by a girl-student at his lectures; she said, very doubtfully: "He looks as if he *might* be interesting"—evidently a different thing from looking interesting. The second came quite casually from the lips of an A.B.C. waitress at the tea-shop where he took a midday roll and glass of milk. I had arranged to meet him there one day and arrived too early; whereat the waitress, who had seen us together before, looked at the clock and said: "It's only seven minutes past one, and he never comes in till ten past. We tell the time by him here." And the third remark was his landlady's. She was a faded, respectable creature burdened by a husband who drank, and to her the young gentleman lodger was clearly the one central rock of stability in a world of bewildering fluctuations. "He appreciates me," she said, with an implied resentment against the rest of the world, "and I *do* like to be appreciated."

III

Mrs. Severn also liked to be appreciated. But she was so well accustomed to admiration that a compliment had to be either very adroit or very original to stir her. If I had told her that somebody had said her singing was delightful, she would probably have shrugged her shoulders and changed the subject. But instead of that, on my next meeting with her some weeks after the party, I told her that the shy man and I had become friendly as a result of our End House visit, and that he had been greatly impressed by her singing. "He said it made him feel uncomfortable."

"Did he?" She was interested. "Did he really say that? ... But—but why is he so easily made uncomfortable? I kept noticing him that night—he *was* unhappy, I could see. But why?"

"He can't help it. Company and crowds make him feel like that. I shouldn't be surprised if women have the same effect."

"You know you're making him sound fearfully attractive. He isn't engaged, then—or anything of that sort?"

"*Engaged*? Good heavens, he never speaks to any woman except his landlady."

She paused in thought for a moment, and then said: "I think Geoffrey had better ask him here again. Don't you agree? ... Some time when we're just *en famille*. You'll come, of course."

I said I should be very pleased to, but that I was rather doubtful whether he would accept the invitation. She replied then, with a touch of imperiousness: "Oh, but he *must*. It is absurd for a young man to be shy. I shall ask Geoffrey to send him an invitation to-night."

The invitation was sent, and I chanced to be in his bed-sitting-room when it arrived. After reading it through very slowly and carefully, he said: "Severn wants me to go there again. On Friday. You're coming too, but there'll be nobody else.... That shows he *did* notice what a fool I was at the party."

"It also shows that he doesn't think any less of you for it," I said.

He was silent for quite a couple of minutes before he announced his decision. "I shall go," he said, "although I don't want to go."

IV

There was certainly no excuse for any guest being uncomfortable at the End House. Of all places I know it was the homeliest; it was, like Hampstead itself, cheerful without vulgarity. Severn's immense wealth (and he was rumoured to be making twenty thousand a year) never bullied or forced itself; it rather hid behind things and came upon the visitor at some moment when he was ready for it. Most wealthy houses make a poor man feel poorer than ever; Severn's made you feel rich.

At the last moment I was ill and couldn't turn up on that following Friday. But from two sources I heard what had taken place. First from Terrington himself, who said merely: "I enjoyed it, and I like Severn ... and also Mrs. Severn."

Mrs. Severn, a few days later, gave me a somewhat lengthier report. "He was quiet," she said, "and he spoke very little, but he didn't look quite so awfully miserable as before. After dinner we even got him to sing—he's got rather a good baritone voice, but he only knew songs like 'Annie Laurie' and 'Auld Lang Syne'.... And then he played with June—*she* liked him. As a matter of fact, we *all* liked him—there seems to be something about him you can't help liking—don't you think so?"

I agreed, and she added, as if it finally clinched the matter: "Have you noticed his eyes? They are rather nice."

It was then that I first of all learned that he was at work on cancer research. Mrs. Severn had been told so by her husband, and he had learned it from one of the senior men at the College; it was typical, indeed, of my entire relationship with Terrington that I acquired this rather important information by such a roundabout route. But when I tackled him on the subject he would do no more than confirm; he wouldn't discuss. He said, smiling: "You're a journalist and everything seems sensational to you. But there's nothing sensational in the work I'm doing.... You and Severn seem bent on making a howling success of me, but I don't want it. I just want to be left alone—to do my own work." He added, in a tone that robbed his words of any sting: "Please don't think I mean anything unkind."

But his summing-up of Severn's intention had been true enough. Severn always wanted to make a howling success of everybody. I suppose, at rock-bottom, it was a form of conceit—an assumption that everybody's ideal must be his own. And yet there was nothing blatant or vulgar in him. His taste was impeccable to the point of being finicky, and he had charming manners. He never in his life bullied either judge or witness, but his suavity was deadly enough; with calm, almost friendly questions, he would lead a man to confess murder or a woman adultery. In private life he was courteous to all; in fact (as somebody once said) he always talked to you as if his life had been incomplete until he met you. It was an oriental gift, and twenty thousand a year was no more than the figure of its rarity.

I owed him then, and owe him still, more than he would ever care for me to say. He enjoyed pulling strings on behalf of his protégés; he pulled the strings for Terrington, though the latter was too innocent to realize it. Severn talked about him to various editors of scientific journals, and the result was a few commissions. He even persuaded the editor of a "daily" to start a popular science "feature," and that Terrington's contributions to this were moderately successful was due to the fact that *I* wrote them. *He* could never have achieved the popular vein, but his science and my journalism made a profitable amalgam. We shared the income, devoting it to more ambitious Sunday rambles, until at last he decided that the job was taking up too much of his time. He was like that—a sudden swerve to right or left, and then an inexorable straight line.

All that time I was getting to know him, and all that time I was liking him more.

11

V

One afternoon of that late winter he came to my rooms and asked me if I thought he ought to return the invitations of the Severns. I told him that they knew he wasn't well off, and that they certainly wouldn't expect to be invited to dinner at an expensive hotel or anything like that. He answered that he hadn't been thinking of dinner, but of tea.

"But I thought tea was always impossible for you?"

"Not if I—if I managed it."

"I see.... Well, I think you'd better manage it. It's a good idea."

"Do you really think so?" He seemed pleased. "As a matter of fact, I met Mrs. Severn in the street just now, and I hinted at it—vaguely."

"Well? Did she accept?"

"Yes. She's coming—next Thursday. And Severn as well."

So it was all settled, and I was merely being asked to register approval. I duly registered, and was then rewarded by an invitation myself. "I'll be delighted to come," I assured him. "But where are you going to have them? You can't very well—"

I paused, hardly caring to stress the unsuitability of bed-sitting-rooms. He saw, however, that Swinton Street would not do. He could have used my own room, but it was not very much better than his; and to take them to some hotel or café would seem rather odd. In the end we decided on the laboratory. "It's a large room," I said, "and it's private, more or less, and there's water laid on, and a gas-ring, and other handy things. Besides, they'll forgive any amount of mess there."

It was fun making preparations for them. We borrowed armchairs from the lecture-platforms, and I carefully selected all my best crockery and transferred it to the top of the Physics building in a suitcase. We cleaned the windows and the lamp-shade, and made the place as habitable as possible. Then we bought the food. Last of all, from half-past three till nearly half-past four on a glowering March afternoon, we waited. He stood by the window keeping an eye on the porter's lodge, while I sat by the fire and tried to think of any possible hitch in the arrangements.

Suddenly he said: "They're here!" and went downstairs to meet them and show them the way. But when he came back there was only Mrs.

Severn with him. She was profusely apologetic. She was sorry she was so late, and she was sorry Geoffrey wasn't with her (he hadn't been able to get away from the Law Courts in time), and she was especially sorry about the toasted scones. "You men oughtn't to have waited for me," she said, as she allowed me to remove her fur coat. Then she looked appraisingly round the room, as any woman will, and made remarks about it. "What a jolly little place! How comfortable you must be here—so high up among the roofs! And all those wonderful-looking instruments—really, you *must* tell me about them."

And the extraordinary thing was that he did. He went round the room with her, exhibiting and explaining, answering in full and patient detail even the silliest of her questions, and all without the slightest sign of either nervousness or reticence. It looked like a miracle. I had been struggling for weeks to overcome the mere outposts of his reserve, and here was a woman who had only seen him for a few hours striding miles beyond me into the unknown territory.

But of course she was no ordinary woman. She was astoundingly pretty, and I suppose that a good many of her most fervent admirers would spend hours in describing her copper-gold hair and her brown eyes with their curious, slanting glint of green; but for me there was always something beyond that. There was a way she sometimes looked, especially if you saw her face in profile against the sky or window—a way that was beyond prettiness. I'm not certain it wasn't beyond even beauty. It challenged, and yet, by some marvellous paradox, it was serene as well.

We had tea. I listened to their talk and said very little myself. It was pleasant to sit back in a chair and, without any effort at all, to add large fragments to my scanty collection of facts about Terrington. She asked him most of the questions I had always wanted to ask him, and he answered them all. He told her, for instance, that his father had been a country parson, and that his mother had died at his birth. He told her also that the total amount he earned was two hundred pounds a year, and that he lived on it. She was astonished. "But of course you will earn a lot of money some day," she said, with vague comfort; and he answered: "I don't want to make a lot of money. I admit that two hundred isn't enough, but I don't want a lot. If I could get two hundred and fifty or three hundred I'd be perfectly satisfied and never want any more."

"You couldn't marry on that," she said.

And he replied: "I don't want to marry."

"You might do some day."

"No."

"How can you be certain?"

"I have my work, and it takes up so much of my time that it wouldn't be fair to any woman to marry her."

"She mightn't let it take up so much of your time."

"Then it wouldn't be fair to my work."

"I see.... You feel it as a sort of priesthood, with a vow of celibacy attached?"

He thought for a moment and then answered: "I don't know—maybe I *do* feel that. I don't very often think about it."

But the oddest thing was yet to come. About five o'clock the tousled head of the laboratory-boy intruded itself round the corner of the door. He was a rough-mannered youngster, and, ignoring the presence of visitors, he boldly asked if he could go home. "I've cleaned all the cages," he said, "and I've fed your mice and Mr. Hensler's cats."

The permission was given him and he withdrew. But I could see instantly that the matter would not be allowed to end there. As soon as he had gone Mrs. Severn exclaimed: "I say, what's all this about cats and mice and cages? Do you keep a menagerie?"

Terrington smiled. "No—only what you said—cats and mice and cages. Oh, and a few rats also, I believe."

"But what do you have them for?"

"We—we need them, you know."

"For your work?"

"Yes."

"You mean you—" The blood rushed to her face and she bit her lip. "Vivisection," she said slowly, after a pause. Then she added: "It's only a word after all—and why should one be hypnotized by a word? I'd like to see your Chamber of Horrors. Will you take me now?"

I tried valiantly to signal him to make an excuse, but he didn't or wouldn't see. He was so transparently honest with her. He replied: "Certainly, if you're really interested. But you'll not find it at all horrible—only just a trifle smelly."

We walked down the dark stone corridor towards the room where the animals were kept. I had a sickening feeling that we were walking into catastrophe—that this part of the programme was going to prove a dreadful mistake; I had certainly seen something in Mrs. Severn's eyes that he had missed. But the room, when he unlocked it and switched on the light, was cheerful enough. It was airy and spacious, and the various cages were placed methodically on platforms all round the walls. The cats had all had their milk and were sleepily washing themselves and blinking their eyes in the sudden glow of light. They purred in joyous anticipation and rubbed their heads against the cage-bars when he went near them. (All animals took to him instantly.)

The dreadful thing was that Mrs. Severn said nothing at all. She had used the word "hypnotized," and that was exactly what she looked—hypnotized. She followed him round from cage to cage, and all the while he kept on explaining just the very things he oughtn't to have explained. "Most of them are strays," he told her. "Nobody seems to know how they're obtained, but they're nearly all half-starved when they first come here. We feed them well, of course—they have to be healthy before you can do anything with them."

Still she said nothing. But suddenly, as by an impulse, she opened the door of one of the cages, and a black-and-white cat squirmed eagerly into her arms—a small, glossy-coated animal with a large shaven patch on the underside of its body. She fondled it for a moment, and then said quietly: "I suppose you can't do anything with the fur on?"

He explained the matter in detail, while the cat purred violently, and, rearing itself up, tried to rub its head against her chin.

"What will happen to it?" she asked, almost casually, when he had finished.

He shook his head doubtfully. "I couldn't say—it's not mine, you know. One of Hensler's—he's our best biology man. I don't know what it is exactly that he's doing at present—some sort of research work, no doubt. The cats and rats are all his—I've only got the mice."

"And all *they* have to do," I said, anxious at any cost to reduce the tension of the atmosphere, "is to feed well and propagate their species. You can't really call *them* unlucky."

But she said nothing; she didn't even smile. And then, by the very greatest of good fortune, he had to rush away to a six o'clock lecture. We hadn't expected she would stay so long, and when the hour came he made rather abrupt apologies and left her in my charge. Her good-bye, as she shook hands with him, was hardly audible.

VI

We went back to his room, Mrs. Severn and I, and sat by the fire. She brought the cat with her, and all the while we were talking it sat on her knee and purred contentedly. After I had offered her a cigarette and lit it for her, she asked suddenly: "Do you think you understand him?"

"I certainly don't think I do," I answered. "But I've been wondering all the time if *you* did."

"Why *me*?"

"Because he tells you more in five minutes than he'd tell me in five years."

She half smiled. "That's true. In some ways I can twist him round my little finger.... But in other ways he's just rock—solid rock—don't you feel that?" She caressed the cat and went on: "I'm not a sentimentalist. I don't believe it's a sin to experiment on animals if by doing so you have a chance of benefiting human lives, and I'm not so absurd as to believe that vivisectors are all sadists. So it isn't anything to do with *that*.... But, all the same, I feel that he's not human. I don't mean that he's *in*human. I mean that he's just *un*human—the humanity in him hasn't ever yet been stirred. He just lives for that high ideal—at two hundred a year. It's splendid, I know, but from a woman's point of view, at any rate, it's just a shade unsatisfactory."

"I don't suppose he ever considers the woman's point of view."

"Of course he doesn't. That's part of the trouble. He's got his eyes fixed on this distant goal and he doesn't see the other things nearer his eyes. He doesn't see that if a man's going to be a success in this world he's got to make friends and go about and not be satisfied with two hundred pounds a year." (The money seemed to obsess her.)

"He'd tell you he didn't want to be that sort of success."

"But he *must* be, if he's going to be any other sort of success in addition. Even the medieval saints, who made a virtue of poverty, used to make an advertisement of it as well. He doesn't do even that. Of course I don't say he need be an absolutely worldly success like Geoffrey. He couldn't be if he tried, I'm sure. But I think he might compromise."

She added after a pause: "It would do him good to fall in love."

I laughed then. "He's not likely to do that. He's scared of women altogether, and—excepting you—I've never known him to be at ease in a woman's presence. When some of his girl students come to ask him about their work, he stammers and looks uncomfortable till they're gone."

We talked on for a short time longer, and then she said she must go. She put the cat into a chair and gave a final stroke to its sleek head. "A saucer of milk after I've gone," she said, "is the best I can do for him, isn't it? Will you give it him?" I promised I would, and then, as I helped her on with her coat, she added: "I'm going to try to convert him. Terrington, I mean, not the cat.... And I shall begin by calling him Terry. Do you think he'll mind?"

I said laughingly that I didn't suppose he would encourage the liberty. We walked out to Gower Street together, and I got her a taxi. "I daresay it'll be a hard job," she said finally, as she shook hands, "but I mean to do it."

VII

I was relieved when she had gone. The whole atmosphere had been curiously tense, and from the moment that the laboratory-boy had made his unwelcome intrusion, I had been thoroughly uncomfortable.

After seeing her off I walked a short distance to buy an evening paper, and it was nearly seven when I climbed up again to the top storey of the Physics Building. The cat was asleep in front of the fire, and when, remembering my promise, I placed a saucer of milk on the floor beside it, one green eye slowly opened and then disdainfully closed again.

At seven he returned, after delivering his lecture on (I think) the Mycology and Bacteriology of Foods. The first thing he noticed was the cat and the saucer of milk. Explanations were necessary, and he accepted them as a wise adult might listen to the charming vagaries of a child. "How like her!" he said, but no more. And within half-an-hour the cat was back in its cage.

I remember that night because then, for the first time since I had known him, he permitted himself to break the iron routine of his labours. Perhaps he felt that since the tea invitation had already interfered with his day, he might just as well walk a further step on the long road to perdition. Anyhow, as I was leaving London early the following morning on some special newspaper work, I asked him if he would come with me to a show of some sort, and, to my immense astonishment, he agreed immediately.

We dined at a small, unfashionable place off Regent Street, and after trying in vain at several theatres, managed to get in at the Coliseum two or three turns late. He was very quiet at first, but the sound and colour of the music-hall roused him completely. He laughed a good deal, and at the simplest things. As we walked home afterwards a reaction set in and he was quiet again; he even went so far as to say that he disliked "gadding about" as a general rule, although it was pleasant on rare occasions. I told him that it wasn't good for anybody to work without any pleasure intermixed, and he retorted, with a curious enthusiasm in his voice: "My work *is* my pleasure. I *mean* that. I'm really looking forward to to-morrow—because I shall be able to work then without any interruptions."

I suppose he remembered that I was going away, for he added hastily: "I don't mean you, of course."

It was so glaringly obvious whom he did mean. Only once did he mention her by name, and that was just before we separated outside his lodgings in Swinton Street. He said then: "Do you think she was bored by all the talk about my work?"

I assured him that I thought she had been very deeply interested, and he replied: "I hope she was. She makes it so easy for me to tell her things."

VIII

I have always kept a diary of sorts, and the tattered and shabby records of those years lie before me now as I write. Many of the days are blank, thus testifying to the uneventfulness of my life in general; for I would never write, even in a diary, merely for the sake of writing. Terrington, or "Terry," as I as well as Mrs. Severn came to call him, makes his appearance on the very day I met him first; I find the record: "Went to dinner with the S's at Hampstead. Met a man there named Terrington. Scientific something at London Univ. Very shy. Took him home afterwards."

The entry for the day on which Mrs. Severn came to tea is similarly brief. "Tea in T's lab. Mrs. S. T. showed her the cats. Afterwards Mrs. S. and I talked about T. Finished up at Frigolin's and the Coliseum. Little Tich and some good wrestlers."

And for the next day: "T. waked me at 6 a.m. Wanted to know my opinion about the cat. Agreed after discussion, though surprised at T. suggesting it. Caught 9.15 to Manchester. Queen's."

The diary, you will observe, is hardly a Bashkirtseff affair. It was written in good faith, not as a literary exercise, and most of its entries are mere reminders, unintelligible to outsiders, but significant to me even to this day. Terry *did* waken me that morning at 6 a.m. And the cat business, with which I agreed after discussion, although surprised at his suggesting it, was simply this: he wanted to give the black-and-white cat to Mrs. Severn. He thought it would be a "nice" thing to do. The principal objection, as I pointed out to him, was the awkward circumstance that the cat didn't belong to him. Technically, it was the property of the University of London, but for all practical purposes it belonged to Hensler, who had prepared it especially for some work he was engaged on. To give it away would be, to say the least, a highly irregular proceeding.

But he wouldn't drop the idea. Hensler, he said, would only suffer a slight inconvenience, for there were other cats that would do just as well. Nor would the loss cause much commotion, for escapes did happen sometimes. Nobody would ever know about it except Mrs. Severn, and she would be *so* pleased.

So we "agreed after discussion." Perhaps it would be truer to say that I was too sleepy to argue the point, especially as I could see he had quite made up his mind. He left me with great cheerfulness, and I finished my sleep. Later on in the day I had misgivings; the cat business struck me as being, on the whole, rather silly. Besides, it might easily be found out, and then there would be trouble with the authorities. I remember, as I travelled up to Manchester, working out the possibility that the cat, strolling in the neighbourhood of Hampstead Heath before its shaven fur had re-grown, might be met and recognized by Hensler himself....

CHAPTER TWO

I

I WAS away about five weeks. I wrote my special articles on the condition of the Lancashire cotton industry (Severn, by the way, had secured me the commission), and from time to time I went into Manchester and called at the post-office for letters. Terry didn't write, but I wasn't surprised at that. What did surprise me was a short note from Mrs. Severn. She wanted me to dine at the End House on the twelfth, if I were back in town on that date. Terry, she said, would be coming as well. (Had she begun calling him "Terry," I wondered?) She went on to inform me about the cat, and she wrote: "I think it is rather wonderful of him to have thought of such a thing. It shows that he is *beginning* to be human."

All the rest of that sombre Manchester day I kept repeating to myself: He is beginning to be human....

When I returned to town I wondered if he was. *Something* had happened to him, at any rate; there was a difference in him, slight, indeed, but plain enough. A sort of eagerness for something.... I reached London late on Saturday night, and early on Sunday he presented himself at my bedside and demanded that I should accompany him on one of his usual Sabbath tramps. For nobody else on earth would I have roused myself that morning, and not even for him, I believe, but for that curious, wistful eagerness.

It was Epping Forest this time. We walked from Chingford to Loughton, had lunch, walked on to Epping, had tea, and then walked on to Waltham—total, fourteen miles. But I enjoyed it more than I had expected, for the day was spring-like, full of blue sky and white clouds and the smell of earth. Most of the way as far as Epping I talked of my

Lancashire adventures, and it was not until after tea that he spoke more than a few consecutive sentences. The dusk sank over us as we walked the last stage through the Forest, treading the sodden leaves of the old year and guiding ourselves by glimpses of Waltham's white tower in the valley below. But I think it was the bells that made him suddenly talk—the Abbey bells that flung us their distant echo as we descended. For he said, when a cool wave of air brought them very near to us: "It's strange how beauty, if you're in a certain mood, comes over you. You can't help it—it comes anyhow, just when and where it likes.... Those bells—to hear them like this—and all this Forest with the winding pathways through it, and the little lamp-lit town that we shall come to in half-an-hour."

A group of men and girls approached, heralded by the glow-worm brightness of the men's cigarettes, and he waited till they had gone past. Then he went on: "Don't you think it's strange that I should talk like this?"

Before I could answer he continued: "It *is* strange. Everything is strange. There's something strange in this Forest to-night—something beautiful, and yet, in a way, sad. I feel that if I didn't fight against it, it would swamp me.... Are you thinking me off my head?"

"Oh, no," I answered. "A trifle morbid, perhaps, but no more than that."

He said slowly, as if talking to himself: "*Morbid?* That's the word *she* used."

"Who?"

"Helen."

I think we both of us then stood suddenly still. We had entered a bright space of moonlight, and we both looked at each other, knowing exactly what we were thinking. I could see from his eyes that he hadn't meant to let me know that he called her Helen.

We took the train at Waltham, and nothing else that he said was of the least importance.

II

I suppose henceforward *I* had better call her Helen. And, as a matter of fact, the first time I saw her after my return she asked me to do so. "Mrs. Severn," she said, sounded dreadfully stiff between friends. Perhaps it did, but I found it hard to break the habit.

I had met her one afternoon on the pavement outside University College. She asked me if I were just going up to see Terry, and I replied, with perhaps an implied rebuke: "Certainly not. Have you just been to see him?"

"Why 'certainly not'?"

"Because he hates to be interrupted in his working hours. But I suppose you *have* been to see him?"

"Yes," she answered, smiling. "But not in the way you think I have. I've been to one of his lectures, that's all."

And then she told me details. She laughed over it in a way that seemed to betray an inward nervousness. She had begun a course in bacteriology. It was interesting. One ought to have *something* serious in one's life, oughtn't one?

"Terry says so, I daresay," I replied.

"*You* call him Terry?"

"I do. Have you any objection?"

She laughed again. "Of course not. I think the less formal we all are the better. That's what's the trouble with him—he's *too* formal—he doesn't seem to believe in any pleasure, or amusement, or—or—" She couldn't, apparently, think of any third commodity that he didn't believe in. "But I think I'm managing to convert him gradually," she added.

"And he's managing to convert you a little at the same time, eh?"

She laughed again in the same curious, muffled-up manner. No, she said; Terry was *not* converting her. Not really. He was only just showing her things that she had already felt or guessed. Bacteriology was a symbol rather than the thing itself.

I asked her whose idea it had been first of all, and she answered: "Not *his*, you can be sure." He, in fact, had been anything but keen about it. Perhaps he thought that her presence would make him nervous during his lectures. (Again the curious laugh.) But of course he hadn't any power to prevent her from paying the fee and joining.

She went on: "It's rather amusing—the way he treats me. Privately, of course, we're friends. But professionally, as a member of his class, I'm nothing. Not a word or a smile. When he's finished lecturing he picks up his papers and dashes out of the room as if he's afraid somebody might follow him."

"Perhaps he is."

She admitted the possibility. "But I have such an absurd ambition to make him take *some* notice of me. *Isn't* it absurd? I feel it would be good for him to be made to break all his neat little rules.... Anyhow, don't forget that you're both coming to dinner on the twelfth. And also, by the way...." And then came her request that I should join in the general informality by calling her Helen. "Or Helène," she added, "if you like to be really correct."

III

There is no entry in my diary for the 12th. I remember why. I had got back to my rooms very late, and was too sleepy to write anything. And the next morning when I looked at the blank space I thought I would leave it blank, to express and symbolize the puzzled blankness of my own mind.

It was a small party—just the Severns, Terry, and myself. The rather sensational Roebourne case had been concluded only that afternoon, and all the evening papers were full of praise for Severn, whose brilliant handling of exceptionally difficult material had brought victory to his side. It had been a fatiguing battle between two great financial interests, and Severn had not only consolidated his already high reputation as a pleader, but had earned also an almost fabulous sum in fees. Naturally his feelings were buoyant, and their buoyancy made him talk in a way which, even for him, was amazing. Before then I had sometimes harboured a suspicion that his knowledge of many things was superficial, but that night the suspicion almost disappeared. He really did seem to have been everywhere, to have read everything, and to have met everybody. One moment he was talking about the queer sorts of *hors-d'œuvres* that he had sampled in various parts of the world; and the next he was discussing medical science with Terry in a way which would have tempted any outsider to assume that he was the master and Terry the rather dull pupil. With the accompaniment of excellent food and wine, the whole exhibition was a sheer delight to the onlooker like myself, and Severn's coal-black eyes gleamed all the while as if he too were thoroughly enjoying it. I believe he was slightly drunk, but that only made his talk better still.

Then, somehow or other, when we were in the drawing-room afterwards, the conversation grew personal. I don't mean "personal" in any unpleasant sense, but merely literally; we began to talk about ourselves. Or rather, perhaps, it was as if Mrs. Severn, Terry and I were suddenly being forced to expose our intimate lives to the full glare of Severn's arguments, while he alone remained aloof—interested but hardly perturbed. It began by his telling me what ought to be the successive stages of my advancement as a literary man. "In a few years," he said "you must have a sub-editorship—I'll see whether I can find one for you. You'll have to work like hell while you're at it, and in your spare time, if you have any, you must manage to write a novel—preferably one that will establish your reputation and bring you in not more than a hundred pounds altogether. After that you must take a flat in either Bloomsbury or Chelsea and decide whether you're going to plod along in Fleet Street, earning a middling salary and work jolly hard for it, or take to the wilder life of the professional fiction-writer, in which you may earn nothing at all or else fabulous sums.... On the whole, I think you had better become the successful novelist who is very shy and unapproachable. In that case you must write a stupid novel about Very Good People and Very Bad People, with a wedge of sex in between, and you must take care that all your most intimate private affairs are reported sensationally in the Press.... After your novel's in its second hundred thousand and your bank balance is beginning to stagger you,

you must marry a society woman and arrange for your name to appear in the next birthday honours' list...."

And so on. Then, filling up his glass, he turned to Terry. The career of the successful scientist, he said, was in many ways a more delicate matter, but still in the main, it was conditioned by the same general principles. "Darwin," he said, "points the way for all scientists. His monkey idea was so simple that only a scientist could have any doubts about it.... Anyhow, you must do your best with the material that comes your way. First of all, you positively must go to Paris or Berlin or Vienna and put yourself under some fellow who, because his name isn't Smith or Brown or Jones, is thereby held in almost mythical esteem by the majority of Englishmen. Then, after picking the other fellow's brains as much as you can, you must launch out suddenly on your own—choosing a slack season when the newspapers haven't much to write about. You must have a new discovery, or a new theory of something—nearly anything will do, provided it is simple enough for the man in the street to misunderstand and laugh at. You might, for instance, discover that to crawl a quarter of a mile a day on hands and knees is a cure of dyspepsia. Get your disciples round you and start crawling—in public—with the cameras all round you! ... Then come back to England and make a fierce attack on the oldest, the most innocent, and altogether the most fatuous member of the Medical Council...."

Terry laughed and said that all that sort of thing was just what he would most of all loathe doing.

"But you *must* do it," Severn urged. "Of course I've been joking about some of the details, but the principle of it all is sound enough. The key to success *in everything* is advertisement."

"Not *my* sort of success," said Terry, doggedly.

"He feels," said Mrs. Severn, "that his work in itself is so important that success doesn't matter. Of course, with you it's bound to be different. Championing one gang of thieves against another is nothing unless it's successful." (She was, I suppose, referring to the Roebourne case.)

Severn retorted by a good-humoured jibe at her recently discovered interest in bacteriology. "I'm sure a gang of thieves is as interesting as a gang of microbes," he said, "and certainly far more remunerative."

She laughed then, but seemed afterwards to grow suddenly serious. "Remunerative?" she echoed after a pause, and added: "Is money *everything*? Oughtn't one to have the feeling that what one is doing is worth while? Do you feel that about the Roebourne case?"

"I'm not sure that I feel that about anything," Severn answered.

"Not even the work Terry's doing?" she queried; and he replied suavely: "I said I wasn't sure. That's the truth. I'm *not* sure."

Then came the argument. I think he thoroughly enjoyed it, and all the more because he could see and watch its effect upon Terry. Briefly, his thesis was that there was no such thing, ultimately, as progress. We were here in the world, and we didn't know why we were here; and there wasn't a scrap of evidence to show that world-movements had any permanent direction. The world had been inhabited for millions of years, and it was merely parochial conceit to suppose that our own civilization was the highest that had ever been known. The Greeks had excelled us in many of the arts; why not some earlier civilization in chemistry or engineering or medical science? It was a fascinating speculation. Quite possibly all the great discoveries had been made and remade over and over again throughout the ages. Nor could it be optimistically assumed that each successive civilization touched a higher peak than its predecessor. It was far more likely that there had been vast cycles of civilizations—some of them with an upward trend, and others with a downward—and that these cycles, in turn, belonged to even vaster movements. It was all, he admitted, very hazy and speculative; but at any rate it gave little support to those worthy Victorians who thought that the laying of the Transatlantic cable represented another step towards the millennium.

"Then," I said, when he momentarily paused, "we might all of us just as well do evil as good."

He demurred to the use of the words "good" and "evil." There were no absolute standards; the world had fashions in such things just as it had in dress and manners. *Anything* was fashionable sometime or somewhere or other—murder in wartime, for instance, or bigamy in Turkey....

"Then what *are* we to do?"

"Do what you like. That's all the advice I can give you. *I* always do what *I* like. I like making speeches, for instance, and getting my name in the papers, and making plenty of money. But tastes differ, of course. And to those who live uncomfortably in this world in the hope of having everything made up to them in the next, my advice is just the same—If you *prefer* having *that* sort of a life and *that* sort of a belief, then have them by all means."

It was all very devastatingly brilliant, but perhaps it was a little too reminiscent of an undergraduate debate. It was Severn himself, rather than what he said, that impressed. He *had* succeeded; he *had* made himself rich; those were the realest arguments. He had, in fact, done just what he liked with the world, and it had rewarded him far more generously than it did those who tamely let it do just what it liked with them. Yet, for all that, I found his arguments stimulating rather than convincing. Perhaps if he had been aiming them principally at me, they would have been different and more effective. But they weren't aimed at me. Terry was the target; and with him they certainly succeeded. Terry hadn't been an undergraduate at one of the older universities, and hadn't ever sat up till dawn shattering morality to bits and remoulding it nearer to the heart's desire. Severn's ideas were different not only in degree but in kind from any he had heard before, and the result was naturally severe.

All this leads up to what Helen did. (Yes, I *must* call her Helen.) Severn, just before we left, had called me into his study for a farewell whisky. He was in high good humour. "You fellows think I've been joking all the time," he said, "but I haven't.... Only *some* of the time." He laughed. "For instance, when I talked about Terry going abroad to Paris or Vienna or somewhere, I really meant it. I think it would be a splendid chance for him.... You might ask him, as you go home, how he'd care to have a few years working with Karelsky. He'll know who Karelsky is."

While we were drinking and chatting he had to answer the telephone. The matter, I gathered, was of a rather private nature, so I edged away towards the doorway that looked into the hall.

And then I saw Terry. His back was towards me, and in front of him, almost hidden from my sight by his tall and upright body, was Helen. The lights in the hall were very subdued, and all I could see of her distinctly was the knuckle of her right hand as she held the lapel of his coat.

She had been talking to him earnestly, and I caught what was evidently a final remark. "... and you mustn't take any notice of him, Terry—you *mustn't*.... I'd *hate* you to be influenced by him at all...." Only that, whispered very eagerly.

He said nothing in reply, and then suddenly, glancing over his shoulder with a little side-movement of her head, she saw me. I know she did, although at that moment I had almost withdrawn myself into the study. It was not deliberate eavesdropping, anyhow.

IV

Looking back on it all now, I can see exactly what was happening. But I couldn't then. It puzzled me that Terry had been so concerned by what had seemed to me merely a brilliant improvisation by a born improviser. But when I told him what Severn had said about Karelsky his manner changed. He seemed rather dazed with the idea, and he insisted on taking me back to his rooms that night and showing me everything he could find that had anything to do with Karelsky. Apparently he was a scientific star of the first magnitude. There was a photograph of him in a recent number of *Discovery*, and an article by him in the *Science Review* on the Function of the Nucleolus in the Life of the Animal Cell. His translated work "Eosinophilic Leucocytes in the Thymus of Postnatal Pigs" was, so Terry informed me, a monument of research; and he had also created a stir in the world of mathematics by a paper in a German journal on "Die Veranderlichkeit der Licht—und Farbe-Empfidnungen." Altogether he was undoubtedly a great man.

We sat up till nearly two in the morning discussing Karelsky and Vienna and so on. Terry's attitude astonished me, yet, in a way, it thrilled me also; it had, if the metaphor isn't too fanciful, the austere beauty of a Greek statue. What I mean is that he was thinking of nothing—nothing at all—except his work. The idea of having anything to do with the great Karelsky had stirred in him something that had always existed but had rarely permitted itself to be seen—a sort of frozen, white-hot passion for laboratory-research. It glowed in his eyes and trembled in his voice; it burned as fiercely as the art of any artist. It would be fine, he thought, to know Karelsky, and not only to know him, but to work with him and learn from him. It would be glorious to sit at the feet of the man who had discovered no fewer than three new species of *spalax monticola*.

V

Helen was a lovely woman. I don't think I ever realized it more forcibly than on the afternoon that followed that End House dinner. She had asked me to tea at Rumpelmayer's, and we sat at one of the tables overlooking the plutocratic hubbub of St. James Street. "I asked Terry as well," she said, "but of course he won't come." She rather overdid the casualness of her attitude, and as soon as I looked at her she began to blush. But she kept her head, adding vivaciously: "I like Rumpelmayer's. It's the only place in London that reminds me of Ostend."

Then, quite suddenly, she began to talk to me with eagerness, bending forward across the table till her head was only a few inches from mine. "You know, Jimmy—(you don't mind me calling you that, do you?)—I believe you're rather clever. Geoffrey says you are, but I don't mean *his* sort of cleverness—I mean *my* sort, which consists in understanding people. I believe you *do* understand people, and I'm certain you notice most things that happen. You noticed, for instance, how I was talking to Terry last night. And you noticed how I blushed just now when I mentioned his name.... Didn't you?"

I admitted it.

She went on: "On the whole I'm rather glad Geoffrey talked last night as he did. I wouldn't like Terry to be really influenced by Geoffrey, but still, Geoffrey's rather good at shaking foundations. And Terry's foundations *need* shaking."

"Were they shaken?"

"Just a little, I think. But *I* did most of the shaking." She added very quietly: "I'm going to be perfectly frank with you and tell you the whole truth. I'm in love with Terry. There now—what do you make of that?"

What *could* I make of it? You are sitting over a cup of tea in a fashionable café when your companion, a pretty married woman, tells you quite calmly that she is in love with one of your greatest friends. What is the correct thing to say? Should you exclaim: "Really? How thrilling!" or adopt an attitude of commiseration?

I did neither. I put into words the thought that came straightway into my head. I said: "Being in love's bound to happen, I suppose. If you keep cool about it, it isn't frightfully important."

"How do you know?"

"Well ... I've always been very slightly in love with you."

"How nice of you!" she exclaimed, with genuine appreciation of what is, after all, the extremest compliment a man can pay a woman. "It's a most wonderful thing to tell me, but I'm afraid it's not much use as a comparison. For you've only got it slightly, whereas I'm in love with Terry just ... just tremendously."

"Are you really?"

"Yes."

It was then that I realized how lovely she was. The admission had brought a heightened colour into her cheeks, and as she sat there, waiting for me to say something, I saw in her again that utmost beauty that includes and yet is beyond the merely physical—a challenge rather than a statement.

She smiled at me suddenly. "Don't look so serious. Have some more tea.... That's right.... I'm glad I've told you, anyway. Do you think it's *very* awful?"

"It may be—for you," I answered.

"For *me*?" She laughed. "Why, I'm not a bit afraid. It's so wonderful and interesting—so far—that I wouldn't give it up whatever happened. Do you know—" her eyes glowed with sharp excitement—"since it began to—to happen—all life seems to have caught fire.... Do you know what I mean? Everything is so—so *different*—so *splendid*...."

There were bright tears in her eyes as she spoke. She went on: "But of course you're thinking of Geoffrey. Well, you needn't worry—*he'll* never need to know anything about it. He's so sure of his own powers of fascination that he'd want a lot of convincing that I could possibly be interested in anybody else."

I nodded. That was shrewd and very probably true. "Well, anyhow," I said, after a pause, "what are you going to do about it?"

"*Do* about it?" she repeated. "*Do* about it? Why, there's nothing to do, except to go on being in love for the first time in my life."

"The *first*? You mean that—"

Yes, she meant it. She had begun by being frank with me, she said, and she might as well continue. No doubt I would be surprised to hear that her marriage hadn't been an affair of love—not on her side, at any rate.... She had been a *midinette* in the Rue de la Paix, and Severn a chance customer. He had taken her about as he would have taken about any girl if he had fancied her sufficiently. "He dazzled me—he was so very charming and delightful, and I liked him because he wasn't a snob...." After the marriage there had been trouble with the Severn family, and— "He was splendid then. I liked him most of all when he hadn't more than five pounds in the world and he *would* insist on taking me to Claridge's. He was always like that—he never feared to do what he wanted. And, of course, you know how marvellously—how *terribly* successful he's been." She smiled and continued: "The quaint part of it is that most people must think me the luckiest person in the world. Geoffrey's so generous—I've nothing very much to complain of. It's just that as soon as I met Terry I knew—" She shrugged her shoulders and added: "Well, you know what I knew, don't you?"

She took a chocolate éclair and delicately pierced it with her fork. "You aren't saying very much," she went on, "but I hope you're understanding.... Try to understand how terrible it is to be married to a man who always gets what he wants. Everything that he said last night was perfectly true—he doesn't believe there's anything very much worth while in the world, except to do what you like and have a good time.... And then, on the other hand, there's Terry...."

"Yes?"

She went on, after a pause: "What seems to me so strange and fine is his way of doing his work very quietly because he thinks it's worth doing, and not because of money or fame or anything like that at all. Just think of it—Geoffrey's made out of this Roebourne case in three weeks as much as Terry may earn in ten years.... It's a shame."

It was, I admitted, but I pointed out that Terry himself would probably disagree. He didn't want a lot of money, and consequently he wasn't disappointed about not getting it. He had often said that three hundred a year would completely satisfy him. To which she replied: "Yes, I told that to Geoffrey not long ago, and he said he'd settle three hundred a year on him if he'd accept it."

"Of course he wouldn't," I answered. "But it was rather decent of Geoffrey to make the suggestion."

"Was it?" She spoke rather sadly. "I suppose it was. But at the time, it just made me feel that the whole world was hopeless."

She meant, she explained, that it hurt her to think that what meant so much to Terry could be bestowed by Geoffrey as a mere whim of the moment. "But there it is," she went on, enjoying her éclair, "Terry's happy, and I'm happy, and Geoffrey's happy, so I suppose it's all right. Being in love—even tremendously in love—seems to be quite a harmless luxury if you keep your head about it. And I'm not likely to lose mine.... Besides, I want to help Terry. I want to make him a little more at home in the world."

"Which is happening faster," I asked, "your conversion of him, or his of you?"

She didn't answer. There wasn't time, for at that moment we saw Terry coming towards us.

VI

He was very shy and nervous. He had decided at the last moment to accept her invitation, but he hadn't known where Rumpelmayer's was, and several bus-conductors had failed to give adequate information. (I think he expected something about as large as Selfridge's.) Anyhow, that accounted for the delay. He was sorry, and he hoped we hadn't been waiting long.

The awkward part of it was that I had to leave them almost immediately for an unpostponable duty in Fleet Street. It was unfortunate, I thought, because Helen might think I had invented the appointment in order to leave her alone with Terry. Perhaps she did; but at any rate she seemed not to care. "I hope you won't be late," she said, smiling as she shook hands with me. And then she summoned the waitress and gave a fresh order.

As I rode back on the top of a bus to Fleet Street, the whole interview seemed almost incredible. It was queer enough to find Terry breaking his cast-iron rules by having tea with her; but it was positively sensational for her to have calmly confessed to being in love with him, and for me to have comforted her with the assurance that being in love wasn't frightfully important. But that was the sort of thing she had power to do; she could have confessed murder, I believe, and have made you feel that murder wasn't frightfully important.

Often since then I have pondered over the matter and wondered what I *ought* to have done. Whatever it was, it was probably more heroic than what I did, which was merely to wait, telling myself over and over again that neither the one nor the other of them was a fool, and that there were certain things which only fools did....

VII

And so it began. The difficulty is to say *what* began. Terry told me so little, and Helen told me so much; and between the two was a vast hiatus of the inexplicable. At first, the affair seemed perfectly harmless. When a man, after habitually working three times as hard as he ought, slows down to twice as hard, there doesn't seem a great deal to complain of. Nor when the same man spends a wet Sunday afternoon listening to a pretty woman play Chopin, instead of drenching himself to the skin on some miserable hillside.

The whole thing is difficult to put into words because to this day I don't really know what happened. All I surmise is that the work of mutual conversion proceeded during the months of late winter and early spring—she attending his bacteriology lectures and he accompanying her to theatres, pianoforte recitals, and so on. Their meetings were frequent enough to stir gossip, no doubt, but hardly scandal, especially as it was so obvious that Severn knew and approved. Helen had always been in the throes of some fad or other, and he probably assumed that Terry was an unusually congenial successor of Christian Science, Dalcroze eurhythmics, highbrow drama, and a dozen other enthusiasms that had had their day and one by one crept silently to rest. It was he, more often than not, who might say to her: "Oh, by the way, I've got a card for Wolferton's private view—it's next Tuesday at the Savile Galleries. I shan't have time to go myself, but you might take Terry and show him the latest painted pot-boilers...." And she would take him, of course.

When I asked him if he had enjoyed going to that or some similar function, he would usually reply: "Yes, very much." Never more, and hardly ever less. It was Helen who assured me that the work of "humanizing" him was proceeding successfully.

"And," I said to her once, "you're still in love with him?"

She replied: "More than ever. Oh, *much* more. And—as I told you before—it's *wonderful*."

"Maybe, but is it wise?"

She pursed her lips and then answered: "Well, what harm can there be in it? It isn't sharing anything with Geoffrey.... It's nothing to do with anybody how I feel—nobody will ever know it except you, and you wouldn't if I hadn't told you."

"Suppose Terry were to find it out?"

"You mean—suppose I'm a fool, eh? ... Well, I assure you, I'm not."

"All right, then—take another supposition. What will happen if Terry falls in love with you?"

"My dear Jimmy—he *couldn't*. It wouldn't occur to him. Oh, don't—don't—" she was beginning to laugh—"don't imagine it. It *couldn't* happen."

"Then what *will* happen—eventually?"

She gave me her loveliest smile. "I shall teach him and watch over him, and then, when the right girl comes along, I shall just hand him over ... in good condition."

"And when do you think that will be?"

She shrugged her pretty little shoulders and laughed outright. "How can I tell?—Perhaps in ten days—or ten months—or ten years. But it will happen—it is bound to happen—*some day*...."

The pages of my diary about this time bear witness to the number of times Terry and I dined at the End House. Generally we went on Wednesdays, and as time passed the "generally" became "always" and the dinners a habit. Once Helen was slightly unwell during one of Terry's Wednesday lectures, and he broke his fixed rule so far as to see her afterwards and escort her home in her car. And then, the following Wednesday, although she wasn't unwell at all, he repeated the courtesy, and that also became a habit.

They were always very jolly, informal affairs, those dinners. More often than not, Severn wasn't there; he was busy at his chambers, or dining at one of his clubs, or on duty in the House. Sometimes, by way of compensation, June, aged eleven, was home from her boarding-school, and Terry used often to amuse her by performing small chemical and physical experiments. I can remember him fixing a Bunsen burner on to the kitchen gas-stove, and to cook's amazement as well as June's, blowing a piece of glass tubing into various shapes. On another occasion he solemnly changed the colour of litmus-paper before our eyes.... He seemed very fond of the child, and she, I believe, thought he was some sort of magician.

All this happened while spring was deepening into summer. Even in my own most unsalubrious district of Camden Town the change of season was unmistakable; nay, even also in Gower Street, and even at the top of the Physics Building and along the corridor where the name "Dr. M. Terrington" rewarded the ardent bacteriological pilgrim after his six flights of labour. But the chief sign of change along that corridor was the fact that sometimes, and more often as the season progressed, the pilgrim knocked at the door, looked inside, and found the room empty.

VIII

He let go his work. It all happened so suddenly—as if some barrier inside him had collapsed. And also, to make the problem of analysis more difficult for me, it happened when I was away. I was only away a week, but a week was long enough to change everything; and when I came back, everything *was* changed.

He would tell me hardly anything, except that he felt he had been working too hard and needed a rest. (And that, of course, was plausible enough.) He also, in an unguarded moment, admitted to a certain spiritual change. "It was what Severn said—that night we went to dinner and we all argued about civilizations and progress and morality and what not—do you remember? Somehow it made me think of things I'd never thought of before.... In a sense, I was blind till then."

That also, I think, may very well have been true. He *had* been blind till then; he had been blind to the beauty of the world all around him; he had shut himself up in his laboratory attic, refusing pleasure and friendship and even, so far as he was able, contact with the world outside. Even his Sunday recreation had, in those old days, been taken medicinally; it had been nothing to him but so many miles walked and so much fresh air breathed. He had been wantonly blind, and it was quite possible that Severn's facile pessimism had given him the first sight-creating disturbance. But was there no middle course between being blind and working far too hard, and having sight and not working at all? And had not Helen helped to remove the blindness?

The weeks passed quickly, and I saw less and less of both of them, for the simple reason that they saw more and more of each other. One felt, instinctively, that whatever was happening could not go on for long. And then, towards the end of July, Severn wrote that he had been in communication with Karelsky, and that the latter was coming to England for a short visit and would be glad to take Terry back to Vienna with him. "It seems a good opening," Severn wrote, "and on the whole I think you would do well to accept it, though of course you must please yourself. Karelsky will be in London this week, and I am giving a dinner to him at the End House on Friday. You will come, of course...."

By the same post an invitation arrived for me, and as soon as I read it I hastened over to Terry's lodgings. I found him reading Severn's letter without, so far as I could judge, either pleasure or displeasure. He handed it to me without comment, and then went on with his dressing, for he had a theatre engagement that night with Helen.

I hardly knew what to say to him. I think I remarked that Vienna was reputed a pleasant city, and then, when he still was silent, I asked him point-blank: "Will you go?"

Almost truculently, as he stood before the mirror adjusting his dress-tie, he answered: "Why *shouldn't* I go?"

IX

I didn't see him again until the evening of Severn's party. I shall never forget that evening. It was, according to the newspapers (which hadn't anything else to make a headline of), the hottest weather for forty-seven years, or something like that. It was a damp and steamy heat, and even at Hampstead hardly a breath of air was stirring when I arrived there about seven o'clock. In those days I couldn't afford taxis, and by the time I had climbed to the top of the hill the boiled shirt was clinging to me like a particularly nauseating poultice.

The party was the sort that Severn loved most of all—a gathering of a dozen or so "big names" from various spheres of activity, with himself as the lowest common denominator—or would it be the highest common factor? ... A sort of social cocktail, to vary the metaphor; and in this particular concoction the preponderating flavour was naturally that of science, pure and applied. It was a distinguished crowd—terrifyingly distinguished. Besides Helen, there were only two women—Doctor

Isidora Hadden (who lectured on anatomy and wrote about six-legged dogs in the scientific journals), and Lady Muriel Spencer, whom Severn had asked, presumably, because of her recent explorations amongst the buried cities of Honduras. Of the men, about three-quarters were sixty; two-thirds wore evening-dress of Victorian design; a half were bearded; and at least a quarter were varyingly deaf. No doubt their combined titles, qualifications, degrees, diplomas, and so on, would have filled a quarter-column of the *Times*. Severn, behind his perfect exterior of charm, was in a sardonic mood, for as he passed me in the drawing-room before dinner, he whispered into my ear: "Beware! Here are lions!"

Terry, perhaps, was impressed. He was also very nervous. He was given a place of honour between Karelsky and Lady Muriel (Severn *would* do things like that), and most of the others were probably wondering who he was and why the devil he wasn't somewhere else. Particularly as he didn't seem able or willing to make the slightest use of his opportunities. Karelsky hardly spoke to him at all, and Lady Muriel tried him once about Aztecs and then gave him up.

As for Karelsky, he was an enigma, and not perhaps wholly a pleasant one. He couldn't help perspiring, I admit; but he needn't have mopped his forehead continually with his table-napkin. He talked most of all to Severn, who was always ready to translate a difficult phrase into German for his comprehension; but occasionally, and with completely bad manners, he shouted across the table in response to some remark, not addressed to him, that he chanced to have overheard. "Dat iss one goot price," he bellowed at a couple of aged professors who were discussing confidentially the amount of money they had made out of certain text-books. But it wasn't hard to believe that he was clever, and he certainly showed signs of being well-informed about other matters besides science. "I haf heard of Hampstead before," he said once. "It iss where—iss it not?—you haf your 'Arry and your 'Arriet on the holiday of the banks." That, I thought, was not bad for a Russian-born Austrian.

My own position at table was between Helen and the greatest living authority on palaeobotany, who, being dyspeptic as well as deaf, must have had a rather miserable time. But Helen talked most of the while to her other neighbour, a middle-aged professor of physics. Once she turned to me and said, very softly: "I don't think I like Karelsky very much.... Is Terry going to go to Vienna with him?"

"I think so," I answered, and then she said, lightly: "I wonder how he'll like it—being abroad...."

X

All that time the temperature was rising. I mean the actual, physical temperature; somebody who, as befitted a scientist, carried a pocket thermometer about with him, informed us that the mercury stood at eighty-three. Because of the heat, coffee and liqueurs were served on the lawn beyond the French windows, and there, without the artificial breeze of electric fans, the air seemed even hotter. Collars were limp; beads of sweat ran down scientific noses and beards; even scientific tempers were not too equable. Only Severn, talking more than anybody, managed to give an impression of coolness; it reminded him, he said, of an evening he had once spent in Colombo. He told an exciting story (possibly a true one) about a Cingalese who, maddened by the heat, ran amok and killed half-a-dozen passers-by. Then Karelsky discussed with him in German-English the effect of intense heat upon the human brain.... Of the whole crowd of us there in the garden, only those two seemed thoroughly alive—Karelsky with his huge face streaming with perspiration, and Severn like a lithe sharp-eyed panther. The rest were puppets, sagging in their armchairs and moving only to sip their brandy and iced coffee. The smell of vegetation rose up like steam out of the warm earth, but even the palaeobotanist was not enthusiastic about it. And Karelsky, with an immense bellow of "It iss verr hot" suddenly tore off his collar and tie and stuffed them in his pocket. I admired him for that; it was the sort of thing that needs courage of the kind that few of us possess. Severn, of course, laughed. It sounded to me like the mocking, diabolical laughter of a madman lost amidst tropical jungle; but that, no doubt, was only the combined effect of brandy, heat, and Severn's story of the maniac Cingalese.

Then at last the first streak of lightning flooded the garden and showed us the heavy trees, reaching over us like gigantic grasping arms. And it was in that sharp and blinding glow that I caught sight of Terry and Helen; they had completely separated themselves from the rest and were walking slowly across the further end of the lawns towards the kitchen-gardens....

The moments crawled on, and each was a little hotter, or seemed it, than the one before. Whenever there came a lightning-flash I tried to take in at a glance the whole vista of lawns and gardens, but I did not see the two of them again. By that time, I suppose, I was partially drunk; and I hardly recollect what happened except that after a seemingly immense gap of drowsiness Severn himself was next to me, dragging his cane chair nearer to mine. "I'm so pleased Terry's decided to accept Karelsky's offer," he said.

"He *has* told you, then?"

"Yes ... Karelsky goes to Vienna to-morrow night, and Terry will accompany him, if he can make arrangements in time."

"That's rather quick work, isn't it?"

"It is, I admit. But it's vacation-time and it ought to be possible.... By the way, what do you think of Karelsky, eh? Rather a rough diamond—"

"I'll tell you this much," he went on, without waiting for my opinion, "Karelsky's a man of business as well as a man of science. He'll get his value out of Terry, you can bet your life. But then, what Terry must do is to get his value out of Karelsky. See?"

"And on the whole you think it'll be a good thing for Terry?"

"If he uses his chances it will be a splendid thing. And, of course, if he *doesn't* use his chances, nothing will do him very much good. I like him a great deal, you know. So does Helen. I'm sure she'll miss him when he's gone.... By the way, where is she? Have you seen her?"

I told him I hadn't seen her for some while, and soon afterwards he had to leave me to bid the first of the good-byes.

XI

I *was* drunk. I had a persistent and rather ridiculous desire to lean back in my chair and go to sleep. This, in fact, is what I actually did, until a terrific peal of thunder awoke me—or was it Severn laughing? Anyway, he *was* laughing. He was leaning over the back of the chair next to mine, like a wild animal waiting to spring; and Helen was standing close to him, with her eyes fixed on me. "So you're another victim, are you?" he said.

I stammered an apology and he interrupted hurriedly: "My dear chap, you needn't say all that. It has been an interesting example of what Karelsky was talking about—the effects of heat on the human brain. Or was it something else as well as the heat?... Anyhow, Professor Foljambe could hardly walk to his taxi. Even Terry the teetotaller had to clear off in a hurry."

"Did he?—Wh—why?"

It was Helen who answered. She said, very quietly: "He said the heat made him feel ill, so he just slipped away without making any fuss."

"And without even seeing me," Severn added.

I said something about calling at his lodgings to see how he was, and Helen remarked: "Oh, you needn't be alarmed about him—it was only the heat."

I wasn't alarmed, but I wanted to see him. Ten minutes later I was on my way to the tube station, and in half-an-hour I was at the door of the house in Swinton Street. It was hotter in London than at Hampstead, and the night was full of lightning and rumblings of thunder. I remember how, in the poorer districts that I passed, whole families were sitting out on the pavement, chattering amongst themselves and waiting for the storm to begin.

CHAPTER THREE

I

THE heat of that night is a sort of canvas on which everything is painted in my memory. Terry, when he came to the door and admitted me, was rather pale, and something in his eyes made me wonder if he were sorry I had come. Probably, if I hadn't been fairly drunk, I should soon have left him; but I was in a talkative, comradely mood, and hints were lost on me. He must have been very patient and forbearing.

We made coffee, I remember, and I smoked cigarettes and chattered about the party and Severn and Karelsky and so on. Perhaps he listened, but I think (and rather hope) that he didn't. He told me that the heat had "got at him," but that after a cold bath he felt much better. All the time we talked the thunder rolled and rumbled over the roofs, and the numerous cracks in the window-blind sparkled with vivid lightning. In the green-yellow gas-light the bed-sitting-room looked dingier and more forlorn than ever. Heaped up in one corner were books and papers that he had begun to sort out in readiness for removal, and about half-past midnight, wanting an excuse to stay longer, I said: "It's not a bit of good either of us trying to sleep on a night like this. We might just as well get to work and finish packing your things. I hear you're going to-morrow night...."

Then came the shock that made me suddenly sober. He answered quietly—almost casually: "No, no ... I'm *not* going."

"Not—not going—to-morrow?"

And he answered: "I'm not going—at all."

I think I was dazed at first. Then I was angry that he hadn't told me before, and then, for a fraction of a second, I was selfishly glad that our friendship had been reprieved. After that bewilderment came again, and finally I was calm but immensely puzzled. I asked him if he meant that the whole arrangement with Karelsky was cancelled, and he said: "Yes—that's right."

"But—but *why?*"

"Because I—I can't go."

"*Why* can't you?"

"I—I just *can't*, that's all."

"But there *must* be a reason!"

"There *is* a reason."

"What?"

"Well ... to begin with ... it was never absolutely settled that I *should* go."

"But you told Severn to-night that you were going."

"Yes ... I thought I *was* going then."

"And you've changed your mind since?"

"Yes ... I suppose I have."

"But—*why?*"

"Well, I've a right to change my mind, haven't I?"

"Of course, but ..."

And so on.... For a long time I could get nothing at all out of him except that he had changed his mind and wasn't going. The cleverest subtleties of cross-examination were wasted on him; whenever I thought I had manœuvred him into a corner, he just shook his head and said: "I don't know what there is to argue about. Severn told me I must please myself.... I'm pleasing myself, that's all." Then, as a last and not too scrupulous resort, I tried a method that had sometimes succeeded before; it consisting in pretending to infer from his silences something that I knew he wouldn't like me to infer. I said: "Well, I daresay you have good reasons, whatever they are. Karelsky seems rather a keen business man, and if the terms he offers aren't high enough—"

"Karelsky," he sharply interrupted, "had nothing to do with it."

"Whether he had or not, you haven't any money of your own, and you obviously can't afford to—"

I guessed that would stir him. He protested with sudden indignation: "I tell you it isn't a matter of money at all. Good heavens! do you think

I'd let a question of money interfere with—with anything I had thought of doing?"

"What *would* you let interfere, then?"

He shook his head. "It's just.... Oh, I can't go—I keep on telling you I can't go.... That's all."

"It isn't me you ought to be telling. It's Severn. He doesn't know yet, does he?"

"Not yet."

"Don't you think he'll be rather disappointed?"

"Perhaps. I'm sorry about that.... But all the same, I can't help it. It's nothing to do with him—the reason, I mean.... I can't help it—I shall tell him I can't help it!"

So the reason had nothing to do with Severn, and nothing to do with Karelsky. Then who *was* the person involved?

II

It took about an hour to extort a few meagre fragments of the truth. Only a few, even then. I talked and questioned, and he answered and sometimes didn't answer, and out of it all, very gradually indeed, there came a very blurred picture of what *might* have happened that night at the End House.... It was obvious, of course, that Helen had persuaded him not to go, and that he had given her a promise. He even admitted as much in the end, in order that he could entrench himself on the much stronger ground that he had pledged his word and must keep to it. He *wasn't* going to Vienna, he said again; that was final; and he didn't see what there was to argue about.

I answered that there was a great deal to argue about. There was what Severn would think, to begin with. Was he going to tell Severn that he had cancelled the arrangement with Karelsky in order to please Helen?... He replied doggedly, as before, that he couldn't help *what* Severn thought; he was grateful to him, but gratitude didn't and couldn't mean going anywhere in the world he suggested. Besides, hadn't Severn urged him to please himself?

Pleasing himself, I pointed out, was a far different thing from changing his mind at the last minute. Then he said, with a touch of sharpness: "Look here, I'm fed up with all this talk. I don't understand what you're arguing about.... What's the game? Why are you so damned keen on getting me sent off to Vienna?"

I told him that I wasn't keen at all, but rather the contrary, so far as I personally was concerned. "It's just," I said, "that I don't want you to make a hash of things."

"A *hash* of things? What do you mean?"

His less passive attitude made it easier for me to come to the somewhat delicate point. I asked him straightforwardly if he were going to continue seeing Helen as much as he had been doing. The question seemed to galvanize him into something like fierceness; he retorted instantly: "Yes, just as much, and perhaps even more!"

We were both silent for a while, and I wondered hazily what I should say, what arguments I could use, how the matter ought to be tackled. In the end I began where the argument should have stopped; I said, almost in desperation: "But, Terry—can't you see how—how utterly *impossible* it is?"

"What is utterly impossible?"

"That you and Helen—should go on—as you are doing." I waited for him to reply, and when he didn't, I continued: "Can't you see that when a woman asks you—makes you promise—to put *her* before your work.... Can't you see that her asking you *not* to go to Vienna is just a reason—an additional reason—why you *should* go?"

He tried to see; I could see him trying to see; but what he saw was something different—some strange and secret vision of his own. "You don't understand," he said haltingly. "There's nothing I can say to make you understand, either. You'd far better not worry about it.... Helen—in a sort of way—needs me—here, and I'm going to stay."

"She needs you?"

"Yes."

"How does she need you?"

He flashed back: "You're forcing me to say something that sounds conceited. But it's true, all the same. She needs me because—because

I'm teaching her—I'm helping her to realize—that life isn't—just money—and pleasure—and idleness!"

And there he was, revealed at last—in his own eyes the missionary, the evangelist, converting her from frivolity to the true faith in Koch, Kelvin, and Lister. There was pride and triumph in his voice, and, looking back on it now, I believe that he was perfectly sincere. But at the time it angered me; I lost my temper. "Damn it all," I cried, "I *will* tell you what I think, whether it offends you or not. You're behaving like a fool—or else like a cad—I can't be quite certain which.... Talk about *teaching* her and *helping her to realize*—why don't you tell the truth and admit that you're head over ears in love with her? ... It's bad enough to play the fool with another man's wife, but to talk highbrow bunkum about it seems to me pretty near the limit!"

He looked for a moment as if he were going to rush at me. But the fierceness soon passed, and behind it was the half-truculent doggedness of his earlier mood. "You don't understand," he said, after a pause. "I couldn't expect you to understand. I don't know why I began telling you anything about this at all...." Then he suddenly stood erect and wiped the perspiration from his streaming forehead. "This heat!" he cried, waving his arms. "Oh, for God's sake, let's get out of it—anywhere—*anywhere*."

III

We went out together into the street. It was nearly two o'clock, and the very slight breeze seemed only to make the night hotter. We walked down Gray's Inn Road and across Holborn and through a labyrinth of alleys and side-streets towards Fleet Street and the river. All the time there was the lightning and the heavy-rolling thunder; the storm would break very soon, and the blackness of the sky was something that could almost be seen. Everything seemed grotesquely unreal, including what he said and what I said. Perhaps we were both possessed; perhaps the whole night was agog with demons and angels, and we, with our problem, were their pitiful sport....

We went on arguing. I told him that if I didn't understand, it was his fault for obscuring everything in a fog of reticence. I had made deductions from what I could see with my eyes, and that was what he must expect other people, including Severn, to do. If these deductions were all wrong, then it was *his* place to assure and convince me of it. But he said: "No, not at all. If your deductions are wrong, then it's your own fault for having made them."

"Will you tell that to Severn, if *his* deductions are wrong?"

"I don't know what I shall tell Severn."

"You admit he has some right to object to what's going on?"

"As much as a man who boasts of doing what he likes has *any* right to object to other people doing what they like."

He was a shrewder disputant than I had suspected. "Look here, Terry," I said, rather more cordially, "why don't you try to see my point? It isn't just nosiness that's making me ask you all these infernally awkward questions. You know that, or at any rate, you ought to.... It's just what I feel—I have an idea—that you may be on the verge of doing something that you'll afterwards regret. Naturally, I want to warn you—to help you, if I can. But you won't let me get near the subject—you won't even let me know what it is you're going to do."

"I'm going to stay in London," he said resolutely. "That's what I'm going to do, and I've been telling you that for the last hour."

"But what does it mean? Does it mean that you and Helen—? ... Look here, will you give me your assurance that there's nothing in your relationship but this—this teaching business that you spoke of?"

"Which you called highbrow bunkum."

"Well, if I did—"

"You *did*, anyhow. And now you want my assurance that there's nothing in my relationship with Helen except highbrow bunkum. Do you really expect me to give it to you? And would you believe it if I did?"

"Never mind that. Come to the point.... Is your relationship with her perfectly all-square and above board?"

"I don't quite know what you mean."

"Is it the sort of thing you could let Severn know about?"

"No.... It isn't the sort of thing I could let anybody know about."

"You mean you're in love with her?"

"No—don't ask me that. Don't ask me any more. I can't and I shan't answer any more."

Deadlock—and then the storm broke. But the rain seemed to change the feeling of the world; it opened, as it were, a window in the sky, and a cool breeze floated through, scouring and freshening every corner. We were cool at last, and then cold, and then, with tremendous suddenness, tired. Too tired to go on arguing, too tired to think of how to get back, too tired to do anything but stand under the Embankment tramway shelter and wait for the clouds to exhaust themselves.

When the rain had nearly stopped we hastened northwards through the swirling and deserted streets. It was three o'clock. We spoke very little on the way, and by tacit agreement the argument was not resumed. Only once was it so much as referred to, and that was when, bidding him good-bye at the door of his lodgings, I said: "I don't retract anything I said a little while ago, but I'm sorry I lost my temper over it."

And he answered, with shy cordiality: "Oh, *that's* all right. Don't trouble about *that*...."

IV

All the next day I was away in the Midlands on newspaper work, but my mind, even when it shouldn't have been, was full of thinking about Terry and Helen and their relationship. I couldn't escape from it; it dominated me like an unsolved word-puzzle. What *had* happened at the End House on that night of the dinner to Karelsky? And what had been happening for weeks and months before? It was, as a matter of fact, seven years later when I found out, and as most of my conjectures were then shown to be wrong, there doesn't seem to be much reason for setting them down. All that need be recorded is that I returned to town late in the evening and found this short note awaiting me:

"Of course you were right after all, and I shall always thank you for what you did and said. I don't know what has been possessing me lately,

but I think I must have been off my head. I'm going to Vienna with Karelsky to-night, and when I'm there I'm going to *work*. Come over and see me as soon as you can spare time for a holiday. Yrs.,
  TERRY."

V

And the next day I saw Helen. I came out of the *Messenger* newspaper-office about half-past three in the afternoon, and found her standing on the kerb outside. "Hello!" I exclaimed. "Fancy seeing you round here. Where are you going?"

She said: "Nowhere. I was waiting for you to come out."

"Who told you I was here?"

"Your landlady. I called at your rooms."

"But why on earth didn't you send up a message to the office? Or 'phone me? I could have been with you half an hour ago if I'd known."

She answered: "I should have done, but—I thought you might not want to see me."

"Not *want* to see you? Good heavens, why shouldn't I?"

She shrugged her shoulder and then said: "Oh, never mind.... Let's go somewhere—where we can talk."

So she wanted to talk. Looking back on it now, it seems incredible that I didn't guess what her attitude would be. I suppose that Terry's letter had made me feel ever so slightly a hero, with its "I shall always thank you for what you did and said." Perhaps, subconsciously, I was in the mood that expects congratulation; at any rate, I wasn't prepared for censure. I looked out for a taxi, thinking I would take her to tea somewhere in the West End; but she said impatiently: "We can go *there*," and pointed to a Lyons tea-shop on the other side of Fleet Street. "But surely—" I began; and she interrupted sharply: "*There*, I tell you. This is business, not pleasure."

We threaded our way amongst the marble-topped tables, and as she passed a waitress she gave a rather defiant order for two cups of tea. Then she selected a table, sat down, and began immediately, with a sort of point-blank hostility: "So—after all—you've managed to persuade him?"

"You—you mean—Terry?"

And she answered, with that peculiar greenish glint in her eyes that made her look rather more wonderful than ever: "Yes, I mean Terry."

She was watching me mercilessly across the table; yet, even then, I couldn't see what cause she had to be displeased with me. I said, with genuine sincerity: "Well—honestly—don't you really think it'll be a good chance for him—going to Vienna with Karelsky?"

And she answered, with a bitter, mocking laugh: "*Honestly*—I *don't* think it'll be a good chance for him—and—*honestly*—I think you'd far better have minded your own business...."

That was a bad beginning. The whole interview lasted less than ten minutes. Then, metaphorically, it broke up in disorder. If she had been a man, we might even have come to blows; as it was, I could do nothing but sit and listen. She wasn't so much burning as burned with indignation; her words came out in an even flow that seemed alternately scorching and freezing. She was passionately certain that I had blundered. "Terry will have *no* chance in Vienna," she said, "except the chance of slogging away for someone else's benefit. You reckon to be a writer and to understand people and yet you don't understand either Karelsky or Terry.... Geoffrey's just as stupid—he thinks it's a great chance for Terry because, if *he* were in Terry's place, he would *make* it a great chance for him. No doubt it is a great chance, for anybody who can watch that he gets as much as he can out of Karelsky, and lets Karelsky get as little as possible out of him.... But Terry's not that sort. It'll never occur to him that Karelsky's out to get all the things in life that *he* doesn't care about at all.... But it's true—I know the Karelsky sort—I've met dozens of him before. All over the world there is the quiet type of man like Terry, and the acquisitive type like Karelsky and Geoffrey, and whenever they meet there's tragedy.... And yet you've deliberately *made* them meet."

She gave me no time either to explain or protest, but went on: "I know, of course, *why* you persuaded him. Not because you had any ideas at all about Vienna or Karelsky (you wouldn't stop to think about *that*), but simply because, with your trained, novelettish eye" (the phrase struck me as rather good) "you scented an intrigue, and wanted to get him out of the way at all costs. I believe you'd have banished him to the North Pole if there hadn't been anywhere else.... As if there ever was, or could have been an intrigue! But *you*, of course—your morality was shocked...."

I couldn't stand that. "Look here," I said quietly, "I'm not going to have you calling me a prig. It wasn't morality at all, though why, even if it was, you should sneer at it, I don't know.... But, as a matter of fact, it was nothing more than simple commonsense. You told me once that you were in love with him. Then, after he had accepted what seemed, on the face of it, a good post, you begged him not to go. And he gave in and promised he wouldn't. Do you blame me if I thought the situation rather dangerous? What *were* you to him that he should change his mind on such an important matter just because you asked him to?"

She answered, with a curious, far-away sadness in her voice: "I wasn't—*anything*—to him—except a teacher. I was teaching him all sorts of little things that he'll need to know in the world—little tricks of the trade of living—I was trying to lessen the probability that wherever he goes and whatever he does, he'll be the prey of men not half as strong and not a tenth as good. And I was trying to show him how big the world was, and how, even with his ideals, it couldn't all be seen from a laboratory window.... I took him to all sorts of places—educating him, in a sort of way—trying to—to—"

Oh, that talk of *teaching* and *educating*! From her lips it exasperated me as much as it had from his; it drove me into saying something that I have regretted ever since. "You may have tried," I interrupted sharply, "but you didn't succeed. Even you can't change the nature of him, and all the time you thought he was learning to be a social success, he was merely learning to love you.... *That's* what you taught him—nothing else. And that's why I judged the situation to be so dangerous that the sooner he cleared out of it the better."

I say I have regretted it ever since, and that's the bitter truth. I began regretting about a second after I had spoken, for she answered, with a calm smile and a thrill of pride in her voice: "I knew, of course, that he loved me, because he told me so. But he didn't tell *you* to tell me, and I despise you utterly for doing it. You have abused his confidence.... It's no good arguing after a thing like that.... I think you'd better get me a taxi and let me go...."

VI

I got her a taxi, and she went, and I didn't see or speak to her again for years. That is the sort of thing which, when one writes it down, gives one a sense of bewilderment. Such a little, paltry quarrel to have caused such a long estrangement! I wrote down in my diary on the evening of the day it happened: "Met H. in Fleet Street. Tiff over T." I was so sure, at the time, that it was only a tiff. I had to leave London the next morning for a week's reporting job in South Wales, and I never doubted that by the time I returned the quarrel would be forgotten.

Yet it wasn't. I remember in particular one hot August afternoon shortly after I came back. Severn had invited me to lunch with him at White's, and during the meal he talked and discussed in his usual brilliant way. But afterwards, while we mellowed ourselves with port, he said suddenly: "I say, Hilton, old chap, what on earth have you been saying to my wife?"

How could I tell him *anything*, much less *everything*? I laughed to gain time to think, and then I asked him rather stammeringly what exactly he meant. He answered: "It's rather queer. She seems to have taken a sudden dislike to you.... I'm giving a farewell party next week—just a little dinner before we go out of town. I suppose you got the invitation?"

"Yes. I was intending to reply to it to-night."

"Accepting?"

"Well—yes."

He filled up my glass and said: "Can't understand it a bit—why she's taken up such an extraordinary attitude. But she won't have you—won't have you up to the house at any price—not even for this party. Says she'll walk out if you come.... Awkward, eh?"

Of course I suggested that I should consider the invitation cancelled, and after formally protesting, he agreed. (It was what he had intended me to suggest, I could see.) "Decent of you not to mind," he said. "If you ever marry, you'll find it's always best to humour a woman when she begins to take absurd dislikes.... We're going for a month to the Canaries—perhaps that'll do her good."

We talked for a while on other topics, and then, just before we separated, he said: "By the way—not been making love to Helen or anything like that, have you?"

I assured him that I hadn't, and he laughed. "Thought I'd just ask you, that's all. Don't know that I'd blame you altogether if you *had* been— she's a wonderful woman, only capricious—absolutely capricious.... Anyhow, no need to worry about it—probably just an attack of nerves. You and I can always meet here when we want, can't we? ... Dam silly creatures, women, eh? Why *do* we marry them? ..."

VII

Letters from Terry began to arrive with marvellous regularity every fortnight. If they were a post late I knew there had been an avalanche in the Tirol or a storm in mid-Channel or some other act of God. They were always very short, and nearly always quite uninteresting. They never mentioned Severn or Helen, and never referred to the argument we had had upon the night of the storm. They were, in fact, the sort of letters a public-school boy might write to his mother. Two items they very rarely lacked—a brief reference to continued good health, and a rough summary of the weather. On the few occasions that the former item was omitted, I was free to guess rather than to know that he had been unwell.

He didn't mention that he had made or was making any friends; but then, of course, that wasn't the sort of thing that he ever would mention. He didn't even say whether he liked Vienna as a city to live in. One or two people wandered in and out of his letters like characters in a Russian play; there was Karelsky, naturally, and Frau Scholz, who kept the apartment-house where he lodged, and "Mizzi," her daughter... Besides these few—absolutely nobody.... Of miscellaneous information, the most frequent reference was to his progress in the German language. No mention ever of theatres or concerts or operas. He was, I gathered, living the sort of life he had had before meeting Helen, and the fact that it had a Viennese instead of a London setting was not, perhaps, so very important.

And meanwhile I, who, thank heaven, am not attempting to present a history of myself, lived on in London, still exiled from the End House, and still seeking a precarious livelihood in the Street of Peradventure. I lunched with Severn at White's from time to time, and I worked hard, so that the months passed quickly; and then, just when I was about to plan my yearly holidays in Vienna, Severn got me a *Messenger* commission that sent me roving round Honolulu and the South Seas instead. And so, without seeing Terry, as I had intended, there came another crowded year of work.

That was the year, you may remember, in which Karelsky burst upon the world with his astonishing Longevity Theory. In a slack season it descended upon Fleet Street like manna from heaven. Karelsky in the course of a lecture at the Sorbonne, announced the discovery of what he called "a new method of revitalizing life-force," and to this he added the startling assertion that, having experimented with it upon himself, he had every hope of beating the famous record of Methusaleh. Naturally the newspapers went wild about it, and so did joke-manufacturers and music-hall comedians all over the world. For a few months Karelsky was almost a household word. Then after a Brixton gentleman had cut his wife into six small pieces, it was generally recognized in Fleet Street that the Karelsky-Methusaleh episode was finished.... I remember asking Terry in a letter what he thought about it all, and receiving a non-committal reply that he couldn't express any opinion because his own work hadn't brought him into any contact with it. Karelsky, I gathered, was a man of many-sided activities.

Severn was more outspoken. "Whether it's all rot or not," he said, "you must admit that Karelsky's played the game rather well. You newspapermen ought to pass him a vote of thanks. He's saved you from having to rake up the Sea-serpent, anyhow."

But all that is really by the bye. The newspapers of the time are full of the Methusaleh business, just as they are of Severn's speeches in the House, and anybody deeply interested in either can search the files and read till he is tired.

VIII

I went to Vienna in the summer of that second year.

Terry had sent me a most cordial letter of welcome; I had engaged through Cook's a room at the Bristol; I had amassed a fair sum of money after a profitable year, and I was prepared to spend as much as need be on a deserved holiday. I chose the middle weeks of July, and it was gloriously sunny on the morning I arrived at Vienna. All the way from London I had been looking forward to that moment, for I felt confident that Terry would be on the platform to meet me. Yet he wasn't. I loitered for a while about the station precincts, thinking he might have been delayed on the way; and then, when he still didn't come, I took a cab to the address in the Laudon Gasse where he lodged.

It was only a short journey, hardly long enough for disappointment to turn into apprehension. I hadn't, of course, *asked* him to meet me, but he knew the train by which I should arrive, and it seemed so very unlikely that, if he were able, he wouldn't turn out for me.

The streets, I remember, were crowded with early-morning workers, and with the sun shining down upon it all, the panorama of blue sky and green trees and red trams and yellow houses might almost have been especially designed to cheer the traveller who hadn't been met. Even the tall apartment-house in the Laudon Gasse struck a cheerful note; it had been recently painted, and window-boxes of bright flowers gave it an almost gay appearance. But there was no sign of Terry. I waited some moments in the hall, and then, just when I was on the point of making as much row as I could on the door-bell, a girl emerged from somewhere in the interior.

"You wish to see Meester Terrington?" she said, with an atrocious accent.

I told her I did, and she answered, with a rather peremptory gesture: "Then you please to come with me."

She led me furlongs, I should think, along winding passages and up and down crooked stairways. Two or three houses had evidently been joined together, and the result, if a trifle bewildering, was certainly homely. I could have been quite happy in such a place myself.

Then, of course, I was thinking chiefly about Terry. "Is he ill?" I ventured to ask, as I followed the girl, and in case she might be unsure of my meaning, I translated the question into schoolboyish German. But she ignored it, and answered, with an absurd but comforting precision: "He iss not ill, but he hass a temperature...."

IX

A minute later I was with him.

I suppose he was bound to look slightly different after two years. He was sitting in an armchair with the sun on his face, and that, no doubt, gave him a look of thinness and pallor that wasn't real. Anyhow, he was delighted to see me. His eyes lit up with his delight—I could see that. He had been perfectly well, he said, until two days before, when somehow or other he had caught a chill. His temperature had been at one time as high as a hundred and two, but was now down to ninety-nine point five, which showed that he was almost better. He was so sorry I had had to find my own way from the station; he had badly wanted to come and meet me, but his doctor (who, incidentally, lived in the set of rooms immediately below) had absolutely forbidden him to go out. But he would be all right, he was certain, in a day or so.

There comes always, soon after the meeting of long-absent friends, a sudden hiatus when the first rapture of reunion is over and the quiet joy of companionship has hardly yet resumed its sway. At such a moment one says anything—*anything*—to break the awkward and intolerable silence. I, for example, when that moment came, made some remark about the comfort of his surroundings. "Better than Swinton Street, eh? ... And even a girl who speaks English—of a sort."

And he said: "Oh, yes, that's Mizzi." (He pronounced it "Mitzi.")

Then we began to talk about his work, and that finally bridged the hiatus. He said that he had plenty to do; and that he was working hard. I asked him if he were doing more than he could have done in London, and he said that he thought so. Then I asked him how he liked Karelsky, and he replied cautiously that he thought he was very clever.... He seemed even more than usually reticent, and when I hinted that I would like to be taken over Karelsky's laboratories, he told me that it wouldn't be possible. They were secret, apparently, and he had had to sign a paper that he wouldn't divulge anything of what went on in them. "Anybody would think you were inventing submarines, not serums!" I said laughingly and there the matter ended.

X

I hadn't seen him for two years. That fact, so simple and so obvious, was yet the hardest of all to realize. I kept on being startled by the revelation of what it meant; it gave me almost a shock, for instance, when I first heard him talking in fluent colloquial German. Those two years ... how *had* he managed to live them through? What had they meant to him?

I should never have known but for Mizzi. Mizzi, I soon found, was a person of great intelligence and even greater industry. It was she who practically ran the apartment-house (her mother being a semi-invalid), and it was under her energetic management that the general tone of the establishment was being constantly improved. She rose at six in the morning and worked till about midnight, and she had sent to her every week from Chicago an immense portfolio of a magazine called *Hotel-Keeping*. In appearance she might have been called good-looking had not that elusive thing, personality, made you forget her looks altogether. She was, as a matter of fact, rather an odd mixture of Latin and Teutonic physical attributes; her broad and essentially German forehead was balanced by dark eyes that might have been Spanish or Italian. But it was her personality that counted. She could bring you a cup of coffee and somehow, by the slightest of gestures, convey the fact that she was not a servant, but rather a hostess honouring her guests.

"Meester Terrington," she told me, as on that first evening she unlocked the front-door to let me out, "iss always at work. Too hard, I think.... You must tell him not to be so hard at work. He wished to go to work even with hiss temperature, but I call the doctor, and he said not. He not let him go even this morning to the station to meet you."

I said that I thought both she and the doctor had acted very rightly, and she went on, aloofly accepting my approval: "*I* would have come to meet you, but I did not know how you looked."

That was our first conversation. We had many others afterwards, and it was from them that I began to have an idea of what had been happening to Terry during those two years.

The *leit-motif* of it all had been Work. He had been working day after day for two years, and except on Sunday afternoons he had taken no holidays and had allowed himself no respite. "I tell him always to go to the Semmering, but he will not, because it iss necessary to go for the whole day." His hours in the laboratories were quite long enough in themselves, but he supplemented them by extra hours of work in his own room at night. He never went to theatre or concert or opera; he might have been exiled in a backwoods village, instead of in the gayest city in Europe. "He says to me that he likes not music," she said. But she thought there might also be another reason—that he hadn't enough money. "Karelsky," she said, "iss a very rich man, but he does not pay much to anybody else. There iss a doctor here who knows him." I said that I didn't know that Karelsky was rich, and she answered: "He gets the money from America—where all the money comes from."

She told me also that Terry had made no friends. "He says to me that he hass no father or mother or fiancée, and I am sorry for that. He also says that he hass no friend except you, but I think that iss his own fault, for there are many very nice people in Wien.... But he will not make friends. I think he likes nothing except hiss work. That iss why I give him the big room at the top of the new house, so that the others, if they come in a little drunken, shall not derange him."

I said to her: "Well, anyhow, he's not going to work so hard while I'm here. And next Sunday, whether he wants or not, he's coming with me to that place you mentioned—what was it?"

"The Semmering," she replied. "It hass wonderful mountains, but—do not forget—it iss necessary to haf the whole day. And he will say to you what he says always to me—that he cannot go because he must feed hiss mice at eleven o'clock.... Every Sunday at eleven o'clock he goes to feed hiss mice! What would you do to him?" There was a touch of indignation in her voice.

XI

She was right about the mice. They put a veto on the Semmering excursion. It was absolutely impossible, he said, to leave the delicate creatures for a whole twenty-four hours. If they were not fed regularly, the whole value of the experiments conducted on them would be destroyed. Could not, I suggested, somebody else feed them for once? He said there was nobody else on the premises on a Sunday. I asked who fed them while he had been away, and he said: "Some of the other men, but it would be impossible for them to do it on a Sunday." And so the mountains of the Semmering lay beyond our reach—barred from us by mice.

In the meantime there were the evenings. He couldn't, he said, however hard he tried, take time off during the day-time. Perhaps, if he hadn't been ill, he might have stolen a day, but as it was …. And so, with a regretful smile, he left me every morning to spend the warm and sunny hours as best I could, lounging about the cafés and boulevards, and occasionally, when such a busy person could spare me a moment, gossiping with Mizzi. Her accent was certainly atrocious, but her knowledge of English idiom and grammar surprised me by its completeness. It was only quite accidentally that I learned that Terry had taught her.

There comes to me now, as I write, the memory of a remark made years afterwards by someone who looked at Terry from a different angle.

"Leave him alone with somebody," was this remark, "and in a quarter of an hour he'll either have said nothing at all, or else he'll have begun to teach. He loves teaching because he loves giving more than taking away, and teaching is *that*."

I wasn't, even at the time, surprised that he had taught Mizzi. It seemed natural, since she had wanted to learn English and he had wanted to learn German. She told me that English was her third foreign language—French and Italian being already known to her. I asked her once why she was so keen to be a linguist. I was standing in the porch, smoking my after-breakfast cigar in the sunlight, and Mizzi's hands, everlastingly busy, were tending the flowers in the ground-floor window-boxes. She said, with a little shrug of her shoulders: "It will be very useful to me—someday...." And then, as if she had suddenly made up her mind that I could be trusted, she added: "I tell you this in confidence. Some day, when I haf the money, I shall buy all the houses along here and make them into one big hotel.... And then I will haf an omnibus at the station, and I will talk to English and French and Italian in their own language, so that it will all be very—what do you say?—*heimlich*...."

XII

The time passed quickly enough, but in a sort of way I was disappointed. I had expected to see much more of Terry; I had had in mind all kinds of excursions, including, if possible, a week-end trip along the Danube to Buda-Pesth. But his Work—his almighty Work—stood in the way. Not, of course, that either he or I was in the least bored. He was so simply and obviously delighted to be with me that I was all the more enraged that he couldn't manage to be with me oftener. But it was no use attempting to persuade him; his Work was a jealous god.

Only once did he mention Helen. It was on the last evening before my return to England, and we had strolled into the Burg-garten, where the heavy dusk-smelling trees were like a belt of magic separating us from the dazzling boulevards. There was a high moon overhead, and an orchestra playing the overture to *Egmont* in the open-air, and a crowd of Viennese, of all ages and classes, listening in silent rapture. Many of them followed the score from large folios, and if a careless foreigner so much as whispered a word or struck a match, shocked eyes stared at him and quelled him into silence. After the day's heat and bustle the kiss of the muted violins seemed to stir the air into cool waves and ripples; it was all delicious, enchanting and utterly unlike anything that could possibly happen in Hyde Park.

After the final chord he asked me suddenly how Helen was. I thought I had better not tell him of our quarrel, so I replied merely that I believed she was all right, although I hadn't seen much of her lately. And then, emboldened by his broaching of the subject, I asked him if he had heard from her.

He said: "Yes. She has written to me several times."

"Recently?"

"Over a year ago was the last time."

"And why not since?"

He shook his head and did not answer for a moment. And then, with the same odd suddenness, he added: "I don't want you to misunderstand.... She gave up writing to me—no doubt—because I gave up answering her."

"Why did you?"

"Because—I *couldn't* answer. The letters she wrote were the sort I didn't know *how* to answer."

The orchestra struck up again, and we walked stealthily away through the trees. It seemed to me that the opportunity had arrived for saying a good deal that I had intended to say some time or other. I told him outright that I thought he was in great danger of making a hash of his life. "Still?" he said; and the word was an answer to everything. I said that perhaps I had put the matter a shade too tragically, although, undoubtedly, it was serious. He was, to be quite frank about it, working too hard. "I don't care," I said, "how important your work is; there are two things you ought never to sacrifice to it—friendship and recreation."

"Well?"

The word was disconcerting. "Of course, I know it isn't any of my business, but still—you *are* working too hard—you *must* realize that. Why don't you take a holiday—a month, say—and come to England? My landlady could easily put you up."

He shook his head. It was good of me, he said, but he couldn't possibly manage it. He couldn't leave his work, and besides that, there were other reasons. It would cost too much, for one thing.... And then (with a sudden agitation of voice) why *should* he go to England? What was there in England for him?

"I'm only suggesting a holiday," I said.

He said that he had no time for holidays, and that if he had he wouldn't think of wasting four days of them in travelling to England and back.

I let myself go when he said that. I told him that it was absurd to say that he had no time for holidays—that a man *must* have time for holidays, unless he wants to kill himself from overwork. "And this extraordinary work of yours—which might be a sort of conjuring trick from the way you're bound to secrecy about it—"

I let myself go for five minutes, and then, for less than one minute he did just the opposite of letting himself go; he spoke very slowly and quietly, weighing up each word as he uttered it. "It's no good," he said, "thinking like that. You don't understand anything about my work.... You don't understand how I've given myself to it. I must give myself to something.... I *must*—always—and that's what you don't understand."

"But I *do* understand it," I answered. "It's simply that I don't agree with it. I say that you oughtn't to give yourself like that.... It would be a good thing if you were married, for then your wife wouldn't let you."

He said, for the second time: "I shall never marry."

"Why not?"

"Because—*really*—I don't like women. And when—if—I *do* like them, I hate liking them.... The ones I don't dislike are the ordinary ones—like Mizzi."

I said that it hadn't occurred to me that Mizzi was at all an ordinary woman.

He said: "Perhaps 'ordinary' isn't the word. What I mean is that we don't—*I* don't, at any rate—think of Mizzi as a woman exactly. She's business-like and does things—she's more like a man."

I said that it hadn't occurred to me that Mizzi was in the least like a man. Really, I must have been rather irritating, but he bore it all with exemplary patience. "She's the sort of woman I can stand, anyhow," he asserted.

"Then you'd better marry her," I replied jocularly, but he seemed to take it in all seriousness. "I don't want to marry at all," he repeated, "and neither does Mizzi. She doesn't bother with men. Her dream is to own a hotel, and she thinks a man would only get in her way...."

XIII

I find now that I have set down everything that I can definitely remember about that visit to Vienna. My diary doesn't help me, because I carelessly left it in London, and when I got back I just scrawled "Vienna" across the blank pages. All I can do is to think of a certain scene or place, and then, nine times out of ten, it's just a picture that comes to me, and not a happening at all. I can see, for instance, the tall yellow-painted houses in the Laudon Gasse, and the "Durchgang Verboten" notice on the door of Mizzi's private entrance, and the masses of velvet-red geraniums on the sills. Almost, as I write, I can smell those geraniums, and also the curious, half-musty aroma that haunts even the cleanest of those old Viennese houses.... I can see the wide, park-bordered boulevards, with the vermilion trams sparkling through the alternate sunlight and shadow, and (most clearly of all, this) the wrinkled old lady at the corner of the Opern Ring, who used to sell me citronnade. And I can see Mizzi standing in the porch to see me off, and automatically (since it was not her nature to waste even a moment) kicking away a few dead leaves that had blown on to the step. It was the night express that I was making for, and the evening sunlight was dancing on Mizzi's sherry-coloured hair as I turned and waved to her just as the car swung us round the corner into the Skoda Gasse. And Terry said: "The next time you come you won't need to put up at the Bristol. Mizzi told me that in future she'd always be glad to find you a room."

That "next time".... We had suggested that it should be at the end of another year, but it wasn't; it was at the end of five. So many things happened in the interval—things important enough in their own scheme of things, but not here. I got a decent sub-editorship, for instance, and chiefly owing to that the vaguely arranged trip fell through. It wasn't postponed; it was just cancelled; for a sub-editorship, more than anything else perhaps, curtails a man's freedom to roam over Europe on visits to even his most intimate friends. I sent Terry, however, a cordial invitation to visit me instead, but he declined for the usual reason—his Work.

To me, of course, those five years are anything but a gap; they're so crowded with business happenings that have no claim to be set down here. More than once I planned a visit to Vienna, but at the last moment something happened to prevent it; nor was I free even on holidays, for I usually combined them with business commissions that took me almost everywhere except to Central Europe. Terry's still regular letters expressed no disappointment, but then, they never expressed any emotion at all. Once he ended with "Mizzi sends you her kind regards," and then, after that, Mizzi always sent me her kind regards. No doubt he acquired the habit of writing it; and, anyhow, I regarded it as no more than an indication that Mizzi was still alive.

My diaries are rather a help to me here. I find in them quite a number of mentions of Severn, and even of Karelsky. Both men were almost continually in the limelight; if you take up any *Messenger* of the period the odds are that you will find either a Severn cross-examination or an account of Karelsky's rejuvenation of some illustrious personage. Fleet Street loved them both, the former for the constancy with which he yielded stimulating copy, and the latter for the uncanny accuracy with which he dropped sensations into the very heart of dead periods. I am thinking, of course, of the great Thibetan monastery sensation. Karelsky travelled, apparently, in Thibet, and somehow or other obtained an entrance into an old and inaccessible monastery in which, to his astonishment, he found that his own methods of rejuvenation had been practised for hundreds of years; so that, in fact, many of the monks were actually in their third and fourth centuries! Fleet Street "wrote up" the story in great glee, with maps of Thibet and excerpts from Sven Hedin and Younghusband all complete; but naturally Fleet Street did not believe a single word of it.

I remember discussing the matter with Severn at a sort of "house-warming" party I gave at my new rooms overlooking Lincoln's Inn Fields. Somebody said that Karelsky would have made a better journalist than scientist; and I think I answered that from my own professional point of view I would rather he remained a scientist, since as a journalist he would only be one liar amongst so many. Perhaps I said outright that in my opinion he was very little better than a charlatan and an impostor. But Severn shook his head. "Karelsky's more than that," he answered. "I shouldn't have recommended Terry with him if he'd been a mere market-place quack. Of course, there is something of the quack in him, and he's obviously running this Thibetan stuff for his own advertisement.... But I shouldn't like to call anything that Karelsky says an absolute lie. In my opinion he's one of the very few first-class geniuses the world possesses...."

"And you really think this story of his—"

Severn smiled. "I prefer to express no opinion," he said. "I am far from saying that Karelsky could not, if he wished, tell the most thundering of lies. But in this case ... well, I just don't know. Oddly enough, I met a well-known Harley Street physician only yesterday and he assured me, from his own personal and rather secret knowledge of Thibet, that Karelsky was perfectly right—although, of course, he deplored the sensationalism of it...."

And there the matter ended. I have mentioned it to show how impossible I found it to make up my mind about Karelsky. He had been, and remained still, an enigma.

During those years Severn and I contrived to meet fairly often—sometimes in town and less often, when Helen was away, at the End House. If ever I were tempted to think the worst of him, I should only need to ask myself the question: Why *should* he have troubled to help me as much as he did? I know, of course, what his reply would be—a suave smile and an assurance that he did it merely for the pleasure he got in doing it, like any other voluptuary. I am to suppose, therefore, that he voluptuously interviewed the editor of the *Messenger* and persuaded him that I was worth a sub-editorship. "My dear fellow," he told me once, "I really do what I like, whatever it happens to be. You'd be surprised if you knew what I was capable of.... For God's sake, don't think of me as a sort of maundering philanthropist."

All this time he was rising rapidly in his profession. He loved publicity for its own sake, and he specialized in cases that gave him it—divorce, criminal, and civil. One year, it was freely rumoured, he earned over fifty thousand pounds. At the same time in the House he had made a first-class reputation, and was almost certain of the Solicitor-Generalship when his party came into office. He had had marvellous, almost incredible good fortune, and *he kept on having it*. He couldn't write a book without it going into seven editions. He couldn't dabble in art without exhibiting at the Paris Salon, and, under a pseudonym, attracting a considerable amount of attention. A newspaper friend of mine once summed him up rather neatly. We were speculating on which of his many activities represented his real natural bent. "All of them and none of them," was my friend's enigmatic opinion. "He's just born to be one thing and one thing only—a *success*. It's only an accident that he paints, writes, and harangues a jury. If he'd been a rag-and-bone man down the Mile End Road he'd have been just as big a success.... While other men, perhaps far better and just as clever, are born to be failures...."

When I look back on those years, I see Severn most clearly of all in his surroundings at White's. It is as if all the memories of meeting him there were laid one on top of another to form a composite picture of a single typical meeting. There were sherry, oysters, port, coffee, cigars, and talk. The talk was always brilliant and the port was always strong. Nothing very much was ever said about Helen, but Severn's attitude to me was so cordial that I knew he must think her's rather absurd. Sometimes he would tell me that she hadn't been well and that she had gone abroad to recuperate. She must have been out of England a very large proportion of those five years. I seem to remember asking the question, "How's Helen?" and receiving always the answer: "Oh, she's at Ostend...." (Or Etretat, Cannes, Biarritz, Palm Beach, or wherever it was.) June, meanwhile, was at her boarding-school, and later on, at Newnham. I met her only once, during a summer vacation; she had grown up into a normal, healthy, sport-loving youngster with freckled cheeks and just a touch of her mother's prettiness. She talked about nothing but tennis.

XIV

And so the gap (if it is a gap) is bridged, and at the further side of it there stands out in my memory a bright June day with the breeze from the river rushing up Bouverie Street and the sunlight glinting in the distance on the cross of St. Paul's. I had lunched at the *Cheshire Cheese*, and when I returned to the *Messenger* office the 'phone boy told me that my man Roebuck (whom, to be quite accurate, I shared with two other tenants) had been trying to get me on the telephone. I rang him up immediately and heard, without the least surprise, that a telegram had arrived for me at my rooms. But then he said: "It's signed 'Mizzi'" (he pronounced it to rhyme with "dizzy") "and it comes from Vienna, sir. And it says, 'Please come immediately Terrington ill'...."

It took me seconds—perhaps moments—to realize what it meant.

"Shall I pack your things, sir?"

I was too dazed to make a decision just then. I said I would get home early and discuss the matter.

XV

In the end, of course, I *did* go. There was never really any doubt about it, when once my mind had grasped the situation. Mizzi was the very last person who would be likely to send for me without reason. Fortunately my editor was able to grant me the necessary vague leave of absence. I rang up Severn at his chambers, thinking to talk over the matter with him, but his man informed me that he was out of town.

Thus, once again, the boat-train from Victoria, the Channel crossing, the dash across Paris from the Gare St. Lazare to the Gare de l'Est, the terrific crawl through the Arlberg, and then, in the sun of early morning, Vienna, with the sky like a blue enamel bowl, and the temperature soaring already.

CHAPTER FOUR

I

MIZZI was there on the platform—a calm, exquisite Mizzi, who seemed to have grown more serene than ever during the five years since I had last seen her. "I knew you would come," she said, pressing my hand, and the accent was better—oh, *much* better. She led me out of the station without saying a word except to hope that I had had a good journey. Then, in the station-yard, she gave the porter a few business-like directions about my hand-luggage, and find imperiously prevented me from summoning a cab. I soon saw the reason why. It came in the form of a smart motor equipage to seat six or eight passengers and emblazoned in gold letters on a blue background, "Hotel London." "You see," said Mizzi, as the chauffeur opened the door for us, "I haf got my omnibus...." Not till we were speeding along the sunlit boulevard did she mention Terry. And then she whispered: "Ever since I sent my telegraph I haf been wondering whether you will be angry."

"Why?"

She said: "I sent it because—because I felt I *must* send it. But you—when you see him—you may think I haf brought you here on—what you call it?—a fool's errand?"

"But why?"

The car swerved round a corner and she almost fell into my arms. "When you see him," she said, "you may say to me, 'He iss not ill at all....' But—we cannot talk about it here.... In a few moments you will haf breakfast with me, and I will explain everything."

"But surely—if we go to your place—Terry will see us?"

"No. He does not know you are coming. You must tell him that you haf come here on some business.... And also, he will be at hiss work by now—he goes very early in the morning."

"He's well enough to go to work, then?"

She shrugged her shoulders, and answered: "That iss what I thought you would say. I am sure you will be very angry with me.... But wait—wait till I haf explained...."

II

The car turned into the Laudon Gasse, but it was not the familiar apartment-house that confronted me when, a moment later, I stepped out on to the pavement. It was the "Hotel London," with a frontage of eighty feet, and an electric sign over the entrance. And also there was an uniformed porter to attend to my luggage, a bureau, an Aufzug fur Personen, a Gastzimmer, and a notice declaring "English Spoken Here: On Parle Français; Si Parla Italiano...." Mizzi could see my astonishment as I penetrated further into such colossal metamorphosis; and I could see her pride. She said, almost apologetically: "It iss a very good hotel. Ass good ass the Bristol, but not so expensif.... My mother—did you know?—died two years ago, and the last thing she said wass to warn me not to do all this because it would not pay.... But—I do it—all the same—and it *does* pay...."

Five minutes later we were sitting together in her comfortably furnished sitting-room, with an English breakfast of ham-and-eggs before us. And she was trying to tell me why she had sent me that telegram.

He *was* ill, she said, whether I thought so or not. His going to work really *proved* that he was ill, because the hours he spent at the laboratories were absurd. He practically lived there. He went very early in the mornings and came back very late at nights, and he had grown very quiet and silent, hardly speaking a word even when he met her, which wasn't very often. He had been overworking for years, but lately he had been more than overworking. She was sure he was on the verge of a breakdown. There had been a doctor staying at the hotel—a German nerve specialist—and his opinion, formed merely from observation of Terry during the few seconds of a lift-journey, had been sufficiently disquieting. "And then once—but that wass many weeks ago—he wass ill when he came in at night, and he began to say things to himself in a very strange way. I would think he wass drunken, but he does not drink.... He talked about hiss work, and you, and somebody named Helen.... Who iss this Helen? Do you know?"

I wonder if the shock of that sent me pale suddenly. She seemed to notice something in my face, anyway, for she went on, gazing at me intently: "I wondered if this Helen wass a lady in England whom he had known a long time ago...."

She paused, and then, as if accepting the fact that there were things I could tell her, but wouldn't, went on: "So you see why I sent for you. I am afraid for him—I am afraid of what will happen. You must take him away—to England—anywhere—anywhere where he cannot work.... Otherwise—I do not like to think of what will happen."

"When can I see him?" I asked.

She said: "He will come back here to-night—probably very late—and you must tell him then, and persuade him, and not go away till he hass given in...." She leaned forward across the table towards me and suddenly laid her cool hand on mine. "Oh, I know it will not be easy for you—I know it iss like trying to move a rock ... but...." An atom of calmness left her as she continued: "I can do nothing. I haf tried, but it iss no use. He takes no notice of me now.... Oh, I know how I haf deranged you—you leave your work in London and come all the way here thinking he iss ill, and then you find he iss not ill as you expect—I know you think I ought not to haf sent this telegraph for you—but I—*I* am glad you haf come—because you can help him. Oh, you *must* help him—you *must* take him away where he cannot work. He iss *worth* helping—he iss worth anything that can be done—*you* know that, don't you?"

I nodded, and she suddenly began to cry. "It iss stupid of me," she said, wiping her eyes. "I did not think I should be so stupid.... But after seven years, I like him very much. I did not ever meet any man—except him—whom I could marry...."

So that was it.

I thought of that afternoon, years before, when Helen had made a similar confession across the table at Rumpelmayer's. But Helen, of course, had told me differently; she had been excited, ecstatic; whereas Mizzi was calm and a little sad. What was it in Terry that could so attract them both—Helen the brilliant, pleasure-loving woman who was still, in so many ways, a girl; and Mizzi, the calm, business-like girl who was almost more than a woman?

And then I remembered how, on my former visit to Vienna, I had jocularly suggested to him that he should marry Mizzi.... Well, why not? If only he loved her a little, it wouldn't be at all a bad match. She on her side had love for him, brains, energy, and a flourishing business of her own. Hadn't he once told me that she was "the sort of woman he could stand, anyway"? ... Supposing they were to marry? The idea curiously attracted me.... Terry as a hotel-proprietor—but no, of course; Mizzi would always be that; she wouldn't be such a fool as to let him have anything to do with the business. He would plod along with his research-work, and she would look after him and see that he didn't overwork, and on fine Sundays she would positively compel him to go with her to the Semmering.... And I should spend my annual holidays at the Hotel London and take the pair of them to all the theatres and operas.... Delightful vision!

I said, marvelling at her: "And yet, although you feel like that about him, you want me to take him back with me to England?"

And she answered: "Yes, if it iss the best for him. I want anything to happen that iss the best for him...."

III

We did not talk for long because she had so much business to attend to. But she had said enough—enough for anger, if there had ever been any—to melt into compassion.

The day was very hot, and I was very sleepy after the long journey. I didn't go out of doors except to send a reassuring telegram to Roebuck;

most of the time I spent dozing in an armchair in the cool lounge. Towards the red-gold dusk I fell asleep, and it was Terry who waked me. I was startled, because I hadn't expected him to arrive so soon. Mizzi must have prepared him about me, for *his* surprise, though obvious, was restrained. "How are you?" he began with an odd sort of calmness. "Mizzi says you're over here on business."

Mizzi had evidently done her work well, which was fortunate in view of my sleepily dazed condition. I could only stagger to my feet and shake his hand and reply: "Oh, I'm fairly fit, I'm glad to say. How are you?"

And then I really saw him. Till then the bright glow of the sunset through the windows and the cloudiness of disturbed sleep had made me stare vaguely without seeing anything at all. But the movement out of the chair gave me sight, and as soon as I saw, I was almost dazed again. For he was *different*. Of course, after five years, he was bound to be different, but somehow the difference was different. It wasn't that he looked particularly ill (though he certainly didn't look well); it was just that he had a look in him of somebody else—somebody whom I had never seen before. Perhaps if I had met him then for the first time, I shouldn't have been in the least alarmed; I should have thought it was all perfectly natural—the blue eyes like sharpened swords, the short-cropped hair with its earliest streaks of iron-grey, the pale, lined cheeks, and the shoulders with their hint of a stoop.... Good God! And he was hardly thirty! He looked fifty to me as I saw him that night. He looked a genius, a poet, a madman, an eastern seer—anything and anybody except the Terry I had known.

Only his voice and mannerisms were the same. He still spoke with an air of reluctance. He still half-smiled. "Extraordinary," he said, "that you should arrive to-day. Really extraordinary...."

"Why?"

"Because to-day"—and he suddenly seemed to grow excited—"I can't explain it to you—not in detail.... But it means—almost certainly it means—success in the work I am busy on—success after all these years—after so many disappointments."

I congratulated him (though I was still too dazed to do anything with much show of fervour), and then he began a slow cross-examination. How long was I staying? Had Mizzi given me a good room? Was my business likely to occupy all or most of the time? I answered as well as I could, and then, with astonishing calmness, he said: "Don't you think that, in the circumstances, I deserve a holiday?"

He went on, before amazement gave me a chance of replying: "Well, I'm going to take one, anyhow. I'm going to take a week—at least a week. And you can combine business with pleasure and come with me. We'll go to Buda by one of the Danube steamers. You wanted to do that trip the last time you were here, didn't you? ... I think the boat leaves about eight to-morrow morning—Mizzi will tell us. And then, after our jaunt, you can go back to London and I can come back here and get to work again."

It would have been positively comic but for the wildness of his eyes and the hectic colour that had suddenly flooded his cheeks. There was I, wondering how on earth to persuade him to take a holiday; and then, before I had even time to begin, he was actually suggesting one himself.... "Look here," I exclaimed rather bewilderedly. And then, very uneloquently, I put it to him that a few days in Buda wasn't my idea of a holiday for him, and that what he needed was a far longer one—months, in fact. Why couldn't he put work on one side for a while and accompany me back to England?

I knew from the way he shook his head that it wasn't the slightest use attempting to persuade him. There was nothing in England for him, he said. He didn't care if he never saw England again. Besides, he couldn't put his work on one side for months at a time—the idea was unthinkable. He could spare a week at most—as a concession to me and in celebration of the success he had achieved—and then he must go back again to the laboratories. Because he had achieved *something* wasn't any reason for resting on his oars; the *something* was only a fraction of what was to be achieved in due course.... He exclaimed, with a curious ecstasy in his voice: "I'm wonderfully happy—just wonderfully.... There comes a time when you turn a sort of corner in life, and see all the road behind you that you have traveled. And to look round and see *that*, if you've slacked, is the most miserable sight on earth—but if you *haven't* slacked—if you've really done anything—it's *great*—it makes you feel"—he laughed and ended up: "that you deserve a short holiday, at any rate."

So (continuing) it must be Buda. The river-trip was very enjoyable, and he was sure we should both have a fine time. Mizzi would tell us of a good hotel in Buda....

We had dinner in his room and talked afterwards until late, and I don't think I ever remember him so garrulous. Yes, garrulous. But he wouldn't, for all that, tell me what his success that day had been. He kept throwing out obscure hints—as if the guarding of the secret obsessed and worried him. Once I mentioned the word "cancer," but he shrugged his shoulders rather excitedly and told me to guess that, or anything else, if I liked. It wasn't *he* who insisted on secrecy, he said, but Karelsky, and of course he was under obligation to obey Karelsky's rule.... The whole matter seemed to me just slightly childish, for if he couldn't tell me anything of importance, why didn't he change the subject? But he didn't; perhaps he couldn't. He kept reverting to it at every pause in the conversation; he kept assuring me that his work had made him wonderfully happy; there was nothing, he said, in the whole world so wonderful as doing what was worth doing. All that sort of talk rather surprised me; it reminded me of a revivalist's rhapsody on the joys of salvation. I'm not sneering—don't think that. It's just that I couldn't have imagined him saying some of the things he did say. He *was* different—mightily different.

IV

We went to Buda-Pesth.

When I think of all that happened as a result of our going, the question occurs to me: What *drove* us there? That we *were* driven, by some kind of ironical fate, is a tempting theory if only because of the numerous reasons against going which were either ignored or overridden. I don't know even now why in the end I agreed to it. I positively loathed the thought of getting up early in the morning and, after two days and two nights of travel, embarking on a third day. Besides, I had left my work to visit a sick friend, not a friend who cheerfully invited me to go on holiday with him. Terry, of course, wasn't to know that. He thought I had come to Vienna on business, and as I had vaguely assured him that the business could be transacted at any time, the main avenue of argument against the Buda trip was closed to me. All I could say was that I was tired after the journey, to which he replied that nothing could be more suitable for a tired traveller than a whole day on a river-steamer. "Besides," he added, "I know how keen you were to see Buda the last time you were here." (That was true enough.) "And—to tell you the truth—I have never quite forgiven myself for not going with you then. It was selfish of me...."

What could I say or do after that? When I told Mizzi we were going she was both astonished and pleased. "And he suggested it himself?" she said, as she wrote me out the address of a hotel in Pesth. "That iss *so* good—and you are evidently such a big influence to him." (I think she was wrong there, whatever it was that she meant.) "But, of course, one week—it iss *nothing*. It iss when you are with him in Buda that you must persuade him again.... I think you know how to do it—oh, I am so glad that I sent for you!"

So we went on board the paddle-boat at the Praterkai the next morning. It was one of those dim preludes to a hot summer's day, when the sun climbs slowly through opaque mists, and the heat seems first of all to rise up like an exhalation from the earth. As the boat chugged its way downstream the air was deliciously cool and fragrant, and there was something indescribably drowsy in the mist-hung panorama of fields and homesteads. Terry sat with me on the top deck, and during the greater part of the journey I was busy making up my mind about him. I think it was his extraordinary buoyancy that was most disquieting, and that made me realize, in the end, that Mizzi hadn't brought me on a fool's errand. He was *too* exuberant; *too* talkative. Again, as on the evening before, the things he said were the things I couldn't have believed he would ever say. He told me, for example (and without being asked), that he had done with women. He liked Mizzi because there was no nonsense about her, because she never tried to "play the woman game" with him. Not that it would affect him if she did, except that he would think less of her.

I asked him if he ever heard from Helen, and he replied, almost triumphantly: "Never. Never since that last letter that I didn't answer."

I told him that she had taken to spending most of her time out of England, and he interrupted, with his triumph fading into mere excitement: "I don't want to hear about her. I tell you—haven't I already told you?—that I've cut myself adrift from all that part of my life? It's gone—it's almost forgotten—and now, with this far more wonderful happiness, I don't want to have anything to do with it—even in memory...." And he added, unnecessarily, that he had changed during those years that I had not seen him.

It was then that I suggested that he should marry Mizzi. Rather to my astonishment he didn't indignantly protest, or even repeat his assurance that he had done with women. He said merely: "It's a hundred to one she wouldn't want me. And, in any case, it seems a pity to interrupt our friendship."

He said that sincerely, mind—without the slightest trace of cynicism.

V

I see now, as I think of it, that gold day of June, with the rippling Danube under the breeze, and the sunshine glinting on the towers and windows of Bratislava. I see the mists lifting towards midday, and the ebb of humanity from the scorching decks to the *Speisesaal*, where the wide-open windows are only an arm's length over the water. Everywhere, like a seething tropical incense, is the tang of paprika; paprika flavouring the soup: paprika stuffed with rice as an entrée; a slice of paprika with the veal and a wedge with dessert; rust-brown paprika pepper in all the cruets; golden Magyar wine and paprika—polyglot chatter and flashing gold-filled teeth and paprika—Heavens, what a meal—a strident C Major symphony of a meal.... And then the beat of the engines suddenly hushed, and the boat gliding against some wayside landing-place where all the local folk are gathered—red-bloused, yellow-bloused peasant women and a *gendarmerie* in blue.... Swift and magical interlude—with the brown-skinned men, waist-naked, rowing in the river, and the boatmen half-singing as they haul in the gangway—"*Achtung—Achtung*...." Then off again into midstream, chug-chugging under the porcelain blaze of the afternoon....

But at last, with tropic swiftness, the sun sinks low and dusk falls; it is the grey Danube, and then the black Danube, with the forests rolling down to the far edge of it. And the tang of paprika, lulled for a while, is spreading and deepening again, until the boat is almost hushed with it—as if the ghosts of all the lunches and dinners that have ever been served on board have come back to haunt.... It is intolerable and unforgettable, with the waiters slinking round and the bald heads, glistening with sweat, and the clink of glasses, and the lights of Pesth already aglow in the southern sky, and Terry lingering over his coffee and telling me how pitiable it would be to interrupt his friendship with Mizzi by marrying her....

All that comes back to me now, as I write, more clearly than I could ever have believed.

VI

We reached Pesth at seven o'clock, and drove to the hotel that Mizzi had recommended—the Andrassy. There we booked rooms, and thence, half an hour later, strolled out into the cool and flower-scented streets. The city was living, enchanted—the pavements thronged, and all the cafés noisy with speech and laughter. At one of them, as we passed, a couple were just leaving, and we eagerly took their places, squirming our way amidst the shrubs and marble-topped tables. Terry had coffee and I a bottle of Tokay, and the orchestra (one fiddle and a piano) played very languorously Toselli's *Serenade*. It was the sort of night when you never dream of asking what time it is—when life seems to rush at you full-tilt and bring the tears to your eyes (or perhaps it is only the wine that does that; one never knows.) And then suddenly, as

I was lighting an immense cigar, I saw a man approaching whose face I vaguely recollected; he evidently knew me as well, for he smiled and held out his hand with great cordiality.... Ah, I remembered—his name was Bentley. I didn't know him at all well, and I daresay if he had seen me in a London restaurant he wouldn't have bothered to introduce himself at all. But Buda-Pesth was different, and my single meeting with him at one of the Englehart parties in Eaton Square gave him ample excuse for affability.

I introduced him to Terry, and he sat down and accepted a cigar. He was pleasant enough company, though no doubt he was better pleased to see us than we were to see him. He was in an English firm of electrical engineers, he told us, and had been sent out to some God-damned spot in the middle of Transylvania to see what was wrong with some equally God-damned turbine. And the God-damned job had taken three weeks, and as he didn't know a word of the God-damned language he had had what might be termed a perfectly God-damned time. But he was on his way back now, thank heaven, and would continue the journey by the Orient Express that evening. "Awfully jolly meeting you in a place like this, eh? Damn it all, it's decent to hear my own voice again, let alone yours. But you're not the only English folks I have seen in this city. There were an interesting couple at the hotel where I stayed overnight—the Andrassy."

"Our hotel," I interpolated, and he went on: "Oh, well, then, you're almost bound to meet them. I didn't—I was only there for a few hours, and the chap was with his wife—very *en famille* sort of thing, don't you know—and besides, I only knew him by sight. But I believe you once told me he was a great pal of yours—Geoffrey Severn, the lawyer johnny...."

I remember saying, very calmly: "Really? How extraordinary! And his wife as well, you say?"

And Bentley's casual reply: "Yes.... Damned pretty woman, too...."

VII

Heaven knows how I got rid of the fellow after that. Perhaps I was discourteous; perhaps he thought I had been suddenly taken ill; more likely, of course, he assumed that I was merely drunk. And perhaps I was. I don't remember what I said to him, or what he said to me either; all I know is that, drunk or not, by the time he had gone, I had reached a very definite decision, and that was that, whatever happened, Terry and I must avoid a meeting with the Severns.

Terry was silent—had been silent, indeed, ever since Bentley's intrusion. As soon as we were alone together I leaned across the table and put the matter to him as carefully as I could. (The orchestra, I remember, struck up with feverish inaccuracy the overture to *Ruy Blas*.) We had better, I said, to avoid any possible unpleasantness, change our hotel. We could cancel the booking if we hurried, and get rooms somewhere else. It was the wisest thing to do, as he would realize if he thought about it. "After all, you can see how awkward the meeting *might* be, can't you?" The trouble was, of course, that I didn't want to tell him the chief reason for the awkwardness—my own seven-years' estrangement from Helen.

I argued for a quarter of an hour at least, and then, inferring from his silence that he was wholly or partly in agreement, I suggested returning to the hotel. He nodded, and I paid the bill. Not till we were outside on the pavement did he speak, and then he said quietly: "*You* can change hotels if you like, but *I* shan't."

And he was adamant. It was as hopeless to attempt to persuade him to leave the Andrassy as it had been to persuade him to come for a holiday to London. He just set his teeth and held firm. He wasn't going to alter *any* of his arrangements—not for her, or Severn, or anybody else. *He* wasn't afraid of a meeting. What had happened to him before couldn't happen to him again—he was proof against it. And he wasn't going to run away and hide as if he had anything to fear.

I pointed out that it wasn't a question of running away, but merely of avoiding possible unpleasantness. He had put an end to the correspondence between them by not answering her letters—would *that* make a reunion very easy? But he said: "I don't care whether it's easy or not. If she goes out of her way to meet me, that's her affair, not mine. *I* shan't make a scene, I promise you. But I won't, whatever's going to happen, skulk round the corner to some other place." He added, apologetically: "I hate to get my own way against your wishes, but I'm afraid you'll have to put up with it for once."

And that was so. I had to put up with it. I had to put up with his determination to have supper in the public dining-room of the Andrassy merely because "we're going to do exactly what we should have done." I couldn't make him budge an inch by persuasion, but I guessed that where argument failed altogether, guile might slightly succeed. Accordingly, when we reached the hotel I piloted him into an alcove of the *gastzimmer*, whence we could see the rest of the room without being too prominently on view ourselves. That was something, at any rate.

I don't think either of us enjoyed the supper very much. Terry was silent most of the time, and I found it hard to keep going a one-sided conversation. I kept looking at the swing-doors that led into the vestibule, looking at the Pesthians remorselessly picking their gold-filled teeth with fibre tooth-picks, looking at the tables as they filled and emptied; and at first hoping, and then, as time passed, even believing that the Severns must be dining elsewhere that night. It was already long past eight o'clock, and the room was getting emptier. The strain of waiting stamped its features indelibly on my memory; I can picture now its rather showy magnificence—panelled walls and gilt-and-white cornice, and so on—and, by way of contrast lower down, a wavy green smear of insecticide running all round the walls just above the floor. I remember that while the waiter was taking our order a large blue-black cockroach crawled sedately from under the table and disappeared into a hole near the skirting-board.

A quarter to nine, and still there was no sign of the Severns. And then, just when I was about to suggest leaving the table, I saw a couple of waiters detach themselves from the serving and rush to hold open the doors with an obsequiousness that seemed to indicate the approach of at least an heir-apparent of a Balkan principality.

But no ... it was Severn.

Severn, in an exquisitely summery lounge-suit, Severn laughing and talking and gesticulating with that queer, panther-like litheness that marked him out from all other men in the world....

But the really odd thing was that the woman who was with him wasn't Helen.

VIII

The two walked to a table at the further end of the room. It was a specially reserved table, decorated with a mass of cut flowers and laid with an assortment of cutlery and wine-glasses that suggested a banquet rather than a meal. Waiters positively surrounded them as they took their seats, and by extraordinary good fortune Severn's back was towards me, while his companion was gazing straight in my direction across his shoulder. She was certainly, as Bentley had assured me, a damned pretty woman.... But, as I said before, the odd thing—yes, the *very* odd thing—was that she wasn't Helen.

We were, I think, as much relieved as surprised, for the moment. I whispered across to Terry: "Severn has just come, but Helen isn't with him. Can you see them? ... It's some woman whose face I don't seem to recognize."

And he replied, quite calmly: "Neither do I. I can see them in the mirror.... What language is it they're speaking?"

We tried to listen, but it wasn't very easy. Terry was certain it wasn't German, and I thought it wasn't French or Italian or Spanish. "Probably," I said, "it's Hungarian—though it's rather an odd language for him to know. And the woman, maybe, is some Magyar countess, if there are such things.... Severn *does* know everybody everywhere, doesn't he?"

For several minutes he didn't answer. Then, with a rather impatient gesture, he said: "I think we've finished. Let's go for a walk before bedtime." So we rose and walked to the doors, and by an especial miracle on our behalf, Severn didn't look round. But the woman was watching us, and with her creamy elbows on the table and a cocktail held languorously to her lips, she looked as exotically lovely as any woman I had ever seen. Severn had good taste.

We went out into the fragrant night-smelling streets, crossed the suspension-bridge over the Danube, and climbed the hill into the old town of Buda. Seeing Severn, after the prolonged tension of expecting to see him, had been almost an anti-climax; indeed, when I thought about it, a meeting with him wouldn't be at all a bad idea provided that Helen wasn't with him. There was no doubt that the rest of our stay in Pesth would be the brighter for his company and conversation. I almost hoped we *should* meet him. And as for the woman, perhaps she would be worth meeting as well.... All these and other thoughts wandered idly through my mind as we strolled about the quiet streets of Buda. It was a Hans Andersen town, with fairy palaces and terraces and castles all hanging precipitously over the moonlit ribbon of the Danube; and for some reason the quiet loveliness of it made me think of Mizzi and of the almost perfect ending there would be to all Terry's difficulties if only he could grow to love her. I even said to him, as we were descending the hill on the way back to the hotel: "Wouldn't it have been jolly if we could have brought Mizzi here with us?"

He looked at me in a way that told me that his thoughts were very far indeed away from Mizzi.

"She could never leave her hotel," he replied, and that, in his mind, was the end of her.

IX

Two hours later I was in bed and asleep, and three hours later I cautiously opened my bedroom door to see Terry standing, fully dressed and very pale, in the corridor. We had been given adjacent rooms on the top floor—furthest from the cockroaches—and I had been very tired and sleepy. Heaven knows how long he had been knocking before I was awakened. "You've not been to bed yet?" I exclaimed dazedly; and he said: "It's not late—not much after one o'clock. Can I come in?"

Of course he could. I switched on the central light and closed the door after him. "I hope you haven't been knocking for hours," I told him. "But, as a matter of fact, I'm about as sleepy as I've ever been in my life...." That was a hint, and when he didn't take it, I went on: "Is everything all right?"

Then immediately I could see that everything *wasn't* all right. He sat down on a chair and clenched his hands between his knees. "I—I think perhaps—I oughtn't to have wakened you," he said at length.

"Oh, not at all—if you want my help in any way. You don't look very well, and I'm glad you came.... What's the matter?"

He didn't, or else he couldn't, tell me for a few moments. I lit a cigarette and made myself as comfortable as I could; I guessed that whatever he had to say would take some time. And then at last he began, heavily: "I've been down to the bureau."

"The hotel bureau?"

"Yes."

"Well?"

"I wanted to .... You see .... I had an idea...." He stopped, as if grappling with some central impossibility. Then he made another beginning. "The clerk knows German—of course—and we had a talk."

"Yes?"

"A long talk. About Severn ... and that woman with him...."

And then it all came out torrentially. "The clerk didn't know he was English. They came here last week—from Belgrade—rolling in money—took the best rooms in the place.... And he—the clerk—showed me the names in the register—not Severn, but some French name—with an address in Paris.... And of course—you see what I mean—they're staying here together—Monsieur and Madame, it says in the register—there's absolutely no doubt about it.... So that...." And he shrugged his shoulders to indicate the inexpressible.

X

Perhaps a seasoned man of the world would have jumped to the incriminating conclusion the moment he had seen them. The idea had, as a matter of fact, occurred to me, though I had at first managed to dismiss it as something that was no concern of mine. Terry's statement convinced me absolutely, yet an almost self-protective instinct made me dispute it. I remember sitting on the bed and propounding a marvellous theory that the man we had seen wasn't Severn at all, but his double—some innocent Parisian whose *bona-fides*, if inquiry were made, would be found perfectly correct. After all, Bentley had distinctly stated that he hadn't *met* him; he had only *seen* him, just as we had. And even we hadn't heard him speak a word of English.... All this, for some curious reason, I expounded to Terry as if I meant it, and after a long pause he squashed it utterly by saying that the handwriting in the register was Severn's beyond the shadow of a doubt.

Even then I went on laboriously arguing. Subconsciously, perhaps, I was gaining time to think. "A mere signature," I remember saying, absurdly, "proves nothing." And I made some vague and platitudinous remark about the necessity of having overwhelming evidence before drawing conclusions.

And then there came a long silence, a silence full of small sounds and murmurs—the creak of a floorboard somewhere, the scutter of a beetle, the distant—the very distant—shouting of late revellers. I was certain—*certain* that the man was Severn, and that what Terry had said was all perfectly true; yet the certainty was outweighed in my mind by the far more momentous revelation that Terry was ill, and that his staring eyes and the hard drive of his breathing could only point in one ominous direction. He was, as Mizzi had said, on the verge of a breakdown. What he wanted was rest and sleep and freedom from work and worry, and he wasn't getting any of it. What an irony that we had come to Buda-Pesth for a holiday! ... He *must* sleep anyway.... I took him by the arm and said, as firmly and calmly as I could: "Look here, Terry, there's nothing to be gained by arguing this out at one o'clock in the morning. We don't actually know for certain that the man is Severn, and even if we did we could do nothing. So go to bed and try to sleep, and then in the morning maybe—"

But he shook himself free and walked across the room to the window. "Moonlight," he muttered; pulling aside the paper blind. He stared hard for a moment at the pavements below, and then, swinging round suddenly, exclaimed: "You say that if we *did* know for certain, we could do nothing?"

"Nothing at all, I assure you, and that's why it's all the more important that we shouldn't discuss it at this hour. So come now...."

Again I led him towards the door, and this time, without further protest, he allowed me to pilot him along the corridor to the door of his own room. He was muttering to himself, as I bade him good-night: "Do nothing.... That's what you say ... just nothing ... nothing at all...."

XI

I oughtn't to have left him. I can see now that I oughtn't, but I had an idea then that if he were left alone he would go to sleep. Not, of course, immediately; I didn't do that myself. I lay awake, I think, for two hours or more, smoking cigarette after cigarette and pondering. But it wasn't Severn who occupied the centre of the stage. Perhaps it was odd that his personal affairs stirred me so little; but then, I had always felt that he was incalculable. There was hardly a thing in the world, good or bad, that I would ever have swore that he wouldn't or couldn't do. I don't mean to assert that I wasn't surprised to find him running off with another woman; I *was* surprised, but, if you know what I mean, I wasn't surprised to be surprised.

What mattered most was Terry's health. His great need was for rest and tranquillity of mind, and it was very evident that neither was to be obtained in Buda-Pesth. We must leave it, therefore; and I fell asleep with that decision firmly fixed in my mind. I think I must have slept heavily, for I remember nothing till I opened my eyes to see Terry in my room again, still fully dressed. It was past dawn, for the window, as he pulled the blind away from it, threw a ghostly spotlight over his head and shoulders. "I'm sorry," he said. "I didn't intend to wake you."

I stammered some sort of enquiry, and he answered:

"I only came in to see if you *were* awake. You left your door unlocked.... Shall we go downstairs and have breakfast?"

"What time is it?"

"Past six."

"Isn't that too early?"

"Not in this country."

"All right, then." I agreed the more readily because it began to occur to me that the earlier the breakfast the less the chance of meeting Severn.

He told me while I washed and dressed that he hadn't been able to sleep a wink, and that the only interesting things had been a couple of cockroaches on his window-ledge. He said, with what was to me the most horrible casualness: "I lifted one chap up to have a look at him. He was much bigger than the English or even the Viennese kind, and had lots more joints in his antennæ. It was odd to see him squirming all over my hand in search of his mate...."

He was very pale, but also very calm.

XII

Half-an-hour later we were breakfasting and discussing, not my decision, but his. That's the way things usually happened. To waiters and cabmen and hotel-porters he always gave a wonderful display of submission to my wishes, but the larger affairs of life he decided for himself. Nor was there ever much hope of persuading him when once he had made up his mind. He told me once that I argued too cleverly; and that he always mistrusted cleverness in argument.

But that breakfast discussion didn't give me even the chance of being clever. He began by telling me, with a terrible sort of earnestness, that he had been thinking all night about Severn. (In the same tone and with the same look might a Methodist preacher have said that he had been wrestling all night with God.) "And—it seems to me—that to say—to be content to say—that we can do *nothing*—is cowardly. We *must* do *something*—we must *help*—if we can."

"Certainly, if we *can*. But how can *we*?"

That also he had pondered over. "First of all," he said, with a slow earnestness that went over me like a steam-roller, "we must have a talk with Severn."

"Good God!" I muttered under my breath. For it was diabolical, almost, the way he had planned everything during that night of sleeplessness. Six hours before, just after his interview with the hotel-clerk, he had been wild and excited; but now he was calm—deadly calm. And I don't know which condition made him look more ill. It was, anyhow, a sombre and unnerving calmness, and it somehow took the courage out of me. I found that I couldn't think clearly in the face of it, much less talk clearly; my mind was overburdened by the knowledge that he was ill. All I could say, when I had to say something, was that Severn's private affairs, however scandalous, were none of our business, and that we had better keep out of them. After all, what could we do? Talking to him wouldn't be much use. "As soon as he cares to tell us to mind our own business, we shall have to slink off. Don't you see?"

"I don't think *I* should slink off," he said, quietly, "if he told me to mind my own business."

"Then what would you do? What *could* you do, anyway?"

And he answered, between almost closed lips: "I know what I—what we—are *going* to do. We're going to make him go back to Helen."

It was the first time her name had been mentioned, and it seemed to give us both a shock to hear it, as if, until then, she had been outside the question—unrealised and unthought-of. Somehow, also, it took away an atom of his calmness, and made me better able to oppose him. For, frankly, the thought of buttonholing Severn and commanding him to return to his wife appalled me; I suppose I wasn't ever meant to be either a judge or a missionary. I couldn't do it. I said: "It's no good, Terry—there are some things I won't agree to, and that's one of them. It isn't that I don't sympathize with what you feel—it's just that it seems to me so—so absurd to suppose that we can achieve anything.... Damn it all, if you or I were cad enough to run off with some woman, do you think we'd welcome a lecture from an outsider about it?"

He said quietly: "It might be the thing we needed most of all."

"You can bet Severn won't need it, anyhow."

"Very well, then, if we fail, we fail. But that's no reason against trying, is it?"

"*I'm* not going to try.... I'm sorry, but I mean it."

"All right then. I'll try on my own."

"Really—I'm sorry—but—"

He smiled. "I don't mind a bit," he answered. "Besides, it may be easier for me than for you. You see, I haven't got your limitations. I don't care about good taste, or what's 'done' in such matters. I just do what I feel I *must* do."

That rather stung me. I said that to me, at any rate, it was perfectly obvious that he was thinking of Helen. Not that there was anything unworthy in that; but it came oddly from one who had not long before been boasting that he had put all that side of his life away from him and didn't want to be even reminded of it. "If you have put it away from you," I said, "why don't you keep it away from you? Why are you so keen to plunge back into the midst of it on the slightest excuse?"

Once again the mention of Helen's name had made him less calm. He told me eagerly that he *had* put it all away from him, but that wouldn't and oughtn't to stop him from helping friends he had known in the past. He said, with eyes burning sharply: "I tell you—in case you're thinking what isn't true—I tell you—I haven't any affection—*that* sort of affection—for her.... Do you believe me?"

"I believe you're speaking sincerely."

He ignored the innuendo. "I'm not thinking of Helen alone," he went on. "Or of Severn.... In a way, they're old enough to do what they like, whatever it is. But ... I'll tell you something about myself—years ago. In those days—just before I came out here—I wanted Helen—you understand?—I *wanted* her. And I'd have done anything to get her, but for—one thing.... Of course I'm not defending myself—there ought to have been a hundred reasons to stop me, but in fact there was only that one.... It would have been caddish and ungrateful to Severn, but *that* wasn't the reason. And it wasn't—just morality.... It was ... it was ... *this* ... I felt I could put up with Severn's reproaches and the world's reproaches ... I could stand everything except—except the thought of June—June growing up and wondering why her mother had left home, and then—some day—guessing or being told or finding out—the reason...." I couldn't stand *that*...." He made an effort to gain completer control of himself, and then, only half-succeeding, continued: "I gave up what *I* wanted for *her* sake, and now—after that—I'm damned if I'll see another man destroy it all! He *shan't*! You say I can do nothing! You don't know what I can do. Neither do I. But I know what I *can't* do—I can't stand by and see things happening as they are happening I tell you I can't—I *can't*—and I *won't*!"

The longest speech, I think, he had ever made in his life, and he was pale and trembling after it. He broke off sharply and stared round at the swing-doors; and no wonder, for at that moment Severn was entering, and with him, lovely to the eye, was this other woman....

XIII

It looked as if a scene was inevitable. Terry's hands gripped the sides of the table and the colour came flooding into his face; he looked like some wild animal about to spring. And meanwhile, breaking into the uneasy silence, came the sound of Severn's voice, smooth and exquisite in a language I didn't recognize, much less understand. He was obviously making some witticism, and the woman answered him by a tinkling little chime of laughter. The very loveliness of it and of her was like a goad. And then, just when I was beginning to wonder if it would be possible to manœuvre Terry out of the room without a disturbance, Severn looked round and saw us.

As an exhibition of *sang-froid* I have never in my life seen anything to equal what happened then. Severn and the woman hadn't quite reached their table when he saw us, and immediately, with a few swift words and gestures, he changed his direction and came over to us, bringing the woman with him. Not a muscle of his face or an inflexion of his voice betrayed the slightest embarrassment. "My dear Hilton, to think of finding *you* here!" He shook hands with me cordially. "And Terry as well—how *are* you both?" Somehow or other he had got hold of Terry's hand and had shaken it. "On business here, are you? Or is it pleasure?

Or both? ... Well, really, things *do* happen, don't they?" (Decidedly they did, I thought.) "Of course you will breakfast with me. You have had breakfast? Then you will have some more coffee, at any rate, at my table ... I insist.... And I must introduce my friend—doubtless her name will be familiar to you—Madame Lydia Danopoulos, the *danseuse*— quite one of the most fascinating ladies in this half of Europe.... She doesn't speak English or German, but just a little French, I think...." He addressed a few rapid words to her, amongst which I could recognize our names, and she favoured us with a graceful but rather distant bow.

A minute later we were all sitting together at Severn's table. The whole thing had happened so quickly that I could hardly realize what it was that *had* happened; and that, I suppose, was Severn's method, as successful with us as it usually was with the most hostile police-court witness. But to have reduced Terry in a moment from the highest pitch of excitement to a calm level of slightly sullen taciturnity was more than a method; it was a miracle.

But now, when I look back upon that extraordinary breakfast-party, it seems to me that it was nothing but a miracle altogether—or rather, perhaps, an infinite series of miracles. Imagine, if you can, a long and brilliant monologue, punctuated by staccato translations into modern Greek and consequent bursts of silvery feminine laughter. Imagine me sitting there making a few interjectory remarks from time to time, and Terry sitting there making no remarks at all, and the waiters hovering round us and wondering (very possibly) why we hadn't made ourselves known to one another on the previous evening.... But the really marvellous thing was that Severn's improvisation wasn't only brilliant and witty; it was also very subtly and dangerously reassuring. More than once I caught myself wondering whether Terry and I hadn't made a thundering mistake. The man's whole attitude was so frank and disarming; he told us exactly how he had met Madame Danopoulos at Bukarest, and how her company had considerably relieved the tedium of the Pan-Balkan Conference, at which he had had the misfortune to be the representative of His Britannic Majesty. Madame had been on her way to Buda-Pesth, and he, after the Conference, had promised to visit some Embassy friends at Warsaw; so what more natural than that they should share together the dust and heat of a midsummer journey? It was sheer luck, he added, that he had seen us, for otherwise his departure for Warsaw that morning would have removed the happy opportunity....

Terry, as I have said, was speechless. Not till Severn rose from his chair did he utter a word, and then, very calmly and deliberately, he said: "I would like to speak to you, if you don't mind ... alone.... Can you spare a few minutes?"

Severn seemed quite genuinely surprised. "Why, of course," he replied. "But why alone? Surely you don't mind Hilton—"

"I want *you* to be alone," said Terry.

"But—surely—if Madame, who knows no English, will excuse us—"

"No, no. It must be alone—if you don't mind. And not here."

Severn glanced at him curiously and then answered after a pause: "As you wish, then. But my train is at ten, remember. Shall we say half-an-hour from now—in the lounge?"

And so it was arranged.

CHAPTER FIVE

I

I DID, after all, turn up at that interview with Severn. It wasn't my intention to take sides; I was prepared to mediate, to put the brake on where necessary—in short, to keep the whole discussion well under blood-heat. Perhaps I succeeded. Perhaps it was really a compliment to my impartiality when Severn exclaimed, about half-an-hour after we had begun: "Look here, Hilton, what *are* you in this game—prosecuting counsel, defending counsel, judge, jury, hangman, or what?"

I might have answered that I held a watching brief, but that's the sort of clever reply one doesn't think of till afterwards. And yet it absolutely summed up my position; I *was* watching, and with a diffidence that gradually, as the affair proceeded, developed into rather dissatisfied disgust. For, as I had feared, the whole thing was almost a fiasco. Terry was sheerly defenceless against Severn; he couldn't think or talk a quarter as fast; he had none of the arts of suavity or blandness; he could only sit there, minute after minute, in a sort of dogged, stupefied silence.... Really, it was no fight at all; it was merely Severn giving a free exhibition of himself.

Perhaps you have heard Severn defending a difficult case in a court of law. He rises quickly to his feet, all smiles and courtesy to everybody; he talks calmly and suavely for a few moments, just to give the prosecution time to reflect what a charming man he is; and then, quite suddenly, he says something unexpected. Perhaps he startles by some unguessed admission, or brings forth a new and unlooked-for item of evidence. But anyhow, after politely upsetting most of the ideas you already have, he proceeds, still politely, to build up in you the ideas he wants you to have. And that is the way he earns his hundreds of pounds a week.

You can picture him, therefore, striding into the lounge of the Andrassy, bestowing on everybody a charming smile, ordering drinks, offering cigars, remarking on the hot weather, and generally, in fact, behaving as if he hadn't a ghost of an idea what we wanted him for. And you can picture Terry, clenching his hands with a queer sort of nervous firmness, declining the drink and the cigar, and going straight ahead to the vital question—was this woman, this Greek dancer, Severn's mistress?

Terry was too nervous to lead up to the question gradually. And Severn was too clever to lead down from it gradually. He answered, as sharply and instantly as a pistol-shot: "Yes. And what of it?"

II

Well, what of it? What could be said by either of us? Severn had won the first round and was fresh as ever after it, while his adversary was driven to the ropes by the suddenness rather than the strength of the blow. It was, indeed, an utterly impossible contest, for while Terry's attitude was rock-still, Severn moved his arguments continually and bewilderingly about in all directions and with all velocities. There was nowhere to grip hold, and besides, Severn was the wicked animal that, when attacked, defends itself. When, for instance, Terry asked if Helen knew what was happening, Severn answered: "Why *should* she know? She doesn't tell me all *her* private affairs." And when I ventured to point out that there was really no parallel at all between *her* private affairs and this one of his, he turned on me with the lightning retort: "Well, *you* ought to know her private affairs, Hilton, if anybody does. *You* ought to know why she hasn't spoken to you for years, and won't even have you in the house.... She won't tell *me*, anyway."

It was a good shot, and it made the second round his as well as the first. Terry, I could see, was utterly bewildered by the revelation; and I, naturally, was nonplussed. In the interval Severn went serenely on with his little game of turning the argument upside down and inside out. It was a fascinating display of dialectic, but I wasn't in the mood to admire it; I wondered why he didn't say: "Look here, I've had enough of this discussion. My own affairs are my own, and you can both clear out and be damned to you." Perhaps he didn't say that because he was enjoying himself so much better arguing.

The interview had begun at half-past eight, and soon after nine I reminded him of his train to Warsaw. And then, with a bland smile, he replied: "Oh, never mind *that*. I'm not going to Warsaw or anywhere else just yet. It was only a blind to get me away from your valued, but in the circumstances, rather undesirable company.... Have another drink, will you?"

I declined one perhaps curtly, and he ordered one for himself. Then he went on, lighting another cigar and making himself thoroughly comfortable: "D'you know, you fellows seems so infernally interested in my affairs that I've half a mind to tell you the whole damn truth about them...."

III

This is the important part. All the rest had been a mere forensic display, and I had already had more than enough of it, dazzling though it was. And yet, even when the whole damn truth came out, it was still marvellously under his control. He played with it; he let us have it in carefully arranged doses; it was the truth only if we cared to believe it was. He began by laughing at us for our unskilful attempts to cross-examine. Logic, he told us, was the great essential, and logic was what we lacked. "If you had attacked the matter logically, you would have deduced two principal reasons why a man can leave his wife. One is that he has got tired of her, and the other is that she had got tired of him.... Why were you in such a hurry to assume the former only?"

The colour rose sharply into Terry's face, but he said nothing, and neither did I. Severn, after looking at us both enquiringly, resumed: "I'm going to tell you very simply what's been happening during the last few years. It really is very simple.... Just this. My wife and I were quite happy together until—oh, a number of years ago. Then—very suddenly—she changed—and we haven't been at all happy since. That's all it amounts to. Didn't I say it was simple?"

Of course it wasn't simple at all, and he knew that as well as we did. And that's why I won't attempt to set down the story in Severn's own words. Like most men of marked ability, he had mannerisms—lightning gestures of hand and finger, sharp changes of tone, tricks of speech, and so on—all, no doubt, accentuated and standardized by his work at the Bar. Normally, in private conversation, he suppressed them, but now, as he told us about himself and Helen, they simply broke out all over the place. It was as if he were savagely and maliciously parodying himself; he pleaded his own case with an extravagant eloquence that was perfectly absurd before an audience of two. Perhaps his most irritating and persistent trick was the rhetorical question; he would say: "Now why do you think Helen changed?" and then, when neither of us answered, continue, as he might have done to a jury: "Well, why *do* women change? Shall we say *Cherchez l'homme*? ... I agree, but suppose you can't find any man—what then?" ... And so on, for well over half-an-hour.

And the upshot of it all was this.

First: Helen no longer loved him. He didn't know why she didn't; but then, neither had he, in former days, known why she did. Perhaps she had just grown tired.... He wasn't blaming her, of course; it wasn't her fault if she had no scrap of affection left for him. Very possibly it was his fault, although she had never said so.... Where her affection had gone to, he couldn't say—but he thought it hadn't gone to any other man. The important thing to him was that *he* no longer possessed it. He had even, he said begun to feel that she actively disliked him, and that something essential and unalterable in him got on her nerves.... Anyhow, what was he to do? Obviously, as soon as he began to realize that she might be happier with her freedom, he must find some way of giving it her. And in law, of course, (as he of all people knew well enough) there was only one way—the way that he had taken. "It isn't," he explained, "that I'm particularly keen on her getting a divorce. It's just that I want her to feel *free*. When I get home, I shall be able to say: Look here, if you don't want me, or can't stand me, or even would rather be without me, here's your grounds for divorce all neatly arranged and documented, so that you can file your petition at once.... Incidentally, there'll be no money difficulties—I've settled enough on her to keep her comfortable, whatever she does."

"And you give it as your honest opinion," I said, "that she'll really be happier divorced from you?"

"That's just what I don't know," he answered. "But I rather think she will, and in any case, it's giving her a chance, isn't it? ... Besides, there's my own side of the question. I should hate you to feel that I'm a mere bundle of altruistic motives. I'm not.... As I used to impress on you years ago, my code of morals is the very simple one of doing more or less what I like. And one of the things I *don't* like is being married to a woman who thinks I'm a scoundrel for being such a great big ugly success while so many other men are such divinely beautiful failures.... Understand?"

I nodded, but he said that he was sure I *didn't* understand. I didn't wish to argue the matter, in case Terry should recognize himself as one of the divinely beautiful failures, so I said, rather curtly: "What I can't understand is why you had to come out all the way here for—for the purpose."

He laughed. "The Conference," he answered. "Didn't I mention it at breakfast? Three weeks in Bukarest, wearing a morning-coat and topper with the temperature at ninety in the shade, discussing places you've never heard of with men whose names you can't pronounce; every damned speech repeated five times, first in French, then in Serbian, then in Greek, then in Bulgarian, and then in Turkish.... God!—it's enough to drive a man to anything.... But, apart from that, I prefer foreigners. When a man is compelled to take medicine, why should he not choose the nicest medicine there is? And where in England could you meet so charming a lady as Madame—in her profession?"

"I'm afraid I don't know any English women in her profession."

He laughed again. "I don't suppose you do," he said, "especially as I haven't been altogether truthful with you about Madame. She doesn't dance—except very badly in a ball-room. Her profession is far better suited to her temperament and attainments.... Understand?"

IV

We understood. He had told us practically everything, and what little he hadn't told us we could guess. Never had the whole interview seemed more pointless than at the end of his explanations; there was simply nothing to be done or said. Except—and it was a slight exception—the matter of Bentley. Severn, most probably, had no idea that he had been seen by anyone who knew him besides ourselves, and I let him know as plainly as I could that whether Helen chose to divorce him or not, his adventures were very likely to trickle across to England through the medium of Bentley's chatter. "And then," I said, "you know as well as I do what will happen."

"Of course," he answered, almost carelessly. "It will mean the end of my political career—perhaps even the end of my legal career as well, though I rather doubt that. But, anyhow, do you think I haven't counted the cost?" His voice became eager as he went on: "My dear fellow, I've counted *all* the costs, and my favourite maxim still holds—I'll do what I *want* to do. I've climbed the ladder because I've enjoyed climbing it, but if the price of staying on top is too high, then damn it all, I'll come down again.... I'll take risks—I'll live dangerously—I'll do any damned thing in the world except be a slave—even to my career!"

Deadlock—complete and absolute. He had his reasons for everything, and most of what he said, whether it convinced or not, was logically unanswerable. I was tired of the whole business, and Terry's silence seemed to show that he was the same. The one thing desirable was to get him away from the brain-twisting intricacies of a situation which had nothing to do with him.

But just then he spoke. He turned to me and asked me very calmly if I would mind if he and Severn were to speak alone for a few minutes. And before I could reply he went on: "Wait for me—in the hall. I won't be long.... And you might—if there's time—look up the return trains to Vienna...."

V

If there were time! There was almost time to memorize the whole timetable while I waited for him. I sat in the coolest corner of the hall and tried to interest myself in a month-old copy of *Lustige Blätter*—the only non-Magyar newspaper on the premises. But it was difficult—as difficult as it is to appreciate the comic papers in a dentist's waiting-room. When a quarter of an hour passed and Terry didn't return, I began to reproach myself with having left him at all; and then, as a relief from that, I tried to analyse, in the perspective of seven years, that early episode with Helen that had so vitally affected his life. What, exactly, *had* happened between the two of them? ...

The clock chiming the hour drove me back again from past to present. There seemed something ominous in his non-appearance—a hint of something terrible that might be happening behind the screened door of the lounge. What might not such a man as Severn do with such a man as Terry? ... The minutes drew towards the half-hour, and I think I should have boldly walked into the lounge when the clock struck, had not Terry, a minute earlier, come out to me—alone. His face was paler than ever, and his eyes—his eyes were just what I didn't like to see. It angered me to think of the strain that all this incessant listening and thinking and arguing was putting on him; it gave me a furious, unreasoning anger with Severn and Helen and Terry himself and the world in general.

His first words were an eager, disjointed apology for having kept me waiting longer than he had intended; and I replied, with perhaps a touch of curtness: "There's a fast train to Vienna at four this afternoon. Shall we go back?"

And he answered: "Yes.... And Severn's coming with us."

"*What?*"

"He's coming with us—through Vienna—on his way to England. He's going back to England—immediately.... He's promised.... He's promised absolutely.... And so—you see—after all—I mean—he—he—"

"You mean he's going back to Helen?"

"Yes—yes—that's it.... He's promised.... He's given me his word.... He wouldn't go back on his word, would he? ... Oh, I *know* he wouldn't do *that*...."

He floundered on into positive incoherence, and then, as if feeling the hopelessness of speech, sank down into a chair beside mine and smiled.

VI

It was true enough that he had done it, but *how* he had done it was just an enormous mystery. All he said to me when he was calm enough to tell me anything was that Severn had "promised." He didn't boast of having persuaded him, though that was what it seemed to have been. "We just talked," he said. "He was quite different after you had gone. You see, you're clever, and in front of you he likes to say clever things, but he didn't bother when he was with me alone, because he knew I wouldn't appreciate them. Of course, I'm not much good at arguing, but then, you see, we didn't argue—we just *talked*."

And that, at first, was all that I could get out of him—the admission that they had just talked. When I pressed for details he said: "Oh, we just talked about things in general, you know—about Helen, of course—and June, and Severn himself...."

The odd thing was that he was no longer even remotely angry with Severn. He was sorry for him; he wanted to help him; he talked almost as if Severn were a pathetic little weakling instead of a man who, whatever his deficiencies, could at least take care of himself. "Severn isn't really a bad fellow," he assured me, and I agreed most cordially that he wasn't. "The real truth is," he continued, "that he's unhappy. He wouldn't let *you* see it, but he couldn't stop *me* from seeing it. He's unhappy because he's really very fond of Helen, and always has been.... And that's why we must help him."

"It isn't much good being fond of her if she isn't fond of him," I said.

He stared uneasily at the floor. "She *might* be fond of him," he replied, at length, "if—if somebody would *help* her."

"In other words, they are both to be helped into each other's arms?"

"That's right!"

"And what does Severn think of the idea?"

"I—I don't know. I didn't ask him anything except to go back to Helen immediately, and he promised to do that."

"So that the reunion idea is entirely yours?"

"Yes."

"And you're going to work it out entirely by yourself?"

"No, no, I'm not. *You're* going to *help* me."

"Another link in this encircling chain of help!"

"Don't—*don't* make fun."

I could have cried when he said that. I hated myself for the sarcasm, but the motive was sincere enough—just anger with him for thinking so much of everybody except himself. I saw him as he was, pale and haggard and on the verge of a breakdown; needing, above all things, rest, and yet, by sheer perversity of fate, embarking upon this grandiloquent scheme for helping people who, if they needed help at all, were very well able to help themselves. It was more than absurd; it was monstrous. And when he said "Don't make fun," it was more even than monstrous; it was pitiable.

I told him contritely that I hadn't been making fun, and that all I wanted was for him to see my point of view. I had always been perfectly frank with him, and—

"Not always," he interrupted.

"What do you mean?"

He said quietly: "You weren't frank with me about the quarrel you had with Helen."

Ever since Severn had revealed the matter, I had been preparing for Terry mentioning it, but I hadn't guessed that he would save it up with such uncanny accuracy for the awkwardest moment of all.

"Why did you quarrel?" he persisted.

I said that the word 'quarrel' wasn't a very apt one; the whole thing had been more of a "tiff"—a minor sort of thing that ought to have been forgotten long before.

"Ought to have been," he said, "but wasn't. Why not?"

"There haven't been chances. Helen's been out of England nearly all the time."

"Not one chance of reconciliation—in seven years?"

"I'm afraid that's the truth."

"It must have been a dreadful tiff."

"Oh, no."

"What was it about?"

"She objected to—to a certain attitude I had taken up. That was all. Nothing very dreadful."

He said: "I suppose the reason you won't tell me is because the quarrel was about me. And I can guess what it was. She blamed you for persuading me to go away."

I said nothing.

"Didn't she? Wasn't that it?"

"Well, if you insist on knowing, that *was* it, more or less.... But what on earth's the good of diving back into things that happened so many years ago?"

"We can't help it," he said, uneasily. "We haven't done with the past yet.... We can't push it away and say 'That's finished with.' It never is finished with." He paused and then went on: "And so she thought that it was *you* who persuaded me?"

"I didn't deny it."

"But why didn't you? You *should* have denied it. It was absurd for you to be blamed. You didn't persuade me at all—I made up my mind myself. It wasn't *your* fault."

"You thanked me in your letter for what I had said, anyhow."

"Did I? Did I?" His eyes sharpened as if searching for something inside his own head. "I don't remember that letter. I only remember sitting up all night and making up my mind that I couldn't—I *couldn't*..." Some spasm of memory seemed to give him eagerness; he went on: "Don't you see why we *must* help Severn? ... *I* couldn't *then*—*he* mustn't *now*—don't you *feel* how it is? ... We *must* help him—he's unhappy—he's been driven into all this by his unhappiness. It's not *his* fault."

At any rate, we had come back to the main argument. That was something. "I'm afraid," I said, "that you're in danger of flying to the other extreme about Severn. I believe, as you do, that he's fundamentally a decent fellow, but the fact remains that he's infernally clever and can lie beautifully whenever it suits him. It seems to me that it's hardly likely that the right's *all* on his side. Most probably Helen has a case, if she were here to tell it."

"Oh, I know ... it's not *her* fault."

"You say it's not her fault, and not Severn's fault either. Then whose fault do you suppose it is?"

I was a fool to ask that question. It made him suddenly crumple up—made him lean forward with his head in his outstretched hands and yield himself up to desolate, hysterical sobbing. "*My* fault," he cried, as soon as he had power to utter a word. "Not his—or hers either—but mine—*mine*—all *mine*...."

VII

And that, after seven years, was what he had been driven to....
No more brave talk about putting all that part of his life away from him; no more assurances that he didn't care, that he had forgotten, that he didn't want to be reminded. He hadn't forgotten; he couldn't forget; the past was all over him, obsessing and dominating. And with the past was bound up somehow or other his own guilt. Wherever and whenever we began to argue, that was always where we ended. *He* was guilty. *He* had been the cause of all the trouble—of Helen's coolness to Severn, of my estrangement from Helen, of Severn's escapade with the 'other' woman, of all that had gone amiss. His guilt forced itself on him—gave him no rest or peace—was both a cause and a symptom of the disaster that was so close to him. He had never been especially religious, in the sense of attending church and so on; yet this consciousness of guilt was a thing of almost religious fervour—but without the peace of forgiveness that religion would have given him. There was some odd streak in him that would never let him do anything by halves; in love, in work, even in repentance, his spirit knew no moderation. When I tried to argue away the extremity of what he felt, he shook his head and answered: "You

don't know what happened.... When we get back to Vienna you can see the letters she sent me. They'll tell you more than I ever can. They'll show you how the guilt of all this is *mine*...."

We missed lunch; we had no appetite. I packed my things, and Terry's as well; Severn was elsewhere, conducting, no doubt, somewhat delicate negotiations with Madame. The time crawled sombrely through that almost impossibly hot day; Terry and I adjourned to the writing-room, where I scribbled a note to Bentley, telling him with an air of casualness that the woman whom he had seen in Severn's company wasn't Mrs. Severn, but a Hungarian friend. Bentley would have no reason to doubt it, and it would prevent him from chattering awkwardly. Terry's idea was that only the three of us should ever know the details, and even we, he said, must try to forget. "He's going back to Helen—that's the main thing. This other business is only an incident—closed from now onwards."

"But suppose Helen doesn't want him?" I said. "What then?"

He shook his head as a theologian might shake away the momentary temptation of heresy. "She *will* want him," he said, at length. "She *must* want him.... When we get back to Vienna I'm going to write to her—about Severn and about you. It's terrible that she's gone on blaming him and you for what is all *my* fault. I shall write to her and tell her *everything*."

"But you can't. You can't tell her about Severn and this woman."

"I can tell her everything *except* that."

"If Severn's going back to her, it seems to me there's no need to write at all. Even to mention him would look suspicious. In fact, to write a letter of any kind, after your long silence, would probably make her wonder what had been happening."

He said, sombrely: "I *must* write—but it's true what you say—I ought to have written before—long before—only I was a fool—a coward—I thought I had done with it all...."

Back again, inexorably and inevitably, at his own guilt....

VIII

Severn agreed with me that he was ill. I had a short but amazing conversation with him as we stood at the bureau counter to settle our respective bills. He began immediately: "Look here, Hilton, has it ever struck you that our friend's not quite himself at times?"

"You mean Terry?"

"Yes. I don't lay claim to be a mental expert, but I reckon I can see trouble when it's staring me in the face.... It struck me he might have been overworking—I'm told Karelsky's rather a slave-driver—and then with this affair on top of it all.... Of course it's all perfectly stupid and none of his business, but then how can you argue with a man whose eyes keep on telling you that he's trembling on the brink of the beyond? ... That's a fact—I'm not exaggerating. He was like that with me this morning when you left us—I felt I *had* to humour him, or else he might have gone right off his head there and then.... And, as it happens, it doesn't particularly matter to me whether I go back now or next week, as I had intended."

So *that* was what had happened. Terry *hadn't* really conquered, and Severn *hadn't* really given in.... I said: "And when you get to England I suppose you'll carry out your original intentions?"

He shrugged his shoulders and replied that he didn't really know what he should do. It all depended on Helen. If she wanted her freedom she'd have to have it. There wasn't much fun in staying with a woman who didn't want you, was there? It was a pity, he said, that there had been this meeting—it would have been far better if we had waited until the sensational news came in the Sunday papers—if it ever did. "You don't suppose I'd do all this without good reasons, do you? The only thing I didn't bargain for was a meeting with a mad missionary. Yes, I mean that. And the trouble is that I like him too much to be able to tell him to go to the devil.... As a matter of fact, the thing's damned serious, by the look of it. What he wants is rest—absolute rest—for weeks and months—otherwise there's going to be a serious smash-up. Know what I mean?"

I said I thought I did, and he relapsed into his semi-facetious humour. "Thank heaven," he said, "that Madame presents no problem. Dear, kind creature—she will be delighted to go back to Bukarest for a slightly larger sum than she charged me for bringing her away.... What a pity we cannot settle everything in life by money!"

Nothing of all this surprised me. It was plausibility itself compared with the theory that Terry had persuaded Severn by some miracle of eloquence or importunity.

Those few remaining hours in Buda-Pesth stay in my memory with nightmarish vividness. The heat—the dust—the smells of cooking; *Blattae Orientales* playing hide-and-seek on the floor; porters sweating and straining under loads of luggage; the Vienna train at the platform like a row of sweltering ovens, reeking with paprika and human bodies and half-molten varnish. Shade temperature in the station—thirty-four Centigrade.... And over and around the torture of it was the tragic atmosphere of illusion—Terry thinking all the time that he had really convinced and converted Severn, and Severn, on his side, having no suspicion of the Terry-Helen episode. Their crumpled heat-soaked unawareness was an infinitely pathetic thing.

Only Severn was cheerful. He talked to us endlessly, and without getting much in the way of answers, for even to open one's mouth to speak a single word was to cause an extra bead of perspiration to trickle disagreeably down one's forehead. But Severn seemed not to care, and when we reached Vienna, with a few hours' interval before the departure of the Paris express from another station, it was perhaps inevitable that he should take command. He knew Vienna well (what city *didn't* he know well?) and I rather wished he were staying on with us. Even the night was almost unbearably warm, and with sure instinct he led us to the cool Rathaus-Keller and ordered iced drinks. Terry spoke hardly at all, and neither did I; the ordeal of the train-journey had been too much for us. But Severn, of all the men I ever met, was the most impervious to physical surroundings; neither heat, nor train-journeys, nor even all-night sittings at the House could disturb that marvellous equanimity. He seemed, indeed, as he sat there in the Rathaus-Keller with his tankard of lager before him, a lithe and entrancingly-mannered boy; and even the stories he told of his life in Vienna twenty years before did not take away from him that extraordinary air of youthfulness. He had spent a year in the city, he said, picking up the language and having a good time. He had *lived*, and his eyes, seeing again the old familiar scenes, shone with it. This Rathaus-Keller—what times he had had there! ... And then on the wall he caught sight of an advertisement of a variety-show at Ronacher's, and it reminded him of the old Ronacher's, where he had seen Rannin, the Cingalese with the Iron Skin, who had climbed a ladder of sword-blades barefoot, and the Chevalier Cliquot, whose pastime had been to swallow twenty-two-inch cavalry sabres, and the Human Ostrich, and Madame Elise, the Parisian Strong Lady, and the rest of them.... Ah, those old days! ...

But the time drew near for the departure of the Paris train. The holiday season was at its height, and when we reached the East Station we found it packed with tourists bound for the Tyrol. Severn had not reserved a seat, and for a few moments it seemed doubtful whether he would even secure a cramped position in a first-class compartment. A berth in the *wagon-lit* was out of the question; all had been reserved weeks before. It was then, faced with these unexpected privations, that he suggested staying in Vienna till the morning train, which would probably be less crowded. "Supposing," he said, "we look in at Ronacher's, and then I'll take you the round of the sights—the Prater's rather worth seeing after midnight...."

"Mizzi could probably give him a room," I whispered to Terry. The postponement of the journey until the morning seemed to me perfectly reasonable, apart from the attractiveness of the alternative programme that Severn had sketched out.

But Terry said: "You promised you would get back at the very earliest moment you could, didn't you?"

And Severn then, with his most charming smile, replied: "I *did*, Terry, and I'll keep my word.... Perhaps there'll be more room on the train the other side of Innsbrück. Anyhow, don't wait for it to go out—it'll probably be hours late. And besides, I'm just as anxious really to get comfortable in my seat as you are to go back to your hotel.... Ronacher's and the rest will do the next time we are all of us here together...." (But there hasn't been, so far, and probably never will be, a next time.)

I liked him at that last moment more, I think, than I had ever done before. It's true, though odd perhaps, that it's not the big things that people do that win your heart to them, but often the very smallest. And so it is that all the big important things that Severn had done to help me hadn't made me like him so much as this gay, almost nonchalant farewell, and the thought I had of him sweltering the night through in a packed train, and then sweltering through the next day and the night after that—and all for no other reason than to help Terry. His last words, as he shook hands with me, were: "Ring me up as soon as you get back to town, and we'll fix up a lunch together."

There was a curious sadness after we had left him, and the warm streets were full of it. We strolled back to the Laudon Gasse with hardly a word between us. I wondered what Mizzi would say to our unexpected return, but she wasn't there when we arrived and the hall-porter told us she probably wouldn't be back until late.

IX

He showed me Helen's letters that night. I had expected a small bundle, but there were only three; and he asked me to read them, not while I was with him, but later on when I was alone. The chance came after I had bidden him good-night; I went downstairs into the lounge, switched on one of the shaded table-lamps, lit a cigarette, and read the letters very carefully. They were none of them long, and all had been written and posted within a month of his arrival in Vienna. It was an odd sensation to sit in a hotel-lounge at two o'clock in the morning and disentangle a mystery; there was something eerie, almost, in trying to build up from a few sheets of handwriting the complete picture of what had happened seven years before. But there it was, in clear focus at last, and one glance was enough to show how wrong my ideas had been.

Those letters were a revelation. They seemed to me the sort of letters that Helen could never have written, but perhaps that is the usual experience of outsiders who read other people's love-letters. Yes, they *were* love-letters, except that the description is a shade too temperate.... And—to put the matter quite frankly—they were *not* the wayward, semi-harmless chits that a married woman might send to a young exile in whom she was sentimentally interested. They were, on the contrary, highly damaging and incriminating documents; and all the time I was reading them I was picturing a packed Divorce Court in which some cool, smooth-voiced advocate (like Severn) was doling them out, sentence by sentence, and pausing with uplifted eyebrows at the end of each.

The earliest of the trio had evidently been written and posted within a few hours of that quarrel with me in the Fleet Street tea-shop. There was, of course, no mention of it in the letter, and at least half the sentences were indignant questions. For instance:

"... Terry, what *does* your scrappy little note really mean? Why have you gone after all? What need was there for you to go? I feel dazed by it, so far; I cannot understand how or why you could have done it, after what we had arranged. Surely it was wonderful enough for us to be together, meeting so often, and with all the summer before us that we had planned—how could you *dare* to break it all to pieces by going away? Terry, I'm angry with you—I *did* think you would keep your word to me. Tell me what made you go—tell me *why*. And for God's sake, if you find there's nothing for you in Vienna, have the courage to come back. I'm frightened to think of you with that man Karelsky—he seems to me to be everything you'll never guess he is till it's too late.... Oh, you *are* a fool for running away like this—it was our wonderful chance, and you've bungled all of it. I don't know whether I can ever forgive you...."

A pause of ten days, and then the next, evidently in answer to a letter from him:

"Your letter arrived this morning at breakfast-time. Geoffrey said: 'Who's it from?', and I said: 'It's from Terry, saying he's arrived safely and is settling down.' Then he said 'Good!' in a loud voice, and I felt I wanted to knife him for saying 'good' when everything was so bad.... Terry, it's almost killing me to think that I could have had you that last night if only I had had the courage. I wish to God I *had* had, but what's the good of that to me now? Terry, there *were* difficulties—money and so on—and you oughtn't to have thought I didn't love you enough, just because I didn't agree straightway. I love you enough for *anything*, and I know it now that you've gone.... I just feel I can't endure it—it's inhuman of you to give me no second chance—and yet you always were like that, I know. Everything or nothing—and now, I suppose, it's nothing.... What you say about being sorry shows how different you are; *I'm* not sorry, except that I didn't seize the chance when it was offered me...."

And as a postscript the single sentence: "I don't think I can ever *live* without you, and you know what I mean by *living*, don't you?"

The third and last letter was the longest. Dated almost exactly a calendar month after Terry's departure, it began:

"Your letter made me feel that I shall never want to write to you again, and if, as you threaten, you don't reply to this, I certainly shan't. What sort of a man are you that you can change so quickly? Your letter might have been written by a parson—or did you, perhaps, get some parson to collaborate with you? Please let me inform you that the old Terry that I loved, and that I love still, was the only man on earth who could ever have made me 'live usefully,' and that the new Terry, with his moralisings and platitudes, only makes me feel I want to go straight to the Devil. How *dare* you mention Geoffrey's career as a reason why *I* should sacrifice my happiness? And even June—what has *she* got to do with it? I suppose you think that the 'che-ild' comes in rather usefully, or else your parson collaborator put you up to the idea.... As for your work—devote yourself to it by all means, but why should you try to make me believe that you can't have more than *one* thing in life? My advice to you (since you have given yours so plentifully to me) is to marry some Viennese girl who loves you and is also a business woman—someone who'll stop you from making an utter fool of yourself. I go white with rage when I read over parts of your letter. What do you mean by saying that love dies soon when the mind is occupied by work? Does *yours*? *Mine* doesn't. And what do you mean by talking of your great sin? There *was* no sin, and if what might have been is a sin, then it was I and not you who stopped short of it. Not that I want any credit for that.... I can't understand you. I can't understand how you could behave as you did that night and then, a month later, send me a sermon. I don't feel that it is *you*—the real *you*—that wrote me that letter at all, but somebody else—somebody I have never known. Did you ever really love me at all, I wonder, or was it, on your side, merely the passion you now profess to be ashamed of? It wasn't that on *my* side; I really loved you, more than I could love anybody else in the world; I loved even your work and your ideals because they were yours.... I *don't* feel ashamed, and you *do*, and there's an end of it...."

X

While I was reading over that last letter for the second time, Mizzi came in. She had seen the light through the window, and had wondered who could be staying up so late. We shook hands gravely, and she said that the porter had told her of our return, and that she was not altogether surprised since Buda-Pesth in midsummer was so hot and—and *unheimlich*. *That*—her using a German word instead of puzzling out an English one—showed me that she was perturbed; and when she asked me how Terry was, a sudden impulse made me place a chair for her opposite to mine and tell her everything about him. *Everything*. And also I showed her the letters.

Perhaps I was wrong to do that without his permission, but there are times when you risk being wrong. I wanted Mizzi to know everything about Terry because, in the end, I wanted her to marry him. I talked to her especially about the letters; they showed, I said, the tragic difference between Terry and Helen. "She was right when she said it was all or nothing with him.... Apparently she was quite willing to carry on a more or less decorous affair with him whilst still living with her husband. But he *wasn't*."

Mizzi nodded and asked me about the 'last night' mentioned in the second of the letters. I described briefly the Karelsky party and the odd way in which Terry and Helen had managed to separate themselves from the rest of the crowd. "I imagine," I said, "that sometime or other during that evening he asked her point-blank to come away with him. No doubt she either refused or else hesitated, and in the end it was arranged that he should decline the Vienna job and stay in London where they could go on meeting each other.... Then afterwards he felt the intolerableness of the situation. He couldn't bear at all what she, apparently, could bear quite easily—the having of things by halves. It wasn't in his nature.... So he cut the knot and came out here."

"I can understand ... I can understand him wanting all of her—or else none of her."

"So can I. And, in a way, I can understand *her* side, as well. After all, he had no money, and neither had she.... It would have been sheer madness for them to run away, and it was her nature to think of that, just as it was his nature not to."

Then we discussed the third and most extraordinary of the three letters. What sort of stuff must Terry have sent her to have evoked such a stinging reply? I suggested that he might have deliberately written her a rather caddish letter in order to kill her love for him, but Mizzi thought he wasn't calculating or clever enough for that. "I think," she said, "that he was perfectly sincere. He *did* think, then, that love would die when the mind was occupied by work. He *did* think that he had committed a sin, and that his love for her had been just a passion.... I think he meant every word of what he wrote."

"It's a pity we can't *see* his letter," I said, but she replied: "I don't think I want to see it. I feel I know what it would be like. Rather stiff and—and awful ... can't you imagine it?"

I tried to, but I'm afraid I hadn't, and never have had, her clairvoyant knowledge of Terry. I went on to explain the difficulties he was in, and how he felt responsible for the trouble between Helen and her husband, as well as for my quarrel with Helen, and Severn's "affair" in Buda-Pesth, and Heaven knew what else. "He's in a mood to take upon himself responsibility for all the suffering in the world," I said, "and it would be comic if it wasn't tragic. Everything is *his* fault—nothing anybody else's."

She said: "I can so easily believe that. He has a spirit in him—that makes him try to do perfect things—and then blames him when they aren't *quite* perfect...."

We were silent for a while, and then she went on: "All through the time I haf known him he has been like that—trying for the perfect goal and flogging himself because he couldn't reach it.... He would have made a great saint—in the Middle Ages ... but not to-day." She smiled as she added: "I remember when he taught me English—he taught me as if I were a sinner, and English the true faith...."

We talked on for a while about what we could do to help him, but at the end of it all only a few desirabilities emerged—that he should take a long holiday and make more friends and work less hard. As we shook hands at the foot of the stairs she said: "It iss so hard to help people who will not haf what they want. If only I could write to this Helen and ask her to come to him! Or if only some fate would send him back to her! ... But no—he will not haf what he wants. Nor will he want what he could haf.... He iss born to be *unglücklich*...."

XI

Sunday.

Terry looked better in the morning; I asked him if he had slept well, and he replied: "Oh, yes, I was so very tired after last night.... *Last night!* Doesn't it seem years away? And isn't it comfortable to be back here?"

"Yes," I agreed. "Mizzi has a genius for making things comfortable."

He seemed surprised at my mentioning her. "I suppose it *is* Mizzi," he said, after a pause, and seemed to ponder over the matter.

Not till breakfast was over did he mention the letters, and then only because I took the opportunity of handing them back to him. He seemed afraid that I might discuss them with him; he told me that he didn't want me ever to mention them; but that he hoped they had made me realize. What he hoped they had made me realize he didn't say, but

I presumed he meant his own overwhelming guilt.... But he wouldn't discuss the matter further. The thing of immediate importance, he said, was the letter to Helen that he was going to write.

I seized the opportunity then of giving him a straight talk about his health. I told him frankly that he seemed to me to be on the verge of a serious breakdown, and rather to my surprise he didn't indignantly deny it. He even admitted that he had been working too hard and that he needed a holiday. "I'll take one," he said, "as soon as all this business is settled. I'll go to Salzburg or Ischl or somewhere—Mizzi will advise me...." He smiled his familiar half-smile and added: "You needn't worry—*I* shall be all right."

He didn't mention his work, and when I ventured a remark, he said: "Just now—for the time—I can't think of it. That's why I daresay you're right—I *do* need a rest.... But before I have it, I must earn it—I must undo, if I can, some of the harm I've done...."

Soon after that I left him to compose his letter to Helen. It was something, at any rate, that he had agreed to take a holiday, but Mizzi, when I told her, was less impressed. "He has promised scores of times," she said, "but always—at the last moment—there has been an excuse."

The morning dragged on, and then literally, as well as metaphorically, came the clouds. It was raining hard at mid-day, and when I went up to his room I found him with a blank writing-pad in front of him and weariness in his eyes. For two hours he had been trying to write, and not a word would come—not a word.

Nor could I help him. The more I pondered, the more impossible seemed the idea of writing to her at all. And yet, for his own sake, it was necessary, his only hope lay in supposing that he could undo what he believed himself to have done. I urged him not to worry about it—to leave it for a while, at any rate. And he turned to me then with a look of sad finality and replied: "But you see, it must—it *must*—catch to-night's mail...."

We had lunch, and then, inexorably, he went back to his desk. I tried once or twice to make suggestions, but he seemed to mistrust them. Words, he said, came easily to me because I was a journalist, but they were no good to him unless they were the words *he* wanted.... He didn't want her to think this ... or that ... but something in between—something elusive and perfect—something in his own mind that ever evaded pursuit. If only he could make her see everything as *he* saw it.... If only the words would come, one after the other in a constant stream, without any agonizing search for them.... But I wondered myself if there *were* any words for what he felt.

XII

The time of posting for the night-mail was seven at the latest, and at five I went down to fetch Mizzi. "For God's sake," I told her, "come up and tell him that letters for England don't go on a Sunday. He's trying to write something, and if he doesn't get it done in time, he'll collapse.... Tell him anything you like that'll put him off."

She did. She did it rather well. She waited for a few moments till after I had rejoined him, and then came up with some idle chatter about the weather. He was still at his desk, taking hardly any notice of anything but the paper in front of him; and at last, with an excellently assumed air of casualness, she remarked that he seemed busy. He said he was writing a letter. And then she remarked: "If it iss a letter to England, you know of course that there iss no post to-night." He turned round suddenly, astonished, but perhaps, beyond his astonishment, relieved. And she went on: "It iss a new rule. No mails for foreign lands from Saturday night until Monday night." Her tone was just right; he put down his pen, walked across the room, and said, with a sort of moody resignation: "Nothing for it but to wait, then." Then a further idea seemed to occur to him; he exclaimed sharply: "What was it you came up to see me about, Mizzi?"

She wasn't altogether prepared for that. She said: "Iss it necessary that I must always haf a special reason when I come up to see you?" And before he could reply she went on: "But of course, I *had* a reason—it was to ask you—both of you—if you would care to come with me now to the Cathedral...."

So we went—the three of us.

It was, as she told me afterwards, the only thing she had been able to think of on the spur of the moment. She even apologized, then, and hoped that the service at the Stefans-Dom hadn't bored me. I assured her it hadn't; but all the same, she might have been surprised if she had known my thoughts during that solemn candle-lit hour. They weren't especially religious, and yet—devout Catholic as she was—Mizzi might have been thinking them too. Perhaps she also, lured by the singing and the twilight, came under the spell of the one perfect solution—that she should become Terry's wife; perhaps she also remembered Helen's advice that he should marry some Viennese girl who loved him and was a business woman.

That night, after we came back from the Cathedral, Terry seemed calmer. I even spoke to him about my return to England, and he renewed his promise that he would take a long and complete holiday "as soon as this business is settled." Then we talked about Mizzi. He thought it odd that she had invited us to the Cathedral with her. "She's rather religious," he said, "but she never talks about it or tries to force it on you. When I first came here she asked me if I were a Catholic, but that was all." He paused for a while, and then, in a different tone, continued: "I suppose a Catholic doesn't care to marry a Protestant?"

I must have shown my astonishment when he said that. "It rather depends who the Protestant is," I answered, hoping he would say more. He didn't, however, and even when I asked him why he had put the question, he only answered that there hadn't been any particular reason.

But there had.

That night was very hot, and neither he nor I was in the mood for sleep. About midnight I left him still pondering over the letter he would write to Helen; I said I would go for a short walk to make myself drowsy. But when I got downstairs the lounge was so cool and so fragrant with the scent of the flowers in the window-boxes, that I sank into one of the largest armchairs and lit a cigar. I didn't trouble to press any of the switches, for the moonlight was streaming in, and besides, I could see through the open doorway the little office in which Mizzi, that night as on most nights, was working late over her bills and ledgers. I didn't wish to interrupt her, yet I was just beginning to wonder if she would mind very much, if I did, when I heard Terry's voice in the hall. He was asking her if she could spare him a moment, and she replied, with her quiet and never-altering cordiality: "Why, of course I can. Come in and sit down."

The office was a small affair of glass partitions, and I could see as well as hear all that took place. I wasn't consciously eavesdropping at first, and later when I must confess to a certain eagerness of ear and eye, I had the excuse that it would have been impossible for me to move away without creating a distinctly awkward situation. So I sat there quiet and still, hardly daring even to smoke lest the smell of the cigar should drift across into the hall and betray me.

For he was proposing to her! There in that little hotel-office, with his face as pale as chalk and his voice half-trembling, he was asking her to marry him! At first he spoke in German, but after a short while relapsed into stammering staccato English.

Most men, when they propose, are doubtless optimists—not only about the proposal, but about themselves and the world in general. But Terry wasn't an optimist. The whole business would have been just comic, if one had allowed oneself to see the joke of it. He informed her in a series of short sentences that he was entirely ineligible—he had no money, and poorish prospects, and it might and probably would be years before he could afford to marry her. Altogether he was a pretty hopeless sort of suitor, and he even reminded her that she could always give him up if she had the good sense to change her mind while there was yet time. All he wanted, apparently, was a vague assurance that some day, if and when he could afford it, and if and when she wished, she would marry him.

While he was talking in this stumbling, sorrowful way, she was all the time sitting at her desk, pen in hand, looking up at him. She didn't say a word; she let him talk on, and then, when he had said everything, she just lifted up her hands and arms and pulled him down to her. I never saw anything so swift and sudden. A second afterwards she was in his arms and kissing him....

Where I was I could feel the sharp slackening of tension as they clung together. And then, after the ecstasy of that first embrace, she seemed to recover a certain self-protective calmness; she was the business woman again, chary of committing herself. "Terry," she whispered, "you must not ask me for an answer now. It would not be possible after this.... Tomorrow I will give it you—when I have thought it over calmly...."

He didn't protest. He didn't seem to care greatly whether she gave him an answer or not. His mind and body were reeling; he could only stammer: "Oh, Mizzi—Mizzi—"

He threw himself into a chair and buried his face in his hands, and she stooped over him like a mother over a child. It was unbearable, somehow, to be spying on them then. I took the risk of tip-toeing out of the room and across to the foot of the staircase. They neither saw nor heard. And it was later—much later—when he came up to bed.

XIII

Monday....

I think I must have dreamed that Terry and Mizzi were married, for I woke up thinking of it. Even now the memory of that morning comes to me enveloped in the dream of the two of them; somehow it is all bright sunlight—the sunlight on the geraniums in the wooden boxes, the sunlight on Terry's face as I left him sleeping, and the sunlight drenching Mizzi's little office....

"*Morgen*," she said, as I entered, and I told her that Terry was asleep, and that I had come down to have a chat with her, if she wasn't too busy.

(I know now almost exactly what I was going to say to her, for I had planned it all very carefully. I was going to talk about Terry—to lead the conversation up to a point at which she might, if she cared, confide in me. I was going to say and do so many clever things, if I had had the chance. But I didn't have the chance.)

She said to me suddenly: "What was the train that your friend Mr. Severn travelled by?"

I told her; and then she said: "Do you think he would break the journey at all—at Innsbrück, say, or Zürich, or Basle?"

"I don't think so. He said he was going to get to England as soon as he could."

"And his train is due to arrive in Paris early this morning?"

"Yes ... I rather think so."

Then she said, very quietly: "I am sorry.... There iss bad news—an accident.... No details yet, but a bad accident—near Paris.... I heard on the telephone just now.... Will you sit down while I ring up again?"

CHAPTER SIX

I

I SAT by the window while she telephoned, and I smoked cigarette after cigarette, and I tried to think—tried to think—tried to think of Paris, and early morning, and what a train-accident would be like, and whether, if Severn.... It was all numbing and bewildering at first; but behind it, amazingly constant, was the thought of Terry.... How would it affect *him*? Somehow I had the feeling that even in a train-accident Severn could be relied on to look after himself.

I think I made some sort of stammering remark about the first reports being probably exaggerated; and Mizzi answered, turning her face momentarily away from the instrument: "It may be. We must wait till there is further news. There will be the newspaper soon."

We waited. I see now in my mind that crowded little box of a room with the sunlight streaming into it, and the map of Austria-Hungary on the wall, and Mizzi's pale-golden hair shimmering against its background of *Jahrbücher* and *Wohnungsanzeiger*, and—most important of all—the telephone. The telephone dominated—was no sooner put down than taken up again; its shrill ringing pitched the highest and most excruciating keynote of tension. "Everybody is telephoning," said Mizzi, after she had rung up the *Stunde* offices. "They do not know much, but it is believed that several Wien people have been killed. Now I will try the railway office."

And so on, telephoning here and there, and then here again, without definite result. And, in the midst of it all, through her little glass partition, she saw Terry coming down the stairs. "You had better go with him," she told me hastily. "He must not know of this. Afterwards there may be need to tell him, but not yet—not till we know ourselves...."

II

Breakfast in his room.... By the most terrible of ironies, he was almost cheerful; he told me he had thought out his letter to Helen and had practically decided every word that he would write. The change in him was extraordinary; the old despondency had given way to a feverish sort of optimism; he saw a future in which Severn and Helen, at his behest, lived happily ever after; he saw himself staying in Vienna to pursue research-work in Karelsky's laboratories; and he saw Mizzi—but how, exactly, *did* he see Mizzi?

He said, anyhow: "Before I write my letter to Helen, I want to go down and have a chat with Mizzi." I suppose he wanted the answer to his proposal. Not that he looked as eager about it as a man ought to be about such a momentous affair. My own impressions of that meal are rather vague, anyhow; I was too agitated to notice anything very carefully. I remember the *Stunde* being pushed under the door; it was my copy, and there was no fear that he would want to read it. I picked it up as casually as I could, and somehow expected to find headlines *in English* about a railway accident.... Ah, a short, dimly printed paragraph in the stop-press column.... Something about "der Pariser Schnellzug" and "schreckliches Eisenbahnungluck".... I remember glancing through it as I had done years before at translation-pieces in examination-papers—with just that feeling of mingled eagerness and apprehension. I saw the words and knew most of them, yet somehow I missed the meaning of the whole.... What did "entgleisung" mean?....

We went downstairs after breakfast, and I was too dazed to have any plans. If he talked to Mizzi and there had by that time been bad news about Severn, perhaps she would tell him; if there had been no news, probably she wouldn't. The matter, anyhow, was in her hands, and so, of course, was the answer to his proposal.... The hall, when we reached it, was unexpectedly full of a chattering crowd, and in the midst of it a news-boy was selling copies of the *Stunde*—a later edition. Terry, who never took more than the very slightest interest in newspapers, asked me what all the commotion was about, and I tried to satisfy him with a vague answer while I led him across the hall towards Mizzi's office.

I might have succeeded—I think I should have succeeded—had not a portly Viennese who was reading the paper muttered something as we passed by. What it was I don't know, but Terry heard it; and the newsboy, with the sure instinct of his tribe, at that moment thrust a paper towards him....

III

That altered everything. He staggered into Mizzi's office reading the headlines incredulously, and I left him there, believing that she would manage things better than I could.

He didn't write to Helen after all. He tried to, afterwards; but when, towards dusk, the news came through that Severn was among the seriously injured, he gave it up in despair. It was hopeless; there were no words in his vocabulary to cope with this new and more terrible situation—no words except the words he kept uttering to me in eager, half-frightened gasps. "She *must* help him now, Hilton—she *must* stay with him and help him now—oh, she *must*—she *must*—she couldn't do anything else.... She couldn't leave him now, could she?" He spoke almost as if he were pleading with himself to try to believe in the essential goodness of her. "He's never needed her before, but he'll need her now, and she'll realize it—she's bound to, isn't she? ..." And then, like the bursting of a dark cloud, came the inevitable—the feeling, deeper and blacker than ever, that *he* was responsible for all that had happened, and especially for all that had happened to Severn. "*I* made him go by that train—you remember? He wanted to go to Ronacher's and wait till the morning train—but I told him to keep to his promise—you remember that? *I* made him go—all this would never have happened to him but for me.... You can see how it is, can't you?"

I was almost impressed myself by the horror of the coincidence, though I took care not to let Terry see it. I told him briskly that it was absurd for him to feel responsible, and that to anybody except himself the idea would appear ridiculous. Severn would be the first to say so.

He buried his head in his hands and was silent. My assurances hadn't helped him. It didn't matter to him what anybody else in the world said or thought. It didn't matter what Severn said or thought. It was he himself who held himself responsible. He was his own accuser. It really seemed to him, in that moment of obsessing guilt, that he had encompassed the ruin entirely by his own tragic efforts—that even, in some dreadfully obscure way, the whole accident, and all its results, lay to his charge. That, of course, was madness; and I think he saw it just in time. He went to his desk and tried again—pitiably, frenziedly—to write to Helen; but everything was wordless, voiceless; there was nothing—*nothing* that he could put down. I said, with an attempt to comfort him, that Helen would almost certainly help Severn all she could; but he answered: "I don't want her just to *help* him. I want her to *want* to help him—I want her to"—he faced me with eyes like swords and added: "I can't tell you what I mean, but I *know* I could tell her."

I asked no questions, for I knew he couldn't say more than he was saying. His nerves were in shreds, racked between that dreadful sense of personal responsibility and the still passionate ideal that made him hope that by some stupendous effort he could put everything right.... And then, quite suddenly, he threw down his pen and walked across the room. "I *will* tell her," he said. "I *must*—there's no hope any other way.... I'll leave to-night—by the express—and be in London by Wednesday.... Oh, I *must* go—can't you see that I *must*—*can't* you?"

IV

I couldn't—I couldn't see anything for a while; it had all happened too suddenly.... And then, when I began to realize, it was too late; arguing was no use. Of the countless reasons why he shouldn't go, not one was apparent to him; he spoke of going as a sinner might speak of his conversion. "Somehow or other," he said, "I shall be able to help." He was certain of it. And with the certainty came, once again, optimism—a childish optimism that made him hope that Severn wasn't badly hurt (although the report most distinctly stated that he was), and that all would be well in some vague and shadowy future. Of course I raised objections; in fact, the more I thought of it, the more monstrous it seemed that he, of all people, and then, of all times, should meet Helen. What good, I asked him, did he think he could achieve by seeing her? He repeated that he could *help*. But how? Was it likely that she would fail her husband in such an emergency, and wasn't it far more likely that she would be insulted at the mere suggestion of such a thing?

He said that I hadn't understood him. He paused for a while, and I could almost see him struggling physically to put what he felt into words. Then victory came to him like a sharp explosion; he went on, with staccato excitement: "You see—I've made such a terrible hash of everything—right from the beginning. It's all led up to this—just one mistake after another.... I began it, and I've got to end it. I tell you, I've *got* to end it. Nobody can end it but me.... We were all friends once, and we've all got to be friends again—whatever happens. It doesn't work—to put people outside your life. You can't do it, even when you try, and you daren't do it, even if you could...."

"So it all amounts to this—that you're going to put Helen back into your life?"

Helen *and* Severn, he replied. And also even *I* was involved, because of my quarrel with Helen. *That* had to come to an end. We were all going to be friends again, and he would show Helen that true affection wasn't narrow and personal, but something that—that—something that.... In fact, to put the whole matter a good deal more plainly than he did, everything that was not perfect was to be summarily abolished, and the reign of universal love to begin forthwith. He was once more the eager missionary; the pendulum of his mood had swung again, and it was the future now that he saw, perfectly obliterating the imperfect past.

V

But everything that night that I shall never forget belongs to Mizzi more than to him. I went to see her in blank despondency and told her what had happened; I expected her to be at least as anxious as I was that

Terry shouldn't meet Helen. But she wasn't; she merely nodded her head and remarked, at the end of it all: "So I had better reserve for you two berths in the *wagon-lit* to-night, is it not?"

"Good heavens, no!" I cried, just in time to keep her away from the telephone. And then I asked her if she really supposed that we *could* go.

She answered: "Well, he's going, isn't he?"

"He *says* he is. But it seem to me we've got to persuade him out of it."
"Why?"

"*Why*? Well, can't you see all the hundreds of reasons why?"

"I can see this," she answered quietly, "that he *will* go, whatever we do or say. Do you remember how—the night before last—I said I wished some fate would send him back to her? ... Well, this is fate."

Her supreme calmness astonished me. I said that whether it was fate or not, his going back could only have the result of turning bad into worse. "Think of it, Mizzi—think of him meeting her for the first time after those awful letters—and *preaching* to her—that's what it'll amount to—about her duty to her husband! ... She'll feel like killing him."

"And if he stays here, he'll feel like killing himself."

"Not if you look after him."

"*I* look after him? How can I?"

"There are ways."

She looked at me with tightened lips for a moment, and then said: "It is what you call an irony—is it not?—that I should have understanding of him but no power—while *she*—this woman in England—has power but no understanding."

"But you *have* power, Mizzi."

She shook her head, smiling. "As much as you have—as much as anybody has, maybe, except *her*. You see, I understand him." She added, with no change in the level calmness of her tone: "You will be surprised, no doubt—when I tell you that last night he asked me to marry him."

I had to try to seem surprised, and I *was* surprised, quite genuinely, at her manner of telling me. She went on, almost casually: "I know why he asked me to marry him. It was so that if I said 'yes,' he would feel bound to *me*—and therefore less bound to her. He *wants* to love me, and he doesn't want to love her."

"I know he's very fond of you, Mizzi."

"Oh, yes, I daresay. But that is not quite good enough for me. I am a business woman, and I do not think the bargain is fair unless he loves me."

"You think he doesn't?"

"I am certain he doesn't."

"Why?"

"Firstly—because he tries so hard.... And then, also, there is another reason. This morning, when I told him that I would not marry him, he was glad."

"*Glad*? No—no—"

"He was. I could see the relief come into his eyes. His mind was full of thoughts about his friends in England, and about the railway accident—he really didn't want to bother about *me*. And when I refused him he looked so grateful. He was glad because it made it easier for him to go to England. He *does* want to go to England. And I—all *I* want is for the best to happen—the best for *him*."

I told her frankly that I was disappointed, and that I thought she was making a great mistake. She ought, I said, to have accepted him; he would soon have come to love her afterwards.

"Or else to hate me," she said quietly.

"Oh, that's absurd, Mizzi."

"No, no. He cannot help loving *her*—maybe, some day, if we were married, he could not help hating *me*. You see, I am cautious. I look to the future."

"And you really think that the best future for him is that he should see Helen?"

"I think the worst future is that he should stay here when all his body and soul are craving to be away."

"But I can't understand why you are so willing to let him go."

She said then, with a half-ironical shrug of the shoulders: "Ah, that is very hard to understand, I know. Maybe it is because I am selfish and care nothing for these two people whom I have never seen—nothing at all in comparison with *him*."

And that was as far as I could get with her. She had refused him, and all the arguing in the world wouldn't convince her that she oughtn't to have done, or me that she ought.

VI

I saw her again for a few moments while I paid my bill. I said that it was quite within the bounds of possibility that Terry would return to Vienna after a short interval, and that therefore it might be advisable to keep his room for him. Would she do this, and let me pay the charge without his knowing?

She told me that there would be no charge, and when I protested she said: "You can think of it, if you like, as my farewell gift to him, for I think I shall never see him again."

I demurred to that, but she only shrugged her shoulders and said: "It is a feeling I have." I asked her then if she would see Karelsky and give him some explanation of Terry's sudden departure; and she nodded all-comprehendingly. Never had she been more the calm, business woman; and it was *that*—the utter perfection of her pose—that I shall never forget.

She came with us to the station and saw us to our places on the train. The temperature had fallen slightly, and there was a cool breeze with the hint of rain in it. Terry, before the train started, thanked her for all the kindness she had shown him during those seven years, and said that he hoped he would meet her again before long. And she answered, in her coolest and most professional tones: "Oh, of course any time you are in Vienna you must be sure to come and see me. I am so pleased you have been satisfied here. Perhaps you will be good enough to recommend me to your English friends." (And yet how well she knew he hadn't any!) She was wonderful then, but the pose, because it was too perfect, gave itself away. The thought came to me at that moment overpoweringly—how extraordinary it was that Terry, with all his *penchant* for self-accusation, hadn't long ago accused himself of making her love him! For she did love him, as much as any woman who ever lived, and the love was like a fire in her eyes as the train began to move. She shook hands with us and said, not "Good-bye," but "Wiedersehen." That, I think, was just the pose, guarding her faithfully till we were gone. And what then? There's no knowing, but I remember that when the train was almost out of the station I looked out of the window and saw her still standing on the platform where we had left her, and I think, though I can't be sure, that she saw me and waved a last farewell.

It was I, perhaps, who was the more depressed during that slow, rumbling night-journey towards the mountains. Terry had his alternate moods of optimism and despondency, but I was uniformly oppressed with a sort of *Wehmut* or *Weltschmerz* or whatever untranslatable thing the Germans call it. The cold dawn came as we ran into Salzburg, and by noon the sun was blazing on the red-roofed chalets above Innsbrück. All the time I was thinking far more of the past than of the future; the parting with Mizzi seemed to me far more pitiable than anything that had or could have happened to Severn. I didn't talk to Terry about it, for he, who never understood a woman at all, had certainly never understood Mizzi. Only once, indeed, was she even mentioned, and that was when he said, quite casually: "Odd, wasn't it, that Mizzi should ask me to recommend her hotel? She might have known I should do, if ever I got the chance. But I suppose the hotel's always in her mind—it seems to be what she lives for, anyhow."

"Do you think so?"

"She told me so herself, only yesterday. She said she didn't care for anything or anybody in the world except her hotel."

I didn't argue the point. But I guessed then (and I still think my guess was right) that that had been her way of refusing him. And perhaps, after all, it was the best way—the best because it could not but leave him with a tinge of disappointment in her. After such words, it would be hard for him to feel pity for her loneliness. Sometimes now I wonder what would have happened if I had said to him outright: "Mizzi loves you, despite her refusal, and her misery now that you've gone is more your fault than any of these other things, and also far easier to undo. Go back and love her and be happy...." He mightn't have believed me, and he certainly wouldn't have obeyed me; but perhaps, in his moments of deepest remorse, he would have tacked on Mizzi's unhappiness to the already heavy enough load of his own responsibilities. And that, of course, was the chief reason why I didn't tell him.

VII

The long journey passed, and by the time we reached the Swiss frontier, we knew all that the newspapers knew, at any rate, concerning the tragedy. It was an ordinary enough story of a driver trying to make up lost time and negotiating a curve ten miles an hour too fast. Result: derailment and a death-roll, so far, of twenty-four. The Basle newspapers, though they took great care to be incorrect about Severn's life and career (one of them even called him "l'avocat général de l'Angleterre"), gave no information as to the nature or extent of his injury. Somehow the absence of detail, and the fact that we were already nearer Paris than Vienna, overwhelmed me with a sense of this sharper and more instant tragedy; perhaps for the first time I ceased to think about Mizzi. I told Terry, as we stood at the buffet-counter at Troyes, that I was glad we had come, because if we could help Severn even a little, it would be worth while. He gripped my arm eagerly and replied: "I *knew* you would think that—I knew you would."

Early in the morning we passed very slowly the scene of the accident (only a few miles from the Gare de l'Est), and saw the gigantic litter of wreckage, and the break-down cranes still working over the shattered and telescoped coaches. A dull drizzling rain was falling, and a grinning baby advertising a famous soap looked down on the scene from the wall of a near-by factory. Ten minutes later we were pacing the long platform of the terminus. The entire station and precincts were packed with English conducted tourists to the popular Swiss resorts; uniformed guides were shepherding them into groups, and I heard one of them promise his party that very soon they would be able to see "the place where the train ran off the lines." A gratuitous tit-bit added by Providence to their Ten Days in Lovely Lucerne.

We joined the crowd of anxious and grief-stricken inquirers in the information bureau. The small, ugly room seethed, as it were, with its burden of misery; and there was something hideously incongruous in the wall-posters of smiling red-cheeked holiday-makers perched on the summits of impossibly precipitous Alps. Women sobbed and chattered amidst their sobbing; men shouted and gesticulated; the whole *ensemble*, with the noises of trains and beating rain as an accompaniment, made me understand how men can sometimes lose control of themselves and run suddenly amok. The waiting lasted three-quarters of an hour, and then, when our turn came, the official would hardly listen when he found that we weren't *related* to anyone concerned. We argued (so far as my limited French would allow), and all the while the official's nerves, as well as my own, were being strained nearer and nearer to breaking-point. Who were we? We gave our names. What was our connection with Severn? What were we—professionally? I took the liberty of labelling Terry "médecin," but when I went on to describe myself as "journaliste," everything everywhere seemed to snap suddenly. The official shouted and waved his arms about; he appealed to the crowd; the crowd shouted; I shouted; and Terry stood by me all the while, silent and very pale. He knew so little French that the row could only have puzzled him. It puzzled me, indeed, until I realized afterwards that I had been mistaken for some newspaper ghoul in search of copy.

At last, after explaining over and over again that we were both near friends of Severn and had travelled from Vienna especially to see him, I was reluctantly allowed to learn that he had been taken to a hospital in the Avenue Friedland. And five minutes after that, as we sat in the cab that was bearing us at breakneck speed along the boulevards, Terry collapsed.

That squabble in the station inquiry-office had been the last straw. Till then he had never wholly given way, but that—that almost trivial thing—shattered all the final strength he possessed. In the semi-darkness of the cab he made total surrender. It seemed a sort of fainting-fit; I wasn't skilled enough to diagnose exactly. But I realized immediately that it was no use going on with him to the hospital. He recovered when I opened both windows of the cab and let in the wind and rain;

and then I shouted to the driver to take us to the nearest hotel. We pulled up almost straightway outside a large establishment in the Place du Hâvre, and for the next hour I worked like an automaton—getting Terry comfortable, calling in a doctor, and making all the necessary arrangements with the hotel people. The doctor reported a complete nervous collapse, and prescribed a long and absolute rest-cure; it was what I had expected. What I had *not* expected was Terry's childlike acquiescence; all desire, it seemed, had gone out of him. He didn't even want to see Severn. "*You* can go," he said, with a sort of tired sadness.

I said that I certainly would, and he smiled and closed his eyes. The doctor had given him a draught, and within a few minutes he was heavily asleep.

VIII

I went to the hospital that evening, and after prolonged difficulties and much tipping of porters, managed to reach Severn at last. He was in a small, comfortably-furnished separate room with a crucifix over the mantelpiece and a view of the brilliantly-lit Champs Elysées through the window. They had stretched him out on a sort of suspended platform, and the whole of his head and face, with the exception of apertures cut for his eyes, was a mass of bandages. Only his left hand was free to move, but as soon as I approached he held it out and pressed mine with the old sharp grip that he had always had. And then, while his eyes sparkled like black gems, he wrote in pencil on a writing-pad: "Delighted to see you. I can't talk, but I'm learning to write with my left hand. What's brought you here? Do you want a special interview with the man who had a carriage-door pushed into his spine?"

I stared at him and saw his eyes dancing (so it seemed to me) with merriment. *Could* it have been that? I stammered: "My dear Severn, I came—*we* came—Terry and I—to see how you were.... Are you—are you very badly hurt?"

He wrote: "There's a nasty kink in my spine, I'm afraid. Also a few face-scratches and a knock on the posterior third of the left parietal bone. Right arm sprained. Spirits excellent. Where's Terry?"

I told him the truth—that Terry was in bed at the hotel (which I named), and that he would have come with me if he had been at all well enough.

He wrote instantly: "So he's ill? I'm not surprised. What he needs is a long rest cure. Are you going to take him back to England?"

Was I? I had hardly thought what I was going to do, but I said: "Most likely, if I can manage to persuade him to come with me." Then Severn wrote: "That's right. We're both crocked up, Terry and I, and you've jolly well got to help us. You're the ministering angel. I'm the interesting mangle. The doctors think so, anyway."

I laughed hysterically. Then I made inquiries about Helen, and he wrote that she and June had been cabled for from New York, where they had been on holiday. They were already on their way. All this questioning and answering took time, for he insisted on writing down everything exactly as he would have spoken it. At the last moment, when the sister had entered to indicate that I must go, I asked him if there was anything I could do, and he wrote, in large block capitals: "Yes. Come and see me again before you go to England. But don't bring Terry—it would only upset him. And also, if you've time, you might run down into the basement of the Magasins du Louvre and buy me one of their BBB pencils with cork holders."

I wanted to laugh again—to burst into loud, unchecked laughter; but the sister was patiently waiting for me at the door. It was she who told me, as she led the way along the corridor to the head of the stairs, that most likely Severn would have to be wheeled about in a chair for the rest of his life. Somehow, even in my most despondent moments, I had never thought of anything so bad as that. I had pictured him dying of injuries; I had been prepared for even amputations and disfigurements; but this grim foreshadowing of death within life struck me with freezing bewilderment.

And so again into the heavy-scented night. The whole visit to Severn had lasted less than half an hour and I have set down everything I can remember of it. If the result seems rather slight and scrappy, make allowance for the fact that I had spent two successive nights in a train, and was fatigued to the point of faintness. I remember standing on the kerb facing the Arc de Triomphe and wondering if I too were going to crock up; I know that I walked the whole length of the Champs Elysées down to the Place de la Concorde before deciding finally that I wasn't. At a café in the Rue Royale I fortified myself with coffee and cognac and was glad of the few moments' rest; besides, I had to make up my mind what I should tell Terry.

He was still fast asleep when I reached the hotel, and I sat up reading and smoking in his room until very late. About two in the morning he awakened, but seemed too dazed to ask questions; I gave him a simple, straightforward account of my visit, stressing what was favourable and ignoring the worst. He thanked me when I had finished, but that was all. No questions; no comments even; it was as if he were too weary even to be interested. I told him that Helen and June were on their way back from America, but even then he only nodded his comprehension. And the next moment, with a whispered "Good-night," he closed his eyes and slept.

But there was no sleep for me. Despite an overwhelming tiredness I lay awake till the early morning traffic made sleep impossible. I smoked cigarette after cigarette in bed; and then, on sudden impulse, I got up and wrote a letter to Roebuck, telling him to prepare a second bed in my bedroom. "It is possible," I wrote, "that when I come back I shall bring with me a friend who will stay some time...." After all, that was the only thing to do. Terry had no English friends except me and Severn, and Severn had enough trouble of his own without being called upon to help Terry. There was really no alternative to his coming to stay with me, unless he went back to Vienna, which he probably wouldn't do in any case. Fortunately my rooms, though few, were fairly commodious, and Roebuck was the sort of man who would rise to an emergency. The only thing I feared was that Terry would find London, and especially the part I lived in, too bustling and noisy for him; apart from that, I was confident I could make him feel comfortable and at home.

The letter to Roebuck was never sent, for before the ink on the envelope was dry, the chambermaid brought me my morning pot of coffee, and with it the following letter from Severn, posted late the night before:

"MY DEAR HILTON,—I must write to thank you for your visit yesterday; it made me more cheerful than any hospital patient has a right to be; but the result, unfortunately, has been a strict order from the doctor that I'm to be kept perfectly quiet and to be allowed no more visitors till Helen and June arrive. He (the doctor) swore that you excited me, and so, by God, you did, and I wouldn't have missed a moment of it. Anyhow, I'm not in any severe pain, and I'm allowed to read and think, so I've nothing much to grumble about. Perhaps, if you remember, you could call at Brentano's in the Avenue de l'Opéra and have sent to me a copy of Brieux's play, *Les Hannetons*, which a friend advised me to read a few weeks ago.

"And now about Terry. I really think you had better get him to England as soon as you can, for breakdowns are serious things, and Paris at midsummer is the very last place to cure them. I happen to have a controlling interest in a small but decent hotel-pub near Hindhead, and if you will send (or, better still, take) the enclosed letter to the manager he will no doubt be pleased to accommodate Terry and yourself for as long as you like. I think it would be a good thing if you took Terry there the minute he is fit to travel.

"Just one thing more. I wonder if you could possibly arrange to meet Helen and June at Liverpool? They are due to arrive by the *Franconia* next Monday, and it would be a kindly act to cheer them on the way here. Besides, you and Helen might make it an excuse for becoming good friends again. Please try to manage it, will you?

"Some of these requests are a sad trespass on your good nature, but, as I remarked before, you're already cast for the rôle of ministering angel! Ever yours,

"GEOFFREY SEVERN."

I have that letter still, and if I'm ever asked what sort of a man Severn is, I should like to show it and say: He's the sort of man who could write that sort of letter three days after being crippled for life....

I read it through to Terry, and when I had finished he looked almost as if he were going to cry. "It's awfully good of him," he said, and I took that to mean that he would accept the hotel offer. So that was one thing settled, anyhow. After a pause I said tentatively that I thought it mightn't be a bad idea if I *did* meet Helen at Liverpool, and I suggested that he and I could travel together as far as Hindhead. He nodded tranquilly, and the whole thing seemed beautifully arranged until the doctor came and absolutely forbade him to travel so soon. In vain my protests about the comparative quietude of Paris and Hindhead; even Paris, he insisted, was better than crowding on trains and steamers. Perhaps by the middle of the following week the journey could be attempted, but certainly not before....

It was Terry, after that, who suggested that I should leave him in Paris while I went to meet Helen. He would be all right, he assured me; he would just potter about the hotel and do nothing at all. And when I looked doubtful he said, with the first sign of eagerness that I had seen in him since his collapse: "Oh, you *must* go, Hilton. It's time somebody did the right thing...."

It was time somebody did the right thing. That, I think, was the saddest thing he ever said, for it showed his spirit at its pitiable lowest—without pride and without hope.

CHAPTER SEVEN

I

FOUR days later I met Helen at Liverpool. She and June were among the first to land, and the meeting was about as casual as if we had been separated for seven hours instead of seven years. She had evidently been wirelessed concerning my arrival, for she said, almost without surprise: "You have come from Paris, I understand, and have seen him? Tell me how he is."

I recited the sentence I had carefully prepared beforehand: "It is serious, but by no means hopeless. We shall reach the hospital to-morrow morning, and you'll find him, I think, very cheerful."

June said, as we walked to the train: "It is ever so good of you to come and meet us like this," but Helen did not echo or assent to the remark. She merely asked me if I were proceeding to London, and when I replied affirmatively, she exclaimed: "I hope you aren't thinking of escorting us back to Paris. June and I have been travelling at all hours of the day and night for the past three months, so I can assure you—"

"As it happens," I interrupted, "I have business in Paris, and must return there immediately." (It was true enough, though the nature of the business would doubtless have surprised her.)

She made no answer, but June smiled and said she hoped we shouldn't have a rough crossing. She, at any rate, was disposed to be friendly.

It wasn't till we were in the railway luncheon-car, with the fields of Cheshire rolling past us, that I was able to take a real look at them both. And then the extraordinariness of it all came upon me—that we three, after seven years, should meet together again like this. June, during that long interval, had grown up; but Helen was almost startlingly the same at first sight, though a sharper glance revealed lines and contours that did not so much detract from her beauty as change the aspect of it. There was little conversation throughout the journey, and I was made to feel that the seven-years feud was by no means ended. June and I exchanged a few sentences—chiefly about America and kindred topics. Only once did she mention Severn, and that was (I noticed) while Helen had left us temporarily. June asked me then if I thought her father would get better, and I replied that it seemed to me quite possible that he might outlive the lot of us. It was a quibble, but she appeared not to notice it. She said, quickly: "Oh, I do hope so. He was always very good to me." And with just the faintest possible accent on the "me."

I am trying, you see, to set all this down as simply as I can. And here, perhaps, I ought to attempt some sort of a description of June. All I can say is that she had reddish hair and clear blue eyes and wasn't quite as good-looking as her mother. One thing she was, anyhow, that her mother had never been; she was English—the independent, honest, freckled product of the English boarding-school and college, plus that shy and unanalysable something that makes the difference between a girl and a woman. All the way to London I had the impression that she was doing what she could to put me at my ease, and that Helen was doing just the opposite.

We reached Euston at five o'clock, dined at the Belgravia, and caught the evening boat-train from Victoria. At Dover heavy rain was falling, and the omens for the crossing were distinctly bad. June was a poor sailor and went below immediately; I secured a cabin for her, and tipped a stewardess to make her comfortable. I suggested that Helen should join her, but she wouldn't; she could stand the roughest passage, she said, provided she stayed on deck in the fresh air. "If you'll leave me here," she said, "with a rug and a mackintosh, I shall be perfectly well. And now you'd better get a cabin for yourself or else stake out a claim in the men's smoking-room."

"You don't wish me to share the wind and the rain with you?"

She replied: "Well, frankly, since you ask me, I'm not particularly keen...."

II

There was no doubt about the weather; as soon as the harbour was left behind, the ship began to sway and shiver sickeningly. I chatted for a while with one of the stewards; he told me uncomfortably that a storm in July was rather rare, but that when it did come it was usually severe. All the time we were talking I could hear the wind rising to gale ferocity; there were also intermittent rumblings of thunder. I felt an obligation to look after Helen, despite her rudeness to me, so I climbed on deck and met her dragging a deck-chair along one of the companionways; she handed it to me rather sulkily, remarking that she was looking for a spot that was better sheltered from the rain and spray. I said I would find one for her, and we staggered with difficulty along the heaving decks. With the port-lights falling on them, the waves looked like rolls of dark moorland peaked with snow. Then, quite suddenly, one of them lifted over the edge and mounted towards us in a huge black wall; we just managed to escape its full onrush, and were immediately and peremptorily ordered below by a ship's officer.

After that the terrible became merely the sordid. In the lower saloons the occupants were horridly inert and comatose; many were engulfed in the varying throes of *mal de mer*; most were grimly unhappy. The smells of oil and stale cooking were all-pervading; intermittent crashes told of casualties in the pantries; the ship's engines groaned like the breathing of a pneumonia sufferer. All this I relate, not as descriptive padding, but to show how force of circumstances drove Helen and me together that night. I suggested first of all that she should share June's cabin, but after visiting it and finding June comfortably asleep, she returned to say that she would rather do anything than lie down. "Then," I said, "there remains the bar. It's probably the most cheerful spot on the whole boat, and French beer isn't a bad sort of tonic."

She said: "You'll have to take me then," and I nodded and took her.

We hung on to the counter and heard the bartender being violently sick behind the scenes. And she said: "I suppose you think you're heaping coals of fire on my head?"

"How so?"

"By being kind to me after I've been rude to you."

"Well—you certainly *have* been rude to me, haven't you?"

"Yes," she replied simply. And after a pause she added: "I rather loathe the sentimental way you assume that everything else is going to be forgotten just because of what's happened to Geoffrey."

"Well?"

"I suppose you thought I was going to welcome you with open arms on Liverpool landing-stage, eh?"

"Not in the least. I only hoped that our desire to help Geoffrey would enable us to treat each other civilly."

Her eyes flashed. "Yes, that sounds as if I'm in the wrong, doesn't it? But let me tell you this—that though I *am* going to help Geoffrey, my feelings towards him remain exactly as they were before."

"And what were they?"

She said quietly: "I don't like him. I don't care what you think of me for saying it—it's the honest truth. And I'm not sentimental enough to think that a railway-accident can make any difference."

The beer came then, and a sudden lurch of the boat sent half of it spilling over our hands. The bartender, white-faced and dishevelled, retired again to endure his sufferings in solitude. She went on, more quickly: "Oh, I know what you're thinking. You're thinking of Geoffrey as *you* know him—how decent he's been to you, and all that. He *has* been decent to you, I'll admit—he's been decent enough to me in *that* sort of way. But—oh, Hilton—I'm friends with you again now, and I must tell you—he's not *straight*—you know what I mean, don't you? He's not the sort of man you can *trust*!"

"Good heavens, I think I'd trust my life to him—"

She interrupted: "I daresay you would. I daresay a lot of people would.... Perhaps I ought to have said that he's not the sort of man his wife can trust."

And then, while the boat rolled so badly that once or twice we were almost battered from wall to wall, she told me. Oddly, perhaps, I didn't realize her complete meaning till she was half-way through—not till she said: "If he only had that one fault in the world (and perhaps he has), it would be enough to make me despise him—for I value faithfulness higher than anything."

Faithfulness! Then she knew ...? *Did* she know? ... Could it possibly have come to her knowledge already ...?

She was telling me how, after her marriage, she had first of all trusted him implicitly. "There were several incidents that made me wonder a little, but I made myself believe that he was *good*. I knew, of course, that women flung themselves at him—*that* wasn't his fault. And besides, he trusted me so much—he never seemed to bother where I went or who went with me. I loathed the idea of being jealous.... And so it went on—for a few years; I just had faith in him—in *us*—and if sometimes I got to hear scraps of gossip, I ignored them.... Then came an affair I couldn't possibly ignore, and there was a fearful row. I nearly left him, but he gave his promise, and I said I'd try to trust him again."

She said, rather pathetically: "You say you'll *try* to trust somebody again, but you don't very often succeed. Personally, I don't think you ever can—it's such a far deeper matter than repentance or forgiveness. There are some people who have it in them to do certain things, and others who haven't—and if you find out that a man belongs to the first kind, then it's final—don't you think so? ... Anyhow, I stayed on with Geoffrey, and, so far as I know, he kept his promise till last year. Then I found he'd been spending week-ends with a girl at Rotterdam.... Do you know, it didn't surprise me a bit.... It didn't even hurt me.... I just felt that I hadn't a scrap of love for him, and that it didn't matter.... I didn't trouble to mention it even; I just let things go on as if nothing had happened, and then, when the fine weather came, I took June with me to America.... And I didn't ever intend to come back."

"But June—does *she* know all this?"

"She knows nothing."

"You would have had to tell her."

"I daresay.... I hadn't made any plans about that. I just made up my mind to leave Geoffrey and never see him again. But of course the accident has altered *that*. I shall stay with him now, but I can't pretend to *like* him any more."

"That seems a hard thing to say."

"Perhaps it *is* hard. You must remember I'm French, and that makes me face the facts as they are."

I said that, however little affection she had for her husband, she wouldn't be able to stop herself from admiring his pluck and cheerfulness. She replied: "It won't matter whether I admire him or not. Admiration is nothing."

"And pity—is *that* nothing?

"I have pity for anyone in misfortune. It is pity that will make me stay with him and help him."

"Perhaps, anyhow, the motive doesn't matter so much. It's what you do that will count, for it's possible—rather more than possible, I'm afraid—that he'll never be able to walk again."

That stirred her, I could see. She whispered, tremulously: "Is that really true?"—and when I nodded slowly, she just bit her lip and said nothing ... nothing at all. It was as if she *couldn't* speak. There came just then a terrific peal of thunder, vibrant above the muffled thudding of the engines, and I think I spoke some word or phrase of reassurance. But she just stared at me blankly—stared *through* me almost; and then, in a queerly casual voice, remarked: "That was loud. I think I'll go down to June's cabin and see if it wakened her...."

She went out, staggering against the roll and pitch of the boat, and not till we were calm in Calais Harbour did I see her again.

III

After that wild scene in mid-Channel, the rest of the journey to Paris lingers in my mind as a quiet and cool aftermath. The train at Calais was packed as only a French boat-train can be packed; I managed to secure seats in the first-class coach for Helen and June, but the latter elected to surrender hers to a lady who had been very ill during the crossing. So we sat on our suit-cases in the corridor, June and I; and there wasn't much room, even there, for the holiday season was at its height, and all the well-known advertised tours to Paris were in full swing. June had passed through Paris before, but had never stayed there or seen the city. "I should like to have done," she said, "but mother was always in a hurry to get through to somewhere else."

"That's rather odd," I remarked, "considering that Paris is your mother's native place. One would have expected her to enjoy re-visiting the old familiar scenes."

June answered quietly: "That's just the sort of thing she would hate most of all. She loathes sentiment about the past. That's why she likes America—because its beauty isn't so dreadfully steeped in memories ... Palm Beach, for instance."

"You've been there? I suppose you've travelled rather a lot?"

"Well, I've always joined mother abroad during college vacations, and now that I've finished my last year I daresay we should have practically lived abroad but for this—this awful accident...." She paused for a moment, and then went on: "Mother hates England, but *I* don't. Do you know, there's one place more than any other that I've wanted to visit during the last few years, and I haven't had a chance yet?"

"Where's that?" I asked, and she replied:

"My own home at Hampstead. I used to love Hampstead Heath and the walk across Parliament Hill Fields to Highgate. I can remember it all from when I was a child."

"And since then you haven't been at home at all?"

"Just odd nights now and then. As soon as the terms were over at school and at Newnham, I've always had to dash away to join my mother in Sweden or Algeria or somewhere.... Of course I've enjoyed it all—immensely—but"—she smiled—"I'd have preferred a week or two in London now and again."

The dawn was stealing in from over the grey Normandy fields, and a misty rain dimmed the windowpanes. We were silent for a few miles, and then she resumed, thoughtfully: "I feel so sorry that I haven't been at home oftener."

"Why?"

"Because I would like to have known my father better."

I looked at her and saw that her blue, tranquil eyes were shining with tears. But the tears did not fall; she had perfect control of herself. She went on: "I don't think it's been quite fair to him to leave him as my mother has done. Of course, he's awfully busy, and isn't home a great deal himself, but still—we *might* have had more to do with him."

I said nothing; there seemed nothing to say. She was evidently eager to pour out her mind on the subject, for she continued: "So you see, my father's almost a stranger to me. I've seen him perhaps once every three months or so during the past ten years, and I've always liked him.... Mostly, though, I *remember* him—just as if he were dead. I remember him teaching me to skate on Highgate Ponds, and I remember him giving me a gold sovereign on the night when he first got elected to Parliament."

"Ah—the Manchester South bye-election. That was a good many years ago."

"But I remember it quite well. I remember you visiting us a lot in those days, and also a man called Terry, who used to do chemistry experiments in the kitchen."

"Terry!" I echoed; and then, before I knew what I was saying, I had replied: "He's in Paris now."

"Is he?" she exclaimed. "Oh, I would like to see him. He must be getting quite old."

"Thirty-one. That's not old."

"It sounds horribly old to me."

I don't know what answer I made; I only know that I was thinking furiously: She's bound to tell Helen that Terry's in Paris, and *then* what will happen? ... The blunder was clumsy and irrevocable, for I dared not face June's puzzled eyes by asking her not to mention Terry to her mother. The only thing to hope for was that he and I would be on our way to England before any complications could ensue.

IV

And that, by the grace of God, was what happened.

We reached the Gare du Nord at breakfast-time and drove straight to the Crillon, where I engaged rooms for them. After hasty cups of coffee we went on to the hospital, and there, in the corridor outside

Severn's room, I left them. The sister said that there was no change in his condition, and it seemed to me that I had better leave them to visit him by themselves. Helen barely nodded a farewell, but June, though her thoughts were obviously elsewhere, was polite enough to thank me for my escort.

And so once more to the hotel in the Place du Hâvre. Terry seemed, if anything, more tired and listless than ever; but the doctor had said he could travel and so, after lunch, we left by the afternoon train for Dieppe, stayed there overnight, and went on to Newhaven by the mail-boat the next morning. Then London at last—after his seven years of absence. I wondered, as we pushed our way into a taxi, whether it meant anything to him—to return after so long an exile. I don't think it did. I think he was too tired to notice any difference between London and Paris. As we drove into Waterloo Station we saw a weekly paper's placard advertising in large type: "Karelsky on the Life-Force," and that—only that—seemed to give him a spasm of recollection. He put his hands to his eyes and said: "I wish I hadn't worked so hard out there. I seem to have made such a hash of things—getting crocked like this and wasting all your time.... It's ever so kind of you."

Two hours later the journey was over. It had been hot and rather tiresome, but it ended at the quaintest and prettiest hotel I have ever seen. It wasn't really more than a inn, and perhaps for fifty or a hundred years it had served mugs of beer to wayfarers on the road from Hindhead to Farnham. Then had come Severn with his "controlling interest," and in a single summer's afternoon a sign-painter had turned the old Brown Cow into the new Valley Hotel. Mercifully the transformation had involved little more than that.

But the interior comfort was as astonishing, almost, as the effect produced by Severn's letter of introduction. We were more than welcomed; we were fêted; and the manager, Taplow by name, assured us with great fervency that it would be a real pleasure to look after Terry and me and, indeed, everybody and anybody else who was a friend of Severn's. Severn, he informed us stoutly, was "the finest chap who ever breathed." And forthwith he served us with a dinner that was at least as good, if not so complicated, as many I have had in first-class city hotels. Even of wines and liqueurs he could provide an amazingly wide selection. "It's Mr. Severn that manages the wine-list, sir," he told me, as he brought my *cordiale Médoc*. "Ah, he's a real good judge of wines—and of most other things too, I should say. He had his ideas about this place right from the beginning—saw it one afternoon as he was motoring past and bought it on the spot, as you might say.... Such a pity about his accident—and I do hope he gets well again. Well, really, sir, it came as such a shock to me when I read about it in the papers, I do declare I couldn't eat my dinner after it—*that* I couldn't...."

V

There comes to me now, as I think of the Valley Hotel, a sense of strange and wonderful tranquillity. For it is here, in Taplow's garden, that I am writing these words; the furious, tragic interlude is over, and all at last seems stilled in the shadow of this English inn. Counting over the pages I have written, I find that more than half are concerned with those days in Buda-Pesth and Vienna and Paris; it would stagger me if I didn't remember how packed with happenings they were.... The miles I covered and the frontiers I crossed and re-crossed—the hotels and the trains and the steamers—the days of scurry and the long nights of wakefulness! ... But all—all are over now, quenched in the glory of this autumn day at Hindhead, with the hollyhocks waving over me and the far brown hills in the sunlight.

But Terry.... After all, this story is about him, not me. The trouble is that I can only describe what he said and did; I can't pretend to see into his mind and describe what he thought. And what he said and did during those first weeks at the Valley Hotel is so easily told; he just said and did nothing. I used to visit him at week-ends, and each time I found him a little stronger-looking, a little less thin and haggard; but in all other respects unchanged. He was cordial enough, but somehow he seemed not to care very much about anything—whether I came or went or even what news I brought him about Severn.

From Taplow came information as to how he spent his time. Apparently he still slept badly, and used often to rise at dawn and take a long walk before breakfast. Then, after that, he sometimes took another walk, but more usually sat in a deck-chair in Taplow's garden and slept for hours with the sun on his face. On wet days he would haunt the sitting-room like a lost soul. "It's like as if he was tired out," said Taplow. "And yet you wouldn't think so if you was to see him walking along the road. Four mile an hour to Farnham and back—that's what he did the other day. And then he wouldn't have any supper—nothing but a smoke and a drop of whisky...."

"Good God!" I exclaimed, "do you mean to say he's begun to smoke and drink?"

Taplow nodded. "But he don't do it like an ordinary human being. Now for myself, I like a cigar and a glass of stout every night before bedtime. But *he* don't seem to have any proper habits—sometimes he'll come into the bar before breakfast and ask for a double. *Before breakfast*, mind you—a thing I've never done in my life. And then, after that, maybe, he won't touch a drop for days and days...."

The next time I was with Terry alone I mentioned the matter, congratulating him on having dropped what I had always considered to be the rather stupid rule of strict abstinence. He answered quickly and almost curtly: "Oh, it isn't *that*—there's no need to congratulate me. It's just that I don't care what I do."

And that, so far as I could judge, was the solemn truth. He didn't care. He had let things go, and there was no more strength of mind in him. Yet all the time, nevertheless, his strength of body was returning. After two months at the Valley Hotel he was changed, physically, almost beyond recognition; his bronzed face and arms and the broadening out of his shoulders gave a splendid impression of recovery until he began to talk. For his talk—what little of it there was—betrayed the truth—that he was tired and sad and melancholy and uninterested. The days came one after the other, an endless dull procession; his body loved the sunlight and the long walks over the hills, but his mind loved nothing, desired nothing. And I, wanting all the time to help him, was powerless to light the fire that had gone out. I remember a Sunday evening when we climbed the long hill to the cross-roads and watched the Devil's Punch-Bowl fill slowly with a vast lake of twilight. I told him then that I had had a letter from June informing me that Severn was shortly to be taken home. "She says he's wonderfully cheerful and full of plans for the future. He's going to write a book about Disraeli."

It was good news (which was the reason I had communicated it), yet it seemed to stir him painfully. He cried, in a sudden rush of words: "Oh, I know—he sent me a letter the other day—said he wouldn't ever be able to walk again.... But he doesn't care about it—or about anything.... Neither do I—it's the only way—not caring.... But *his* not caring is somehow like bright sunlight, whereas mine's like a heavy cloud pressing down on me.... *Do* you know what I mean?"

"Perhaps," I said, "you mean that not caring comes naturally to him, but not to you?"

He wouldn't, or couldn't, think that out. "I *don't* care, anyway," he almost shouted. "I've done enough caring.... If I could change places with him and take his injury, I'd do so gladly, but I can't, so what's the good of caring? It won't help him, or me either."

"And is it helping you not to care?" I asked, but his burst of confidence was over, and all he gave me was a doubtful shake of the head. We walked back to the hotel with hardly another word, and later on, as I strolled down the lane to post a letter, I caught sight of him whisky-drinking in the bar.

VI

Severn was taken home at the beginning of September, and a few days later a letter from him invited me to dinner at the End House. He wrote that he had stood the journey very well, and was delighted to be back in his own home.

Helen and June were both in the drawing-room when I arrived, and if Helen's attitude was a shade cool, June's was a shade warm to make up for it. I did not see Severn himself till we went into the dining-room; the butler then wheeled him in on a specially-constructed chair and placed him at the angle of the table that was most convenient. He was a good deal paler than I had seen him before, but his spirits were high as ever. He said that of the two occupations, walking and talking, he very much preferred the latter, which was lucky, in view of what had happened. "Fortunately, also," he added, "I was always extremely lazy, and never walked an inch when I could possibly find a vehicle of any sort to ride in. Now I can even ride in and out of my own dining-room...."

The dinner itself was quite up to Severn's usual high standard. He and I lingered over our coffee while the others took theirs on the verandah. His peculiar pose (the only unusual feature of him) suited the informal stage of the meal and made him seem almost his old self again; even when he discussed his changed future with me I found it hard to believe in the tragic reality that was behind it all. He said that the accident had settled one thing, at any rate; it had put the veto on his political career. "I might fight the next election as a *tour-de-force*, but I could never dream of taking office—that goes without saying.... Anyhow, since he who runs may read, I suppose he who cannot run may write. There are a few much-maligned characters in history I've always had a fancy to defend, so now's my chance.... Disraeli for one ... and Machiavelli, and Robert Walpole ... and perhaps even Pontius Pilate...."

He went on: "There's another matter which has perhaps been settled by those scoundrelly French railways ... I mean—about Helen."

I said "Of course," hardly knowing what I meant; and he rejoined: "She won't leave me now, whatever happens—women are like that.... So perhaps, in the altered circumstances, it would be rather needlessly cruel to supply her with hotel evidence from Buda-Pesth."

I said eagerly that I was very glad, and hoped that he and Helen would learn to be very happy again, and so on. He soon interrupted me. He said: "You know, Hilton, you're too damned sentimental, that's what's the matter with you. You've still got the idea that I'm a very moral fellow at heart, and that all my talk is just a sort of cynical pose to cover up the gold underneath.... The fact is, you're born, in my opinion, to be a successful novel-writer. You've just got the right mixture of brains, sentiment, and conventionality."

We laughed together, and then he asked me to tell him all the news about Terry. I did so, and at the end of the recital he said: "He's an extraordinary puzzle. What possessed him to work himself to death in Vienna? What possessed him to preach at me like an infuriated missionary? What possesses him to do anything?"

"*Something* possesses him," I admitted.

"You reckon you understand him?"

"A little, perhaps."

"Then perhaps you'll be able to understand this letter. It reached me yesterday."

He took it from his pocket and handed it to me. It was on Valley Hotel notepaper and ran thus:

"DEAR SEVERN,—Thanks for your letter telling me the bad news. I'm no good at writing, but you'll know what I mean when I just say I'm sorry. If there were anything I could do, I'd do it, but there isn't anything. You've been right and I've been wrong in our ways of looking at things, and I can see that now, though I couldn't years ago when we argued about progress. Please don't ask me to come to the End House yet—I don't feel I *could* come. All you have done for me—and especially the chance you've given me of being here—makes me feel ashamed and a prig. Sincerely yours,

"TERRY."

Severn was smiling when I had finished reading. "Can you give me some or any idea what it's all about?" he asked, with a whimsical lift of his eyebrows.

I read it through once again very carefully before I replied. Somehow I *felt* the meaning of it right enough, but to explain it to Severn was another matter. Nor was I at all sure that I would explain it, even if I could. I said at last: "I think it shows the state of his mind more than anything else."

"Do you mean that he's off his head?"

"Oh, no—not that, by any means."

"Then what?"

"I don't know that I can tell you exactly.... It seems to me that he's in a sort of slough of despond—he's overworked and over-worried himself into a state of acute mental and spiritual depression—do you know what I mean? I can imagine he's on the verge of anything—he might suddenly take to drink, or religion, or fall headlong into some love affair, or even kill himself.... Or, of course, he might—and probably will—just do nothing at all."

Severn laughed. "Your explanation is even more bewildering than Terry himself."

"I daresay it is. It's hard to put into a sentence something that could only be properly explained by giving you the whole history of the man's life."

"All right. Give it to me. I've heaps of time to listen."

"I'm afraid it would take too long.... Oughtn't we to be joining the ladies?"

"Oh, never mind the ladies. For the moment they aren't half as interesting as Terry.... You said just now that the true explanation of him is in his life-history?"

"I certainly think it is, but I didn't say I could give it you off-hand. As a matter of fact, a good deal of it's so complicated that I don't think I *could* tell it—though I might manage to put it down on paper."

He was silent for a moment, and then the idea came to him. "My dear fellow," he exclaimed suddenly, brandishing his cigar, "the solution's staring us in the face and we haven't seen it! ... Man, it's a great notion! ... *Put* it down on paper, as you say—put down every word of it! Then spin it out, or cut it down, as the case may be, into a full-length novel! ... I told you years ago that you'd have to write a novel some time or other—it's expected of every literary man. Now's your big chance—a novel about Terry, giving a rational and coherent account of all his virtues, vices, and vagaries!"

I laughed, and said that the trouble would begin when other people's virtues, vices and vagaries invaded the story, as they certainly would. He answered: "That doesn't matter a bit. Change all our names and nobody will be the wiser."

"Except ourselves."

"What do you mean?"

I said, rather carefully: "Well, there are certain things that you and I know, and that Helen doesn't know, aren't there?"

"I suppose there are."

"There are also—maybe—things that Helen and I know, and that you don't know."

"*Really?*" His eyes suddenly sparkled. "But, my dear chap, what a splendid reason for writing the novel! Pour all these strange and exclusive secrets into the melting-pot—let's all of us know the plain unadulterated (and, if possible, unadulterous) truth about one another, and damned be him that first cries, 'Hold, enough'!"

Argumentatively it sounded all right; in practice, as I could see, it bristled with dangers and objections. And yet the idea of setting down the truth about Terry began to be just slightly fascinating, and all the rest of the evening it was vaguely on my mind. So also must it have been on Severn's, for the last thing he said when I bade him good-night was: "As soon as you get home, take a pen and a clean sheet of paper and write 'Chapter One' at the top left-hand corner.... I'm serious, mind; in fact, I shall ring you up in the morning and ask if you've done it...."

VII

Of course I didn't do it. And when, as he had promised, he rang me up the next morning, I told him that even if I did tackle the novel (which was by no means decided), it was unlikely that I should begin for some time. It was a big undertaking, I said, and would need a good deal of planning and thinking over before even a word was written.

And yet I wrote the first sentence that very evening. It was Saturday, and I had motor-cycled over to the Valley Hotel. Terry was out when I arrived, so I sat in Taplow's garden waiting for him. And there and then, since there was nothing else to do, I thought I would make a few rough preliminary notes, and I wrote, on a sheet of hotel writing-paper the words: "First met him outside the Tube Station at Hampstead." After that I felt I wanted to go on in straightforward narrative form, so

I stuck an "I" in front and continued. And so, on that sudden impulse, it began.

On an equally sudden impulse I decided I wouldn't tell anyone about it—not even Severn. Secrecy seemed the only way to escape a constant battery of worrying and perhaps embarrassing questions; it would also give me freedom to throw up the business if at any moment I chose to. A secret, therefore, it had to be, and when Severn asked me about it, I lied to him quite emphatically. I told him (and his hero Machiavelli, at any rate, would have condoned the falsehood) that I was really so busy that for the present I couldn't possibly undertake any additional work. He laughed and protested and told me I was missing a grand opportunity. And I laughed and said I didn't think so, and all the time went on (in secret) adding to the pile of manuscript in my bureau drawer.

But I had to lie to Helen as well. It was at the End House one evening, when I arrived and found her playing the piano alone in the drawing-room. That, in itself, surprised me, for since our talk in mid-Channel she had carefully avoided any sort of tête-à-tête. But she began, more surprisingly still: "Is it true that you are going to write a novel about Terry?"

I shook my head and asked her (rather weakly, no doubt) who had been spreading false rumours. She answered: "It isn't a rumour. Geoffrey says he's been persuading you to do it, and I know how clever he is at persuasion."

"But not clever enough to persuade an innocent journalist into attempting what is utterly beyond him."

She struck a harsh random chord with her left hand. "I'm glad you think that. It *is* utterly beyond you." Then suddenly, swinging round on the stool to face me, she asked me how he was and whether he were getting on well.

I said that physically he was recuperating splendidly though, owing to the slowness of his mental recovery, it would be a long while before he could resume work.

"And then he'll go back again to Vienna?"

"I don't know. He hasn't any definite plans."

"Do you think he wants—he would like—to be invited here?"

"I'm rather afraid he doesn't want to go anywhere."

"Or to see anybody?"

"Not at present."

I suppose my answers gave her an impression of hostility, for she said, bitterly smiling: "You don't particularly want him to see me, do you?"

"I'm not very keen, I admit."

"Why not?"

"Need you ask?"

She laughed and retorted: "Don't be afraid.... I haven't the slightest desire to see him. There are some things I can't forgive."

"Neither can he."

"What do you mean? What are the things he can't forgive?"

"The things he has done himself."

"Such as?"

"I don't think I can tell you. As you said just now, I don't know enough about him."

"Is he sorry he ever met me?"

"Maybe," I said hastily, as the entrance of Severn in his wheeled chair put an abrupt end to our conversation. Heaven knows where and how it would have ended but for that.

I didn't understand her. Perhaps I never have understood her; perhaps, if and when this manuscript is finished, she will seem a kind of incomprehensible mystery, without clue or key.... All I can set down are the things that happened, and these, it may be, are not always very significant.... One of them, fortunately, is beyond controversy—the change that took place in her way of life from the moment that she brought her husband to England. It was extraordinary; she became all at once the model wife, avoiding all social engagements and spending most of her time dutifully at home. Severn, if he had been less abnormal in temperament, might have been gratified by the change; as it was, he did his best to persuade her to enjoy herself as usual. But she wouldn't; she would stay and look after him whether he liked it or not. He on his side accepted the novel situation in a spirit of slightly sardonic good-humour. "Women are sadists," he told me once. "They love men most when their bodies are broken and helpless...." And when I suggested that there might be some other motive besides sadism, he retorted laughingly: "Oh, yes, there *may* be. But I wouldn't take *your* word for it—you're such a thoroughgoing sentimentalist...."

Sentimentalist or not, I found some of those evenings at the End House almost more poignant than I could bear. They were poignant, if you know what I mean, because Severn wouldn't let them be sad. Never had he been more cheerful; never had his wit shone more brightly; never perhaps in my life had he made me laugh so much. He made Helen laugh, and June too—we all laughed. And then suddenly, there would come a second's silence, and we would glimpse him, as it were, behind and beyond the laughter—a spirit tragically brave, chained to that wheeled chair for life.

Once he gave me a long medical lecture on the injury to his spine. It was, he said, in the opinion of every leading authority save one, entirely and absolutely incurable. The exception was a young and adventurous Chicago surgeon named Hermann. "Unfortunately, Hermann's gone with an expedition to the head waters of the Amazon, and won't be available till next year at the earliest...."

VIII

And Terry, meanwhile, lived through the summer and autumn at the Valley Hotel. Every Saturday (with few exceptions) I went down to see him and every Monday I came away; and yet, even after so many visits, the picture of him will be rather blurred. Physically he was all that he had ever been, and more; the weeks of sunshine and fine air had left a splendid mark upon him. But in other ways he seemed hardly to have begun to recover at all; indeed, it was as if the full extent of the trouble were only just being revealed. He was intensely quiet and melancholy; nothing interested him or stirred him to any expressed emotion; he had the look of one who has lost his way and doesn't particularly care whether he finds it again. All his habits were listless and slack; his not-caring invaded even the most trivial things. It was not-caring, also, that had made him take to drinking; and, since his drinks were obtained from Taplow, he very obviously didn't care how much he was costing Severn. I don't think he ever troubled to realize that a record was kept of everything he had and a bill made out in the usual way. My own habit, when accepting Severn's hospitality at the hotel, was to pay for the drinks I had, and I rather wondered why Terry didn't do the same. Then I found out one reason, at any rate.

It was a Monday morning and I was preparing to leave on my motor-cycle for town. Terry walked with me as I wheeled the machine into the lane, and then, quite suddenly, he asked me to lend him half-a-crown. It was a simple, almost a half-hearted request; there was certainly no trace of either shame or truculence in it. When I had mastered my surprise I made him take a pound, and then, leaving my machine where it was, I led him away from the hotel and asked him to tell me frankly about his financial position. He confessed (as if it didn't trouble him much) that he hadn't any money at all, and after much questioning I gathered that the journey to England and the hotel expenses in Paris (of which he had insisted on paying his own share) had swallowed every penny he possessed. Then I asked him what his salary had been in Vienna, and he named a sum which a skilled artisan would have scorned.

Even my indignation didn't stir him. But after further cross-examination I found out something of more immediate importance—that Karelsky hadn't paid him for that last and unfinished quarter. "I suppose he forgot to send it on," Terry said listlessly, and was obviously prepared to let the matter drop. But I wasn't. I said I would write to Vienna as soon as I reached town, and that until Karelsky's cheque arrived he could draw on me for whatever sums he wanted.

Karelsky didn't answer my letter. After ten days I wrote to Mizzi, asking her if she would interview him on Terry's behalf, and she replied almost by return as follows:

"DEAR MR. HILTON,—I went to see K. as you asked, but he was away, so I had to talk to his chief assistant, Herr Schubert. He said there was no money at all owing to T., because he left without giving notice. I explained that he was ill, and then S. showed me an agreement signed by T. seven years ago, when he first came here. I am afraid that this agreement, though very unjust, is quite legal, and will give T. no chance at all of getting any money. S. said that T. had caused great inconvenience by leaving so suddenly, and that K. will never have him again. If you like, I will see K. personally as soon as he returns, but I do not think it will be much good.

"S. sent me some of T's books and papers that were left at the laboratory, and these are now with the rest of T's things in his room here. Shall I have them all packed up and send them to you or to T. himself? Please do not think I mind keeping his room for him; it is just that I think, if he cannot return here, he may soon want his books again in England.

"I should like to know about T., and also about Mr. Severn. Things are just the same here, and I am quite well and remain—*Deine treue, mit den herzlichsten Grüszen,*

"MIZZI."

That letter reached me on a Saturday morning, and I read it a second time by the roadside near Ripley, on my way to Hindhead. I remember smoking a cigarette and deciding that for the present, at any rate, I wouldn't tell Terry the disappointing news. I decided also that I would give him the quarter's money in cash, and let him think that Karelsky had sent it.... The plan would have been easily carried out but for a single act of carelessness; in changing my clothes when I arrived at the hotel, I chanced to drop the second sheet of Mizzi's letter on the floor of the room which Terry and I were sharing. He picked it up when he entered some time later, and, I suppose, he recognized the handwriting; anyhow, he read it and understood it quite sufficiently to learn all that I hadn't intended him to learn. He met me afterwards in the bar-parlour with a quiet, almost a bored—"So Karelsky's given me the push?" I stared at him in astonishment, and then he added: "You left part of Mizzi's letter on the floor. I didn't know it was yours till after I'd read it.... Anyhow, it doesn't really matter, does it? Have a drink?"

He didn't care! I don't know whether I was more glad than sorry that he didn't, or more sorry than glad. I was glad, at any rate, because I didn't want him to begin worrying about the future, and I was sorry because his not caring seemed such a tragic thing in itself. Not to care that he had lost his position, that he had been virtually swindled out of the money he had earned, and that for seven whole years he had been giving out his best and deepest in the service of an unprincipled rogue! Naturally I didn't lay stress on the matter, nor did I give my opinion of Karelsky. But I couldn't help protesting when he said, as if he were calmly thinking it out: "I suppose Karelsky found I wasn't any use. After all, I'd been seven years on the job and hadn't much to show for it."

I said sharply: "You know perfectly well that you *had* something to show for it. You told me yourself that you'd nearly finished something important."

"Oh, never mind about it now," he replied, almost peevishly. "Take me on the back of your bike into Guildford and let's have a canoe out on the river."

We went, and the odd thing was that for the rest of the day he was actually more cheerful than I had known him since the beginning of his illness. The weather was perfect, and we splashed about in the Wey for an hour or two, had tea, and then returned along the Hog's Back and through Farnham.

"When you write back to Mizzi," he shouted into my ear as we were doing forty against a strong wind, "tell her to send on all my books and papers to the hotel, will you? ... Then on Guy Fawkes' Night we'll take them into Taplow's garden and make a damned great bonfire with the lot...."

He laughed loudly, and I think I have never heard so eerie a sound as his laughter then, borne far away from me by the wind and the speed....

CHAPTER EIGHT

I

I WAS out of town a good deal during that early autumn, and I saw very little of anyone. That Severn was getting more resigned to his unhappy condition I gathered from the brilliantly vivacious and epigrammatic letters he sent me from time to time. He was hard at work on the Disraeli book, which he hoped to finish soon after Christmas. "It will be something rather new in biographies," he wrote. "I shall show, if I can, that all genius has in it a touch of the flamboyant, the charlatan, if you like; and that the contrasting scrupulousness of, say, a man like Gladstone, is merely the absence of genius. No genius, for instance, can be entirely honest, or entirely truthful, or entirely faithful in marriage, or entirely anything—entireties being the stock-in-trade of the second-rate. That is why it is so astonishing to find a genius in politics, where, as everybody knows, mud is thicker than water, and a good deal easier to sling...."

Some of the letters are well worth publishing, and perhaps, some day, this may happen. The thing I remember best in them is a phrase about Terry. "He hasn't," Severn wrote, "quite got the knack of living in an imperfect world." That, I think, was the best summing-up I ever heard.

All this time Terry was still living at Hindhead, doing nothing and caring for nothing. And yet, looking back on it now, I have an idea that the sight of all his old books and papers stirred him to some sort of emotion, even though he showed none. They arrived from Vienna one roaring October afternoon of high wind and creaking trees—a Saturday, and the second unforgettable day of that autumn. I had motor-cycled from town in the morning, barely fighting through in the teeth of the gale, and after lunch Terry climbed with me to the lip of the Punch-

Bowl. The wind there was terrific; the whole landscape of hill and valley seemed foundering like a ship in a wild storm. After a few shivering moments we walked briskly back to the hotel, and there, waiting for us, was Mizzi's parcel. I unpacked it for him in his room, while he sat on the bed, smoking and watching me with a curious detached interest. He made no comment except, when I had finished, an almost embarrassed: "It's awfully good of you to do all this.... The things aren't much use, but I suppose they may as well stay here as anywhere else."

We had tea, and afterwards I wrote a few letters while Terry went out, as he said, for another blow on the hill. It must have been about six o'clock when I finished writing, for I remember hurrying out into the lane to catch the last post of the day. I had walked a few hundred yards with eyes almost closed by the piercing wind, when I heard the sharp hoot of an approaching car; I should have been run down if the driver hadn't swerved smartly to avoid me. The car just grazed a gatepost and then stopped; I stopped also, composing in my mind the most handsome and abject apologies. The first thing I noticed (rather to my relief) was that the driver was a young woman; and the next thing I noticed was that the young woman was June. She climbed out of the car and viewed critically the long scratch on the door-panelling. Then she turned to me. "I suppose you know that you've had a narrow escape?" she said, before recognizing me. She added, a second later: "Oh, it's you, is it? Well, you ought to be ashamed of yourself."

"I not only ought but am," I replied, and she said: "That's right.... I suppose you're staying at the hotel?"

"Yes."

"I'm just going there. There's something the matter with the car—apart from the scratch on the door, which is your fault—and Taplow's a bit of a car expert.... Where are *you* going?"

"Only to post a few letters."

"Up to the cross-roads? ... Jump in, and I'll drive you up; then afterwards we'll go back to the hotel together. I can turn the car at the next corner."

"Sure it won't be too much trouble?"

"I shouldn't offer, if it were. I've just come over from Petersfield—had quite an exciting drive. Falling tree missed me by inches near Liphook, and I nearly ran over another man just before I met you.... But there was some excuse for him—he was drunk."

I got in the car and in a couple of minutes we were speeding up the hill at thirty miles an hour. We chatted desultorily during the short run, but all I remember is that when we were nearing the summit she suddenly cried out: "Ah, there he is—the man I nearly ran into.... Why doesn't somebody take him home, I wonder?" And she pointed ahead to a man who was staggering drunkenly along the middle of the road towards us.

I shouted: "Good God, it's Terry!"—and nearly, in my astonishment, jumped out of the car. She braked sharply to a standstill, and nothing, I think, was ever so typical of her as the calm way in which she did everything and said everything then. "Terry?" she echoed, and then added: "Oh, yes, I know about him. We'd better tell him to get in, hadn't we?"

She left the car and came with me, and in the end it was she herself who made the arrangements. She didn't wait for me to introduce her; as soon as we were barely within speaking distance she said: "You're Terry, aren't you? I remember you years ago—you used to do chemistry experiments in our kitchen at Hampstead.... But I don't suppose you know who I am."

He wasn't too drunk to answer; the drink had, in fact, rid him of his usual shyness at meeting a stranger. "I know who you are," he said, with a sort of truculent facetiousness. "You're the young lady who nearly ran me down just now, aren't you?"

"Serve you right," she retorted brusquely, "if you *will* get drunk and go rolling along the roads.... Get in the car now, and I'll take you where you belong. Otherwise somebody else'll drive along and knock you down."

He obeyed without another word, and I sat with him in the rear seat while June drove us up to the post-box and then back to the hotel. She was the embodied spirit of calmness; it struck me then that she had all her father's coolness without any of his cynicism. And, incidentally, she was the only woman-driver of a car who ever made me feel perfectly safe in her charge.

At the hotel she paid little attention to Terry and me, but sought eagerly for Taplow; and the chief impression I have is of the two of them stooping to examine the car's interior mechanism and exchanging technicalities. The trouble, whatever it was, did not take long to rectify, for at seven o'clock I heard her asking Mrs. Taplow to make her some sandwiches for the journey. She wanted to be in Hampstead by nine, she said, and would have no time for dinner.

Before leaving she came hurriedly into the sitting-room where I was reading and Terry was dozing in a chair. "Good-bye," she said to me, taking off her furred gauntlet glove to shake hands. Then she went over to Terry and touched him sharply on the arm. "Wake up," she cried, "and thank me for saving your life!"

He opened his eyes and stared stupidly at her; I daresay he was as surprised as he had ever been. "Do you play tennis?" she asked, before he had time to speak.

He stammered that he didn't, and she said: "Well, you ought to—it's better than boozing, anyway ... Good-bye—I'm off now."

She waved her hand and hurried out, but even her hurry had in it some curious quality of calmness.

And that, grotesque as it may be, is a plain account of their first meeting since she was a child. Taplow told me afterwards that Terry had had no more drink than on many previous occasions—certainly not enough to make an ordinary man stagger along a road. But perhaps he had been—just then, at any rate—an extraordinary man. Perhaps, as I suggested awhile back, the receipt of Mizzi's package *had* stirred him, and at a time when any sort of emotion was rather more than he could bear.

He made very little comment when June had gone. In no way did her visit seem to affect him; he just lived on as usual, letting the days slip idly by, with no care for what he did with them or for what they did with him. Anything, almost, would have been a welcome change from the monotony of his indifference; I would rather have had him swear vengeance on Karelsky, or even steep himself in despair because June had seen him drunk. But he had no energy for either; and all the while the bill for Severn to pay was piling up to quite a formidable sum.

Chiefly, of course, I was concerned for what Severn might think; the money itself was of small consequence. I should have tackled Terry pretty frankly, had he not been overwhelmed by a belated realization of the facts. News of that reached me from June, whom I chanced to meet one frosty morning in Piccadilly. She said instantly: "Come for a walk—I want to tell you something." We strolled into Green Park, and she told me that she had just met Terry.

"In Charing Cross Road," she said. "He was trying to sell some books, and I watched him go in and out of half-a-dozen shops without any luck. Then I went up and spoke to him. At first he wouldn't tell me what he was doing, but I asked him to tea and wriggled it out of him."

"Well?"

"It was a good job I *did* ask him to tea. Otherwise he'd have gone without—for he hadn't a penny on him—nothing but the return ticket to Haslemere.... He'd thought he'd get quite a pile of money for the books, but the dealers wouldn't even make an offer—no market for scientific treatises in German, they said.... He couldn't understand it."

"But why did he want to sell the books at all?"

"That's what I asked him.... It seems he saw the bill that Taplow was making up for father to pay. He hadn't had any idea he was costing so much. He said he felt it couldn't go on any longer—that he must find work of some sort and put an end to it."

"But surely he would need his books for his work?"

"No.... He wasn't thinking of *that* kind of work. He was prepared for anything—to take a job in the colonies—to go to sea—*anything*...."

"That would be no use."

"I know. I told him he had far better stay at the hotel till he was well enough to carry on with his research work."

"And what did he say to that?"

"Nothing. You can't get him even to *think* of his work—not yet.... But I made a beginning. I said I would go down to Hindhead next Sunday and teach him tennis...."

II

There was a hard court within a quarter of a mile of the hotel, and on this she gave him his first lesson. I was away that week-end, and when I returned to town there was a short note from her awaiting me on my desk. Nothing sensational. Just to say that she had tried him, and that he would probably make a decent player after practice.

And he did practise. I don't know quite why. I don't think it was because he was at all keen to become a decent player. I don't think it was even to please *her*. Maybe he found that the hard use of his body helped to calm his mind, or perhaps it was just that he had nothing else to do.... Anyhow, he practised, and when he couldn't find a partner, he 'served' over the net by himself. As always, he went terrifically to extremes; the hours he spent on that tennis-court must have made many people wonder what had happened to him. Whenever I paid him visits, it was to the court he led me straightway; it was as if he had no thought for anything else. On those scowling December afternoons we played for hours, with hardly a word between us; he always beat me, for I am excessively bad at all games. When one set was over, we began another; and so on, until dusk made play impossible. It was martyrdom of a sort for me, but what was it for him? That's what I find so hard to decide.

June, however, seemed satisfied with the progress he was making. She spoke of it so much from the point of view of the athletic coach that I told her candidly on one occasion that it wasn't his body that needed help, but his mind. "If your tennis means nothing to him but just tennis," I said, "then it's not much better than getting drunk, or taking long walks over the hills, or other things he used to do. What he wants is a new mental eagerness—something that will send him back to his work."

That was during a motor run from Hindhead at the beginning of the following March. June, furred and gauntletted, and driving very prettily as usual, shrugged her shoulders and smiled. "I'm afraid I'm not such a subtle analyst as you are," she said. "I can't help being glad that he's improving his game."

"Oh, of course." And I disclaimed all intention to sneer at tennis in any way. "All I mean," I said, "is that when you tell me his volleys are getting faster, it doesn't make me want to caper about and cheer enthusiastically."

"No?" A little laugh and several miles of silence. And then, as we were nearing Ripley: "By the way, what *would* make you want to caper about and cheer enthusiastically?"

I said it would have to be some news that showed a complete change in Terry's *mental* attitude.

"Such as a return to work—even in a small way?"

"Well, yes. That would be the best sign, no doubt."

We travelled on a few more miles, and it was in the main street of Cobham that she remarked: "Suppose I told you that he *had* already begun to work again?"

"I should be delighted, of course, if it were true."

"It is true."

"You *mean* that? You mean that he's actually gone back to his books—his old research work—"

"He's *beginning* to go."

"How—*beginning*?"

"I'll tell you in a minute."

She drove on till we were out of the village, and then, on the straight stretch of road between Cobham and Esher, she gave me details. "We were playing some hard games yesterday," she said, "and for the first time he beat me—and I'm pretty good, you know." (It was like her to say that, so calmly and confidently.) "I told him that if he went on improving he'd have to enter for some tournaments when the season began, and he said he'd most likely be at the other side of the world before then. We argued about it, and I found out he'd been answering all sorts of advertisements for jobs. Nobody, of course, would have him—without experience, references, or anything.... So after a while I just said—'Look here, Terry, why don't you carry on for the time being with your old scientific work? It's the best job you can do, and probably also it's the only job you'll get....' Better to be frank with him, I thought. He said he'd think about it, but I didn't want him to think about it—I wanted him to begin right away. So when we got back to the hotel I went up to his room (what on earth Taplow thought I don't know), and we began sorting out all his old notebooks and papers. There's at least a fortnight's job in that."

"And you really think that he intends to get on with it himself?"

"We're both of us going to get on with it. It looks to me as if he's done quite a lot of work in Vienna, only it wants getting together, classifying, typing out, and so on."

"And *you're* going to do it?"

"No, *no*.... We're both going to do it, I tell you. I shan't do more than *my* fair share, anyway. He'll have to dictate while I do the typing. Taplow's lent us a downstairs room, so that we shan't shock the proprieties."

And there it was, so calmly settled by this girl with the blue eyes and the reddish hair and the brown, freckled face. She did everything so simply and directly; she was an angel rushing in where fools feared to tread. I hoped, without really believing, that she would succeed.

III

I wish I had seen them at work together. Circumstances prevented me, and it is only from Taplow that I know anything of what happened. He told me that June used to come two or three times a week and stay for the whole day, alternating the typing with fierce bouts of tennis.

Was she succeeding? There came an evening in early April when she banged at my door and demanded an interview. "I want to talk to you about lots of things," she said, settling herself in my bachelor-armchair and accepting a cigarette. The first thing, apparently, was Karelsky's approaching visit to England. Had I heard about it?

I hadn't.

"He's due to arrive next week. There's going to be an international medical conference, or something of the sort, and he's one of the star turns.... Another is Hermann, the spinal fellow—you've heard of him, haven't you? Father's going to consult him, and if there's the least chance of a cure by operation, he says he'll take the risk."

She went on: "I suppose I'm getting to know my father for really the first time in my life. It's queer ... I keep on thinking—'What sort of a man *are* you?'—and I can't *quite* make up my mind.... But I like him. He's *game*." She gave me a sharp upward glance and added: "Perhaps you think I'm heartless to be able to talk about him so calmly? Most people seem to imagine I ought to be coddling and making a great fuss over him ... I *couldn't* do it—I'm not made that way. And neither is he."

That was as much as I ever heard her say about him. I don't think she would have said even that but for an unwillingness to drive too abruptly to the main object of her visit, which was to ask me questions about Terry. And the first question, when at last she came to it, was: "What's happened in his past life to make him like—like *this*?"

"Like what?"

She paused for a short while and then said: "It's as if he's had one blow after another until he doesn't care any more about anything—that's my impression. He does what I ask him to do, but still he doesn't care."

"And you want him to care?"

"Of course I do. And you can help me—you've known him for years. Tell me what's happened to him. What's been the real cause of his breakdown?"

I gave her as carefully as I could a summary of all that I could possibly tell her. I stressed the hard work that he had been doing, and Karelsky's shabby treatment of him, and the shock of hearing about her father's accident. And when I had got to the end, she said quietly: "Is that all?"

"I think it is."

"Won't you tell me the rest?"

"The rest? I don't know that there is any rest."

"All the same, I have an idea there is." She stared at me unflinchingly, and then added: "Never mind—if you won't tell me, then you won't. Let's talk of something else."

And we did.

IV

Throughout all the early months of that year I was almost heading for a breakdown myself. I certainly hope that I shall never have to work so hard again. In a sort of way it was Severn's fault, though he meant well enough, just as he had meant well enough in getting Terry fixed up with Karelsky. But Severn was like that; he'd help you so carelessly that unless you used remarkably shrewd judgment of your own the help might turn out to be a hindrance. On this occasion he got for me the editorship of a rather decadent weekly that had already killed or bankrupted my predecessors and would have done the same to me if I hadn't thrown up the sponge after three months' hard labour. The wretched thing gave me no proper time for meals and sleep, let alone for Hindhead week-ends and the novel about Terry. From Christmas till Easter I don't think I added a word.

There was, perhaps, another reason for this besides pressure of business. Terry's continued slackness and inertia disappointed me, and (I may as well confess it) I began to wonder if he were altogether the man I had taken him for. Anyhow, if he were going to stay on indefinitely at the Valley Hotel, I didn't see how I could write a readable novel about him, unless I chose to end it fictitiously. I remember, during the few spare moments I had during those days, making drafts of such possible endings; one of them was that Severn should die under an operation, and that Terry and Helen, after suitable novelistic adventures, should marry and end the book happily. Another dragged Mizzi back into the story, and I think this was the one I should have favoured, chiefly because the character of Mizzi always appealed to me But I hadn't time for any of them, which was perhaps just as well.

Karelsky landed, I recollect, in mid-April, and from his first moment on English soil was never without a posse of newspaper-men at his heels. I had several chances of meeting him professionally, but avoided them all; it wasn't possible, unfortunately, to avoid the constant references to him on placards, in the press, and from platform and pulpit. For over a week he had Fleet Street positively begging him for copy, and all he gave in return for fabulous cheques was a vast quantity of worthless self-advertisement. I found myself loathing the man and his methods so intensely that I even tried to persuade my proprietors to let me run a campaign against him in my paper; fortunately for me, in view of what happened subsequently, they refused.

On the opening day of the Conference the furore of newspaper adulation rose to an impassioned shriek. In my little office in Gough Square I took as small notice of it as I could; I wanted to forget, if possible, that Karelsky existed. But when I went out for my usual cup of tea in the afternoon, the newsboys were rushing up Bouverie Street with placards announcing "Karelsky's Great Speech" and "Sensational Scene at Medical Conference." For the first time for many years I didn't buy any evening paper at all; I felt that to read of some new self-advertising stunt of his would be almost unendurable. I worked at my office until nearly eight, and then strolled quietly through Lincoln's Inn to my rooms. There was a strange peace in that walk; the old Inn buildings and the trees just budding into leaf were everything that Karelsky was not.... I was calm by the time I climbed my own staircase and unlocked the door. Roebuck was out, and in the letter-box there was a telegram.

It had been handed in at Glasgow at six-thirty that evening, and ran: "Can you meet me four a.m. to-morrow Crewe Station urgent will look out for you June ..."

V

Of course I went. As I packed a small hand-bag I thought of that other telegram that had summoned me, less than a year before, to Vienna. Crewe, at any rate, was not so far, and there was a suitable express that left Euston at midnight. But I hadn't the faintest idea why June could want me, and why she had been to Glasgow, and why she was coming back to Crewe, and why, above all, she had thought the outrageous hour of four a.m. most convenient for the appointment.

Nor is Crewe Station an altogether delightful rendezvous before dawn on an April morning. My train dumped me down soon after three, and for over an hour I walked up and down enormous lengths of platform and watched mysterious shunting operations that seemed to provide the maximum of noise with the minimum of result. Then a train came in from the north, and out of it stepped June.

"I knew you'd come," she greeted me, smiling. But the odd thing was that she was nervous; I could deduce that from the way she talked. "It's so good of you," she went on, "although in the train I was wishing you wouldn't be here, and that I hadn't sent you that wire, and—oh well, you *are* here, anyway, and it's no use arguing about it."

"The question is rather why *you* are here."

"*Me?* Oh, that's easily explained. I've been doing business for my father in Scotland, and to-day I've got to do some more for him in Liverpool. I thought Crewe would be a good meeting-place."

"Charming," I assured her, and then we both laughed and said no more till we were at a table in the refreshment-room. There her manner altered; she became more serious and less nervous; her cheeks, too, were slightly pale beneath their open-air tan. She declined food, saying that she would take an early train to Liverpool and breakfast there. And so, over cigarettes and cups of that dark and bitter liquid sold by railway companies as coffee, she told me why she had sent for me.

"You've seen the papers, of course," she began.

I said I hadn't. The answer seemed to put her off; she replied, almost resentfully: "I never thought you'd have missed them. About Karelsky, I mean."

"*That* man?" I told her frankly that I was sick of hearing and seeing his name, and that I had deliberately avoided the papers because I knew they were all full of it. She nodded slowly and said: "I'm afraid you'll *have* to read about him, all the same. Unfortunately I didn't bring a paper with me.... It's this speech he made at the Conference yesterday."

"What about it?"

She stared at the table and said, after a pause: "I don't suppose you'll believe me—especially as you haven't read the papers.... But what happened—roughly—was this. Karelsky announced in his speech a new discovery—about cancer—and everybody clapped and cheered and made a hero of him. Apparently it's a big thing—this discovery."

"Well?"

She tried hard to be calm. "But the fact is—the fact is—it's not really Karelsky's discovery at all!"

"No?"

"Not his, I tell you."

Even then I wondered what she was driving at. "Then whose is it?" I asked.

"It's Terry's."

"*Terry's?* ... You mean—"

"Just exactly what I say. It's Terry's discovery."

It was minutes before I grasped what she meant, and then only hazily. She had to keep on saying: "Terry's—not Karelsky's—don't you see what I mean? Karelsky's stolen it. I've proof—loads of proof. I've been copying out for the last month the very same stuff that Karelsky gave to the Conference yesterday...." She tried to give me details, but they weren't very coherent; she could only assure me that the theft was flagrant and indisputable.

"Of course you don't believe me," she said. "I don't blame you. I hardly believed myself when I found it out.... But it's true, all the same."

"You mean that what Karelsky's getting all the fame and credit for now is something that Terry found out while he was in Vienna?"

"Presumably."

"Then, by God, we'll expose the man! We'll fight it out in the courts, and we'll—"

"I guessed you would talk like that," she interrupted, half-smiling. "But for the present there's an even more urgent matter to be settled. And that's to do with Terry himself."

"He doesn't know yet?"

"Probably not. He doesn't read newspapers—perhaps it might be weeks before he'd hear about it at all. But he's bound to know some time, isn't he?"

"He *ought* to know—so that he can fight it out—"

Again she half-smiled, and again, so it seemed to me, she had to make a great effort for self-control. "I told you a little while ago," she said quietly, "that he gave me the impression of having suffered blow after blow. This is another blow—and perhaps the worst. How do you think he'll stand it?"

I didn't answer, and she continued: "It's rather an awful thing—to have your life-work stolen and used by somebody else. I wonder if you can imagine it. I've tried to—and I think I can—just a little.... And I pity him when he finds it out."

"How do you think he will find it out?"

"I'm going to see him the day after to-morrow."

"And tell him?"

"Yes. He'll have to learn—somehow and from somebody. And I think I can tell him better than anybody else."

Then she told me why she had sent for me. "I felt I had to tell somebody about it," she said, "and you were the only person I could think of." She added: "That's a compliment, though it mayn't sound one. You can guess how I felt—reading that speech and recognizing parts of it.... I'm so glad—*now*—that you came—it's doing me good to have this talk with you...."

We talked on, but there wasn't much else to say. The Liverpool train came in at an adjoining platform; I wanted her to stay for a later one, but she wouldn't. Then I offered to go with her to Liverpool, but she said (sensibly enough) that I had my own work to do and must get back to it. Just before the train started she leaned out of the window and touched my arm. "We mustn't let Terry go under, must we?" she said eagerly. "This *may* seem—when he hears about it—the last straw—but he won't go under, will he?"

"Not if you can stop him, I know."

"And you," she insisted. She went on quickly: "I don't want to have all the job to myself. You've got to help—we've all got to help.... You *will* help me, won't you?"

"All I possibly can," I answered, and she smiled happily as the train separated us.

VI

I went back to town by an express that had just come in. At Rugby the bookstalls were open and I bought half-a-dozen morning papers, of all kinds and sizes from twenty-four-page Diehard Conservative to the daily pennyworth of revolution. I don't think I realized the full significance of what June had told me till I had thoroughly digested at least a score of their closely printed columns. First of all I read Karelsky's speech verbatim in *The Times*. It was just what I expected—noisy, blatant, self-assertive, full of impertinent jibes at other investigators, and enlivened by quips that would have done credit to a Hyde Park orator. The whole thing gave me the impression of being addressed to the man in the street rather than to the Conference members; there was hardly a sentence that the layman could not *think* he understood. Theories which most men would have advanced cautiously and modestly, Karelsky hammered out with a sort of slanging, impudent dogmatism; there never could have been, I think, such language spoken to a scientific assembly before.

In a long leading article *The Times* struck a note of cautious approval. "The fact that Herr Karelsky's methods of obtaining publicity savour rather of the market-place than the laboratory, should not blind us to the possibility—nay, even the probability—that he has made a noteworthy contribution to the alleviation of human distress.... It would seem that, if the cases he cites are authentic, he has indeed made an important discovery.... Investigators in all countries will not be slow in examining carefully all the details, many of which, in his desire to tickle the ears of the groundlings, Herr Karelsky has doubtless withheld...."

All the other papers had leading articles, but the tone of them varied from straightforward approval to positively ecstatic adulation. It was sickening to wade through some of the pages, especially those of the picture papers, in which Karelsky's face, fat and smiling, stared out from amidst a journalistic rake-up of all his earlier stunts—rejuvenation, Thibetan monasteries, and the rest. "Hats Off To Karelsky!" shouted the *Daily Wire* rampantly, and even went so far as to praise Karelsky for "talking to the public in words that the public can understand." The *Messenger's* stuff was evidently the work of old 'Pot' Higgins, for it quoted Tennyson, Goethe, Peter the Great, and (incorrectly) Disraeli.... And to think that it was Saturday, and that the scribes of the Sunday papers were already at work! Oh, my God....

Perhaps it is rather silly to have written that. But I am feeling now, as I write it, what I felt during that journey from Rugby to Euston—not so much hatred of Karelsky for being a mean thief, but disgust at the way everybody was taken in by him. Perhaps I am prejudiced. Perhaps I am bound to be. And, anyhow, it doesn't matter....

I reached London in time for a very late breakfast, and in the early afternoon I went up to Hampstead to see Severn.

CHAPTER NINE

I

MIDWAY through that April afternoon at the End House I thought: I shall feel like continuing the novel to-night.... I didn't do so, as a matter of fact, because I was too sleepy; but the desire was there, reawakened by the extraordinary way in which events were developing.

Helen was out when I called, but Severn himself, reading in his invalid-chair, was delighted to see me. I think he was still more delighted when I recounted to him the full details of my interview with June. His eyes quickened with excitement, and when I had finished he said: "Well, Hilton, it all sounds most decidedly queer, but let's join in thanking Heaven that *something* has happened. If you only knew how bored I am in this chair all day, you'd understand my deep gratitude to Karelsky."

"To *him*?"

"Yes. For doing something interesting at last. When I read his stuff in the papers last night, I said to myself—'Ah, the usual thing—some discovery that will either be discredited within a fortnight or superseded within a year....' But it *isn't* the usual thing, if he's stolen his ideas from Terry.... By Jove, it's going to be interesting—damned interesting." He asked me to get him a box of Havanas from a cabinet nearby, and when I brought it to him I saw that his eyes were filling with tears. "*Interesting!*" he repeated, offering me the box and lighting a cigar for himself. "D'you know—I've wondered some times if I should ever have to use that word again? But *this* news—well, it deserves it. And it's jolly good of you to use up your valuable time in coming to tell me about it."

"It's more than interesting," I said. "It's serious. And it's going to be made serious, too—for Karelsky."

He laughed then. "What are you going to do—murder him?"

"It will probably be sufficient to bring an action against him."

"What for?"

I said that I wasn't a legal authority, but that it seemed to me that Terry would have a good case if he took the matter to court. "As a matter of fact," I added, "I rather wanted your advice about it."

"My advice is never to expect to win an action because you've got a good case."

"No?"

"The case doesn't matter. It's the lawyer that counts. That's my experience, as a man who's won hundreds of bad cases and made other people lose hundreds of good ones."

"It sounds rather terrible."

He laughed again; I think he would have purred if he had been able. "Shall I tell you," he said, "what I would say if I were defending Karelsky in an action brought against him by Terry?" He paused for a moment, and then, with gleaming eyes and the old professional note in his voice, continued: "Gentlemen of the Jury,—my client is a scientist of world-wide reputation. His honour is assailed by a man of whom none of you, I am sure, have ever heard before. Let me tell you something about him. He was formerly in the employ of my client. After being granted full access to all the privacies of the Professor's laboratories, he left suddenly, breaking his signed contract and leaving behind him not even a word of explanation. Since then he has done no work of any kind, but has been content to live mainly on the charity of friends.... And this is the man who, according to the prosecution, has made a discovery to rank with those of Kelvin and Lister!"

"There are the note-books and papers to prove it," I interjected sharply.

"Ah yes—the so-called evidence of the prosecution. Gentlemen of the Jury—what is it you are asked to believe from this *evidence*? I will tell you. That this man—a failure—penniless—unemployed—an unsuccessful applicant for dozens of jobs in all parts of the world—that this man kept in his possession a secret which any day, if he had disclosed it, would have made his pocket full and his name world-famous! ... No, gentlemen, the idea is *too* absurd. I suggest that this action is entirely malicious. I suggest that it is the plaintiff, and not his illustrious employer, who did the thieving. I suggest that while the plaintiff was in Karelsky's employ in Vienna he made copies of his employer's private records, and then, nearly a year later, when he read Karelsky's speech, realized the significance and the possible value of them.... It was a silly, futile scheme, my friends, but was it not the sort of one that a man of good education, crazed by failure and disappointment, might devise?"

"This is absolutely monstrous!" I protested. "Do you really mean that the truth could be so diabolically twisted round—"

"The truth," he interrupted cheerfully, "can always be diabolically twisted round, or how else would lawyers get their living? ... Mind you, I'm only telling you the particular twist that *I* should give it if *I* were handling the case.... As a matter of fact, there are one or two points in Terry's favour."

"You do think that?"

"Oh, yes. There's his breakdown in health, and the rather shabby way Karelsky treated him about his money—we should require evidence from your friend Mizzi about that.... And then there's Karelsky's general reputation, which isn't too high amongst the sort of people who don't believe all they read in the newspapers. And of course he's a Russian-born Jew naturalized an Austrian—that can always be made to sound rather terrible to a jury...."

"And the note-books and papers—wouldn't they count?"

"Undoubtedly, though we should have to be damned certain of every detail beforehand. For instance, how did Karelsky make the theft? Did he get hold of Terry's books and make copies? Or were there duplicates left behind in the Vienna laboratories? ... And also—a rather important matter—what exactly were the relations of Karelsky and Terry in Vienna? Supposing that Karelsky, when the action is tried, should say blandly: 'Oh, yes, it was this man who kept my records and looked after my mice and generally made himself useful. But he was under my supervision, and it is outrageous that he should claim credit for doing things that I expressly told him to do... What should we say to that, eh?"

"Surely we could bring witnesses to prove that Terry was an independent research-worker?"

"Could we? I doubt it. And, in any case, Karelsky could bring other witnesses to say he wasn't."

"The disgracefully low wages that Karelsky paid would show the jury what sort of a man he was."

"Not at all. They would show what kind of a man Terry was. Karelsky would say—'These are good wages for a mere laboratory assistant—a man who takes temperatures and cleans test-tubes.'"

I said (and regretted it immediately afterwards); "It seems a pity Terry ever had anything to do with Karelsky."

He replied instantly: "It is. And, of course, it's my fault in the first place. Fortunately I've no conscience. If I troubled about all the thousands of things in the world that are my fault, I should never have a minute's peace."

We talked on until after tea, and he was (or seemed to me) most irritatingly cheerful about it all. There was even a faint undertone of admiration in his voice when he spoke of Karelsky; and my own indignation grew with his calmness. Couldn't something be done, I implored him. Was Terry to stand by helplessly and do nothing at all?

He remarked that Karelsky was clever—*damned* clever.

"I daresay he is," I retorted, "and I believe you admire him for that, whether he's a rogue or not!" He laughed then. "I'm afraid it's a shade more subtle than that, Hilton. You see—I like things that make me happy. Being interested makes me happier than anything. And Karelsky interests me.... Therefore—you follow? ... I'm sorry if it seems to you rather callous."

"It's Terry I'm thinking about," I replied. "It's terrible to think that there's nothing really that can be done. Surely there's *something*—some law or other—"

"Oh, there may be—I certainly don't say there isn't. All I want to make clear is that if he goes into battle against a man like Karelsky he'll have to fortify himself with something more than a few note-books and an immense quantity of moral virtue. Do you think you understand?"

I thought I did. I thought that Severn had made up his mind to stand aside, an amused and cynical spectator of a drama so rare as to be especially worth the seeing. Severn, I decided, was going to be neutral, being bound to Karelsky no less than to Terry by ties of 'interest'. It was a disappointment, but, in any case, what *could* he have done? Beyond advice (which he had already given freely enough) there was little that could reasonably be expected from a man unable to move out of his chair without skilled assistance. He had done and was doing his best, and it was perhaps too much to wish that he had shown my own particular brand of indignation.

And yet in most of those thoughts I was entirely wrong. That night, as I was working late in my room, one of the End House servants brought me a note that showed me how wrong I was. Written less than an hour before I broke open the envelope, it was as follows:

"MY DEAR HILTON,—June arrived about half-an-hour ago, and told me over again most of what I already knew from you. She happened to have some of Terry's papers locked up in her room (she had been copying them out at home), and a glance at them convinced me far more (if you will forgive me for saying so) than the combined oratorical efforts of you and June from now until Domesday. I am sorry to appear so distrustful, but the fact is that temperamentally and from experience, I never *really* believe extraordinary yarns until I get proof.

"Not that anything I've seen so far is *legal* proof; it isn't that at all, but it shows me pretty clearly that K. has been up to his tricks. I doubt if we shall be able to trap him; indeed, I reckon that he wouldn't do a thing like this unless he had a good many safe cards up his sleeve. But even if we don't *win* the action, there's no reason why we shouldn't *have* it, provided we go about it in the right way.

"See what I mean? First of all, we'll work up a damned great newspaper campaign; I'll have the *Messenger* editor to dinner next week and see what I can do with him. It's my belief that an anti-Karelsky campaign is just what the country is *subconsciously* ready for; the 'great man' stunt has been overdone lately. Then, too, there's the psychological value of Terry himself—he's young, handsome, and English. All that will count.

"Eventually, of course, we shall begin the action (unless K. frustrates us by a libel charge, which is what I would do in his place). I don't think we shall win, but we'll fight like hell. Besides, if once the dear old British public takes Terry to its ample bosom, it doesn't matter whether we win in the courts or not. Anyhow, I shall take up the case for Terry; and it'll be fearfully impressive when they wheel me into court. By God, it gives me a thrill to think of it! William Pitt the Elder did something rather similar, I believe, in 1778, but that was in the House of Commons. Won't it make a grand subject for next year's Academy—'The Last Speech of Geoffrey Severn'—purchased for the nation by the trustees of the Chantrey Bequest! The really perfect thing, if only Providence could be prevailed upon to oblige, would be to die just after the last word of my final speech. I'd give at least ten years of my life to die at that particular moment.

"June goes to Hindhead to-morrow to talk over the whole matter with Terry. After that, things ought to move quickly. Can't you imagine how I feel, with the prospect of being drawn so soon out of the Lake of Existence into the Whirlpool of Life? In great haste, yours,

"G.S."

II

I have that letter by the side of my typewriter now, and I have copied it word for word. It takes up three sheets of Severn's best parchment notepaper, and each sheet has been torn across into four pieces. And that, even if there were nothing else, would bring back to my mind the Sunday of 'the Karelsky week-end.'

So Fleet Street called it, and with good reason. Never in all my experience have I known such a frenzied chorus as went up from the newspapers on that first Sunday after Easter. From the rolling periods of Mr. Garvin down to the silliest paragraph of the silliest columnist, the theme was just Karelsky—Karelsky—Karelsky.... It was more than infuriating; it was sickening. I remember strolling across Lincoln's Inn

Fields in the morning sunlight and asking myself the question: What would you think of all this if you had never met Karelsky and if you didn't know that he was a rogue? I decided that, even so, I should have reacted against the stupendous publicity that the fellow was getting. Severn was right; the 'great man' stunt *had* been overdone.

Something lured me to mention Karelsky's name to people I met. The match-seller in Holborn told me that he hadn't read the papers and had never heard of Karelsky. The policeman at the corner of Kingsway said: "Seems a lot o' fuss about one man, don't it? Time enough to shout when 'e's really done something, *I* should think." Both answers gave me such keen pleasure that I warned myself against letting my feelings develop into an obsession.

In the afternoon I read over all that I had written of the novel, and then tried to resume where I had left off. But I kept thinking: June is at Hindhead now, talking to him, telling him what has happened…. The thought was a disturbing one. At tea-time I gave up the idea of writing any more until I heard from her. And then, in the evening, Helen came.

We hadn't met for weeks, and the sight of her, so sudden and unexpected, made me think, for the first time without an effort, of her age. It wasn't that she looked old; it wasn't that she looked even her age; it was rather that there was some curious expression in her eyes that could never have belonged to a younger woman. She looked—it is the only word—tragic. And she began, without preamble of any kind: "I've just been told about Terry. Is it true?"

"About Terry and Karelsky?"

"Yes."

"It is true, I'm sorry to say." I offered her a chair, and she sat down with a sort of sweeping dignity I have often seen on the stage, and which, until I saw *her* with it, always struck me as overdone.

"Geoffrey told me," she went on. "He's wild with delight. It will give him *such* a chance of making a show of himself."

I said nothing.

"It's what *he's* going to do—his own future success that he's been talking to me about. Never a word about Terry's tragedy."

"And never a word about his own tragedy, either," I put in. "You may as well be fair."

"*Fair?*" The word stung her, I could see. "*Fair?* It doesn't matter about being fair to *him*. *He* can defend himself. None better. Even stricken as he is, and with the whole world against him, I believe he'd be more than a match for it."

"You ought to admire him for that."

"Ought I? One gets tired of admiring a man for the same thing. I've admired him for his brains and his power so long that I'd like a change."

"And you don't feel sorry for him, lying in that chair all day and positively aching for something to happen?"

"I feel sorrier for Terry—giving the best years of his life to a thief and a fraud."

"I don't see why you shouldn't feel sorry for both of them."

"*You* do, I suppose?"

"Yes."

"Equally?"

"Roughly so, I daresay." I went on, taking advantage of her silence: "Look here, I'll tell you frankly what I think about Geoffrey. He irritates me by his calmness just as much as he irritates you, but I try to look behind it all, and there I see a stoicism that bears his own misfortune just as bravely as he expects other people to bear theirs."

"That's very nicely put."

"It's *true*. Do you suppose the man's happy, chained to a chair for the rest of his life? Can't you forgive him his delight at the prospect of once again playing his little piece under the limelight? Maybe it isn't what you or I would crave for, but still, *he* wants it badly enough, and what right have we to be so confoundedly superior about it? *He's* a pagan, frank and unashamed, and we're pagans, maybe, with the cloak of hypocrisy thrown over us."

"You're getting quite eloquent."

"If I am, it's because I feel what I say. I *like* Geoffrey, and I'm damned sorry for him. I don't know which of the two I'm sorrier for—him or Terry. And especially after the letter I had from him last night.... He's going to put up the biggest fight he can on Terry's behalf, and if he can manage to enjoy himself at the same time, I for one am very glad.... Anyhow, here's the letter—you can read it if you'd care to. It may, of course, strike you as something absolutely diabolical and callous, but *I* think it's rather pathetic."

She read it slowly, and then deliberately tore it twice across and dropped the pieces on to the floor. "*That*," she said, with deadly quietness, "is what I think of it.... And now, if you've quite finished defending a man who's well able to defend himself, perhaps you'll tell me what's going to happen to Terry?"

III

When I look at those torn fragments now, I think how excruciating must have been the tension that made her do a thing so pointless and silly. I oughtn't of course to have shown her the letter at all. It merely infuriated her; she didn't and couldn't see in it what I have seen.

I think I never realized fully before then what a difference the years had made in her, and how changed she was from those early days when she had been the charming and immensely popular girl-wife of the successful careerist. She was still good-looking, but there was a growing bitterness in her that was killing the charm, as her altered habits had already killed the popularity. People had admired her in a vague sort of way for sticking to her husband, and then after a time they had forgotten her. She never troubled about her old friends, and when she met them she gave (as she gave me) an impression of grim implacability.

Implacable she was that night when she asked me what was going to happen to Terry. "When he learns how he's been duped and defrauded, how will he stand it? And what can he do? He won't win the action against Karelsky (Geoffrey's been frank enough to tell me that)—the action's merely to give Geoffrey a chance of amusing himself. After Terry's served his purpose in contributing to that noble end, what on earth is to happen to him?"

Implacable....

I said quietly: "One thing at a time. It's no use looking so far ahead.... June's telling him to-day."

"So I gathered."

"She's discussed it with you, no doubt?"

"She discusses nothing with me. She prefers her father as a confidant."

Implacable again....

"Well, anyhow, we can only wait."

"*Wait*? We've waited long enough.... Seven years—for the inevitable to happen.... I'm tired."

"Of waiting?"

"Of everything."

And that, I saw at once, was the look in her face that no younger woman could easily have had—that look of being tired of everything.

The anger that had made her tear up Severn's letter had spent itself, and for over an hour we talked together very quietly about Terry and what might happen. She, like June, was fearful that the blow would be too much for him. I tried to reassure her by saying that lately there had been distinct signs of the beginnings of recovery, but that seemed to make her more apprehensive than ever. "To hit a man when he's down isn't as bad as to hit him when he's just coming up," she said. And then there was the strain of the fighting campaign that Geoffrey was planning for him—how would he stand that?

How *would* he? I wondered myself. I wondered how soon I should hear the result of June's momentous interview, and what degree of catastrophe there would be to learn.... And then, at the moment of deepest gloom, there came a sharp knock on my outer door. I went, and found one of the End House chauffeurs with a letter in his hand. I thought immediately of Severn—that the letter was some urgent summons from him, either to me or to Helen. Yet he would have telephoned if anything had gone seriously amiss. A dozen vague alternative conjectures suggested themselves; and all before the man said: "From Miss June, sir. She told me to bring it to you."

"Miss June? I thought she was at Hindhead?"

"So she is, sir. I drove her down this morning, and she sent me back this evening with the car and this letter."

"She's not coming back herself, then?"

"Not to-night, at any rate, sir. She's staying at the hotel."

"I see...."

But I didn't see. I stood under the light in my small lobby and tore open the envelope. The letter was pencilled and very short. Just this:

"DEAR HILTON,—The most extraordinary thing has happened, and I want you to get down here to-morrow morning if you possibly can. I'll meet the 10.15 at Haslemere. I don't think it's any use my trying to write any details, but I'll tell you this much to reassure you—it's good news. At least *I* think it is. Do come to-morrow.

"JUNE."

Helen entered from my sitting-room, and before I had time to think, I said: "It's from June."

"June?" she echoed; and then, with what may or may not have been sarcasm, added: "If it isn't *too* private, may I see it?"

I gave it to her, and just for a moment while she was reading I wondered if she were going to treat it as she had done Severn's. But at last she handed it back to me, saying sharply: "It tells us nothing."

"Most likely whatever has happened is too complicated to write down," I answered. "Anyhow, June says it's *good* news."

"She says *she* thinks it's good news."

"Which you fear may not be quite the same thing?"

"*Fear?*" There was fear in her voice. "I think I fear everything."

"Even after June's reassurance?"

"June? June doesn't understand—doesn't understand *anything* in this business. She *couldn't.*"

"Why not?"

"Because, for one thing, she's only a child, despite her adult ways of managing things. She hasn't the faintest idea of what sort of a man Terry is—oh, it's absurd—*too* absurd...." She broke off suddenly and added, after a pause: "You'll go to-morrow, of course?"

"Most likely."

She shrugged her shoulders almost contemptuously, and then decided to return to the End House in the car that the chauffeur had driven up. I wasn't altogether sorry; somehow she was just beginning to get on my nerves.... On the pavement, as I saw her into the car, she said, finally: "I'm glad you'll go to-morrow. Then you'll find things out for yourself. June's too young—too unsophisticated. She means well, but she *can't* know—she *can't* understand—she must be making terrible blunders about him all the time. It was all right her teaching him tennis—she can do that well enough ... but now...."

The chauffeur had not heard us talking, and drove away in the middle of that sentence. I have often wondered how, if at all, she had been going to finish it.

IV

And the next morning....

It was one of those cool, sunlit days when to leave London for the country is more than a pleasure—it is an intoxication, an orgy. During the journey from Waterloo there seemed but one rift in the whole sky of optimism—and that one rift was Helen. She *had* been getting on my nerves. I had already learned to dislike her attitude towards Terry and her husband, and now, it seemed, I was beginning to dislike her attitude towards her daughter also.

Her daughter met me at Haslemere, cool and pink and smiling in the sunshine. It is the loveliest picture in my mind (no, *nearly* the loveliest) that quiet country railway station with June and the sunshine mingling together into a blaze of welcome. We conversed for a few moments in that eager unimportant way that always heralds the important. Had I minded coming? Should we hire a car to take us over the ridge to the Valley? *She* preferred walking—it was only three miles or so.... Very well, we would walk.

And we walked. Everything she said and everything I said has that winsome background of sunlight and red roofs and green lanes. We were in shadow when I said: "It's good news that I'm to hear, anyway. That relieves my anxiety, but not my curiosity."

Then we came out of the shadow into a yellow blaze of roadway, and she answered: "Yes, it's *good* news. It's more than good—it's marvellous."

"He took it well, then, when you told him?"

"Oh." And we passed into the shadow again. "I didn't need to tell him. He knew already."

"Really?"

"He'd seen one of the newspapers.... Odd, wasn't it?" She glanced at me quizzically. "*You* said he never read them."

"We both said so. The headlines must have caught his eye.... But tell me what happened."

"I will, if you'll give me the chance." She paused, and for a moment we walked on in a rather queer silence. Then suddenly the trees by the roadside gave way, and a blaze of sunshine enfiladed us. That seemed to give her impulse to continue. She said abruptly: "The fact is, Hilton, he hasn't the remotest idea that Karelsky's been thieving from him at all."

"But—"

"It's no good protesting. I know it all sounds incredible. But it's true enough.... When I got here yesterday he was different—utterly different; I knew something had happened the moment I saw him. I thought he was hysterical at first.... Then I found he was absolutely wild with delight."

"*Delight?*"

"Yes; and I mean it. He thinks—oh, it's so difficult to tell you *what* he thinks. But—somehow or other—he regards Karelsky's speech as a sort of justification of all the work he's done. He says it shows he's been working on the right lines."

"He recognizes his own work in Karelsky's announcements, then?"

"Oh, yes.... That's the queer part of it. Maybe he thinks Karelsky was entitled to do what he did.... I don't know. He doesn't talk about that. He's just pleased (he says) because his work's been worth doing."

"Worth stealing, anyhow."

"Yes, I know.... It's easy to be sarcastic. I tell you—it hasn't occurred to him that he's been let down at all. On the contrary, he thinks it's great that his seven years of hard labour should have led to such a magnificent result."

"Now *you're* being sarcastic."

She shrugged her shoulder. "I'm trying not to be. I'm trying to look at it from *his* point of view. He really is sincere. I'm certain of that, because of the difference in him. *You'll* notice that. And he's working again like mad—trying, he says, to make up for a wasted year."

"But surely, when you put it to him, he could see what had happened?"

She said quietly: "I didn't put it to him. I didn't put anything to him.... And that's just what I want to talk to you about...."

We talked. That quiet country lane, dappled in sunshine, wound upwards to the windy cross-roads, and all the way we argued whether a man who had been the unknowing victim of robbery should be told about it by his friends. Perhaps it isn't fair to put it like that. She wasn't arguing the general case; it was only of Terry that she was thinking. Briefly, her idea was that we should leave things where they were. Since the truth hadn't occurred to him, what was the use of trying to prove it to him?

I answered her as well as I could. I told her that my whole mind and soul revolted against letting Karelsky go scot-free. We ought to fight, and Terry ought to fight—even if we didn't win. Severn thought so, anyway, for he intended to back Terry in a law-suit....

Then she said: "Damn the law-suit. If father wants one to amuse him, he can denounce Karelsky publicly and get himself sued for libel. There's no need to bring Terry into it at all. He's happy—because he thinks he's succeeded in something at last. What's the good of convincing him that what *he* thinks is a success is only another failure?"

Put like that, it sounded fairly unanswerable; nevertheless, I wasn't by any means convinced. All I promised was that I wouldn't attempt the process of disillusionment till I had discussed the matter with her at least once again. She smiled and answered: "I'm satisfied with that. I'm so certain you'll agree with me when once you've seen him."

And just then I did see him. He was coming up the lane to meet us.

V

He was different. It isn't easy at first to say anything but just that. He came to me with outstretched hand and gave me a quick smile and a grip of iron; with his superb physical fitness there seemed now another and more potent sort of fitness. By God—June was right about him!.... All the way down the lane she and he were talking, but I didn't hear a word: I was desperately trying to size things up for myself. He *was* different; the cloud had passed from him; he looked as he had looked in those old days when we had tramped for miles on those Sunday afternoons.

And at the Valley Hotel we went into the small ground-floor room where June's tidy hand had exercised careful restraint over the litter of his books and papers. But there were signs visible enough of what had been happening—a typewriter, a paper-perforator, and stacks of typed manuscript. I said, cheerfully: "Well, I see you've begun work in real earnest."

And he looked almost embarrassed, as if he had been found out in a guilty act. "I'm just gathering up the loose threads," he replied, and changed the subject.

It was all wonderfully, *miraculously* different. Under that clear brightening sun we strolled over to the tennis-court, and there June and he played a few games together with me as spectator. He wasn't dressed for it; that, apparently, didn't matter.... I suppose the play was rather good; but I am no judge of tennis, and the game, like most games, bores me to desperation. All that interested me that morning was Terry's extraordinary physical agility—yes, and June's too. It was hard to realize that he was a decade older than she; and yet, when you did realize it, there seemed something curiously right about the gap. A girl of twenty *can* be a woman, and very often is; but a man of twenty is never very much of a man....

Then came lunch, and the sort of lunch that Taplow, alone of all the hotel-keepers I know, can serve at short notice. During the meal the talk was all of tennis and walking and the beauties of the locality and nothing in particular—not a word about anything more important. But afterwards June made an obvious excuse to leave me alone with him, and then, at my suggestion, we went out into the sunlit lane. "Let's climb to the Punch-Bowl," Terry said, and I agreed, as I would have agreed to anything.

That afternoon! It was a time of almost sheer happiness, for I took thought of nothing but the clear truth that somehow or other the miracle had been accomplished. He was *keen* again, filled with the old zest for life and work; and he told me, embarrassedly at first, but with eagerness after a while, the things that were in his mind.

First of all he thanked me for the way I had managed to put up with him. That was rather an unnerving experience. Then he expressed his gratitude to Severn, and said that he would visit him soon and thank him personally. "To think," he exclaimed, "that all these months he's been ill, and I haven't even visited him!"

"He'll certainly be glad to see you," I said, and rather oddly, perhaps, I didn't think of Helen.

"I want to repay him," he went on. "And also—I must have a job. Do you think he could help me again?"

"What sort of a job?" I asked, and he replied confidently: "There's only one sort of a job I'll ever have, whether I starve or not. And that's the job I've been successful in already."

It was fine to hear him talk like that; and yet, when I thought of Karelsky, it was infuriating. *Successful?* He really thought he *had* been. He said: "I *must* work. I feel there's work that only I can do. That's conceit, I daresay, but I can't help it. I feel I must get on with the job. I'd go back to Vienna if there were nowhere else."

Before I could check myself I had exclaimed: "Indeed you won't do *that*!" and he looked up with such sharp surprise that I knew then, as June had known earlier, the utter impossibility of telling him the truth. She had said that I should agree with her, but it wasn't exactly that. I knew he must find out the truth in time; but I felt that *I* couldn't tell him—not just then, at any rate. I even, in a sort of way, joined in the deception; I felt that for the present he must be helped and not hindered in his dream. I told him I was sure that Severn would manage to find him the sort of post he wanted, and that probably it would be a good deal nearer home than Vienna.

"I don't care where it is," he answered. "Anywhere will suit me—provided the work's there." And he added, with particular intensity: "Thank God I'm not married, or anything like that.... As it is, I'm free—absolutely—to give my whole life to the sort of things I want...."

VI

In the cool twilight of that evening June and I began our journey back to town. Taplow drove us to Haslemere station in his dilapidated Ford car, and Terry sat with June in the rear seat. All the way she was talking and laughing, and he was evidently saying things that made her laugh. It was an aspect of him that I had never seen before, but when June and I were alone in our compartment she made me realize that I had. "Do you remember years ago," she said, "when he used to come round to the End House and bend glass tubing and mix sulphuric acid with ammonium carbonate and things like that? I was a child then, and he always tried to amuse me.... I'm afraid he still thinks I'm a child."

She was pensive for a while, and then went on quietly: "Of course you've kept your word about not telling him. I knew you would. But I've an idea you haven't even *wanted* to tell him. You agree with me, don't you, that it's better to let him keep his illusion?"

"I quite see that it would be very difficult and unpleasant to tell him," I answered. "But, on the other hand, I don't see how he can live very long without finding out."

"Why?"

"Because, for one thing, your father intends to push on with this legal action against Karelsky."

"Then we must persuade him to drop it."

"Do you think *you* can persuade him?"

And she answered: "Yes, I think I can." So quietly, so serenely; there were no limits, apparently, to the things she felt she could do.

"Very well, then," I said, and we left the matter at that. It was dark when we reached Waterloo. She took the tube, and as we shook hands gave me her final message.

"You're on my side," she said. "Somehow I *know* you are. My idea, *our* idea, in fact—is that Terry mustn't be told. It might just smash him if he realized.... He mustn't know, and we mustn't let anybody tell him. Just let things go on quietly for a while, and the danger will be over."

"Masterly inactivity?" I suggested, and she answered with a smile:

"Yes, if you like. And *I'll* persuade father."

CHAPTER TEN

I

NOTHING happened for nearly a week. Terry stayed at Hindhead; the Karelsky sensation died down a little; and I, after my adventures at Crewe and elsewhere, had no time to visit the End House. On Friday, however, Severn telephoned me to come to dinner the next day, and by the late evening post there came this note from June:

"DEAR HILTON,—I hear you are dining with us to-morrow, and I want you to be on your guard. Father is sure to ask your advice about the Karelsky affair. I've argued with him for hours over it, but it hasn't seemed to be much use so far; and apparently he's rooted out some discreditable part of K's past, which of course makes him keener than ever on action. He likes Terry, and wants to help him, but it's so hard to get him to understand how things are. I think, though, that if you back me up, as you promised, we may just manage it. Yours,

"JUNE."

But I *hadn't* promised! At least, I ransacked my memory for any word or incident that might have given her such an impression, and I couldn't find any.... Even when I sat down at Severn's table the next night, I was by no means certain what I would do. There was nobody there but the four of us. Helen was very quiet and June rather nervously subdued; only Severn, in his febrile way, possessed any degree of vivacity. There was something slightly horrible in the contrast between the intense activity of his mind and the dead incapacity of his body. During dinner he talked principally politics, but afterwards, when the servants had disappeared, he announced his newest Karelsky discovery. It was pretty shady—some business about a student whom Karelsky had tricked and who, in despair, had drowned himself. The affair had been partially hushed up at the time, but under Severn's skilled manipulation it could doubtless be made to live again. "It's just the very thing we wanted," he exclaimed rapturously. "Nothing could have been better—except a scandal about a woman.... It's just possible we might even get a verdict—you never know. Anyhow, we shall certainly achieve our object, which is, I take it, to give our hero a good boost at the expense of our villain."

"No," said June quietly, and looked at me.

He smiled. "June," he went on, quite good-humouredly, "has some rather peculiar ideas on the subject. May I assume that she has hammered them into you as well as into me?"

She said (and I could feel before she said it, that it was what she was going to say): "Yes, I've told Hilton what I think. And he agrees with me, too. Absolutely."

"*What?*" And Severn laughed. "What's that? *Do* you agree with her? Do you agree that we should all do nothing and say nothing and let Karelsky go on his way rejoicing?"

And the extraordinary thing is that I heard myself answering: "Well, you know, there is something in what she says."

It astonished me; it was as if something sudden and impulsive jerked me into position—into position by her side. I even began to argue the matter—at first as an impromptu defender of something I wasn't very certain about, but later on with conviction and even enthusiasm. I think I made an impression on Severn, for he heard me very attentively. I assured him that, from my own knowledge, Terry was quite ignorant of the fact that he had been duped. "Not only that, but he's actually delighted—because he sees that the work he did is really of value. Probably the idea that he has any proprietary right to the results of his own work has never occurred to him."

"And you don't want it to occur to him?"

"Well, as things are, I feel that I don't. The thought that's he's scored such a success has worked a miracle with him, and one's always rather afraid of a relapse after a miracle."

"Do you think he can possibly go on without knowing?"

"There's an odd chance that he might."

He made a grimace. "All these arguments, you know, Hilton, are June's. I've heard them over and over again during the past week.... Haven't you anything new—something you've only just thought of—something bright and original—anything—anything—I don't care a damn what it is so long as I haven't heard it before?"

I thought he was sneering until I saw his eyes. They were full of a curious, child-like eagerness—an eagerness that almost *tore* through them. Something new—something bright and original—something he hadn't heard before ... it was his heart-cry always.

I said: "I'm sorry. There isn't anything new to say. It's just that, quite sincerely, June and I believe that the best service we can do for Terry is to leave things alone."

"You've changed your mind, then, since the last time we talked about it?"

"Yes, I have."

Then he said, quietly and almost casually: "Very well then, we'll drop the matter."

II

Drop the matter! And June was speechless. She went towards him as if she would have hugged him, but remembering his fragility in time, kissed him warmly on the lips. It seemed to please him; he patted her head and told her that he quite realized her little game of throwing me into the fray at the last minute, as Napoleon threw in his guards at Waterloo. And all she could reply then was: "You dear—*dear*—to have given up your beautiful trial-scene—for I know—I understand—how much you were looking forward to it."

He said, patting her head again: "Wait till that Chicago fellow has finished with me. Then I'll have all the trial-scenes I want."

She couldn't reply to that at all; I could see her eyes filling and brimming over with tears. I intervened then myself, telling him how glad and grateful I was, and how much I hoped that the future would bring recovery to him. And when I had finished he said, quite in his old half-mocking tone again: "That's very nice of you. Now let's be as sentimental as we can about it—and, to begin with, let us all cry."

Perhaps we should have cried but for his saying that. As it was we laughed, June, he and I; and then suddenly I noticed Helen. She wasn't laughing and she wasn't crying either; she was just looking dreadfully in front of her, with cheeks pale and lips tightened; and when she caught my eye she said, quickly and sharply: "So you're *not* going to tell Terry?"

We looked at her, all of us; the centre of gravity had suddenly shifted.

"That's what we've decided," I said.

"You're satisfied for him to get what happiness he can out of ignorance?"

"Well—if you put it that way—yes."

She bit her lips till they were almost white. Then, in the midst of the tense, expectant silence, she retorted: "I'm *not* satisfied, and I never will be. And if you aren't going to tell him the truth, then I am...."

It was a far bigger surprise than Severn's capitulation; it staggered us all, and even Severn was less ready for it than for most things. And before we could collect our scattered wits, she was going on—ranting, if you like—telling us what she thought of us, of Terry, of everything else, and of the world in general. She had hardly spoken all the evening, and it was as if the words had been heaping themselves up behind her barrier of silence, and that now the barrier had given way.

I wish I could have taken down in shorthand everything she said, for it was an impressive tirade. It held us spellbound while it lasted, but the spell is over now, and all that memory yields is a few scraps and sentences.

"Ever since you knew him," I can remember her saying, "you've been planning things out for him and settling things that he ought to have settled for himself, and the result has been just disaster—disaster—over and over again.... And now you're planning that he shan't discover the mistakes you've made.... But he *shall* discover them, and the sooner the better. Let him know the truth—let's all of us know the truth—let's know the truth about his life and your life and my life....

"You're afraid it will make him ill? Then let him be ill—better that he should be ill of the truth than smiling in your fool's paradise. Let him know everything. Even if Karelsky's fooled him, *you* shan't!"

June was white-hot. "We don't want to fool him, mother. We want to help him. Why should *you* interfere?"

"*Interfere?*" Her bitter laugh was more than words. "*Interfere?* That's a strange word to use about me and Terry."

"Is it? I don't see why it is. If you deliberately tell him things that you needn't tell him, that's interference, isn't it?"

"All right, then. I'm going to interfere."

"You're *really* going to tell him?"

"Rather."

"When?"

"As soon as ever I can. He's staying at the hotel at Hindhead, isn't he?"

"You'd dare to go there and tell him?"

"It doesn't strike me as particularly daring."

"Oh, but ... mother.... You *shan't* go—you've no right to—you—"

"Haven't I? How do you know what I've a right to do? Perhaps I've a right to do what *you're* doing, anyway. *You* visit him, don't you? *You* talk to him, and tell him what you want to tell him, don't you?"

The two were facing each other dangerously—June flushed and angry, and Helen with an ashen-pale mask of curious, half-contemptuous calmness. And then, in the midst of the almost ugly tension, Severn thought fit to fling his own delicate and carefully-prepared bombshell.

"You won't need to go anywhere to see him," he announced, looking at Helen. "He'll be here any minute...."

"*Here?*"

I think we all said that. He watched our bewilderment, enjoying it as a conjuror enjoys the mystification of his audience. But we had had already such a surfeit of surprises that perhaps we showed less than might have been expected. He told us then that Terry had written to him, suggesting a visit, and that he (Severn) had invited him for that night without any anticipation of "this delicious little family contretemps."

Helen remained calm, saying merely: "I don't care. I can tell him here to-night as well as at any other time and place. It makes no difference to me."

And then the butler entered and spoke the name that seemed so strange to us because we never used it ourselves.

It was like a play—one of those rather obvious, melodramatic plays in which, as soon as a character announces that he is expecting somebody to call, there is always a deafening ring of the doorbell.... It was, anyhow, far too "pat" to have been an entire coincidence; and my theory is that Severn, who had exceptionally sharp ears, must have heard or seen Terry approaching along the drive....

There is a sense in which the long-deferred answer to any question is always something of an anticlimax. Often, for example, during the long interval of years, I had thought: Will he ever see her again, and if so, how and when and where?

And here, after a few moments, he was, standing before her with his bronzed face and his keen eyes and his shy, boyish smile. He didn't speak; she didn't speak; it was their first meeting since that storm-riven night eight years before.

Then he went across to Severn. To him more than to her he seemed to show emotion; he said, with almost a child's wistfulness: "Severn.... How *are* you?"

And Severn replied: "Much better for seeing you. Why the devil haven't you come here before?"

"I couldn't," he answered simply, and then he looked round the room and completed his salutations. To me he gave a cordial nod, and to June a curt quick smile which she returned instantly. He was one of us again.

I remember feeling an almost overmastering desire to make some trifling remark—something like—"Extraordinary how the years have flown, isn't it?"—anything, however stupid, that would in some way acknowledge the central fact of that eight years' interval. I don't know whether anybody else felt like that—quite probably not. Except for Severn, they all seemed stricken with a desire to say nothing at all.

Strange—that he should have met her again in that room, and with all of us looking on.... I had pictured so many places—some flower-decked railway-station in the Tirol, a Viennese boulevard at nighttime, some winding, hedge-bordered English lane, even Charing Cross Station—but never that room at the End House, with the port on the table and the twilight creeping over the cold lawns outside. It was disappointing, almost; it seemed to be making such poor use of a romantic opportunity....

The situation, however, was interesting, the more so as none of us knew what would happen.

For quite ten minutes nothing happened at all, and we just sat round the table making remarks as conventional and featureless as if the occasion had been the state visit of a grand-duke. Terry sat at the table with us, and though he declined a glass of port, he pulled a pipe out of his pocket and asked if he might smoke. We chaffed him a little about letting go his good resolutions, and he answered, rather cryptically: "You have to choose what you'll let go and what you'll hold on to."

For a time I allowed myself the faint hope that Helen, after all, mightn't carry out her threat, but her attitude soon dispelled it. "So you're working again?" she remarked, while he was filling his pipe. (And those were her first words to him.)

He replied that he was. He also gave a perfectly natural explanation of everything that had happened to him. "I worked a bit too hard in Vienna," he said, "and the result was a sort of break-down. But I think I've got over it now—at the price of a year's slacking." And he smiled.

She went on, with no more beating about the bush: "What do you think of Karelsky's latest discoveries?"

He looked up sharply, but without perturbation. "They're interesting," he said, puffing contemplatively at his pipe.

And we, as spectators, looked on. June and I lacked the power to intervene, and Severn, I think, was too fascinated by the spectacle to wish to do so. She continued her cross-examination.

"Karelsky's been working rather on your lines, hasn't he?"

"We've been investigating the same subject."

"Do your conclusions tally with his?"

"Some of them."

Pause.... Then: "Karelsky seems to have got the most tremendous publicity out of it."

"Yes. It's the sort of thing he likes."

"And you don't, I'm sure."

"I should hate it."

"It's a good job, then, that he never mentioned you in any of his speeches.... I suppose you helped him?"

"Oh, yes, I was paid to help him."

She wasn't getting on as easily as she had expected; I could see that. I could see the calmness of her eyes turning gradually to exasperation, especially when June put in, rather coldly: "I'm sure Terry doesn't want to answer all these questions, mother."

But it was his casual, "Oh, I don't mind in the least," that stung Helen to absolute desperation. "You don't mind, eh?" she cried fiercely. "You don't mind anything, do you? ... You're a fool, Terry—and I'm going to let the truth into you even if nobody else here has the courage to do it.... These discoveries Karelsky has made are yours, if you only had sense enough to realize it—they're *yours*, and he's stolen them off you, knowing what a little fool you are!"

He put down his pipe and stared at her, and I think we were all slightly relieved that he didn't go off immediately into acute hysterics. He just said—almost quizzically: "But really—to tell me *this*! What grounds can you possibly have for saying such things?"

"You needn't ask me," she retorted. "Ask June—she's had access to all your papers. It was her discovery in the beginning."

He turned to June, wordless; and June smiled at him. "Don't get alarmed, Terry," she said quietly. "It's true what mother says, though I wouldn't have bothered you about it if I'd been her. I *do* think Karelsky's stolen your work. I don't see how anybody could help thinking so who'd gone through it all in detail as I have.... There's not much doubt about it, Terry—you've been done ... but never mind—it doesn't really matter...."

And then, to our complete astonishment, he replied, taking up his pipe again: "I daresay you're right. But, as you say, it doesn't really matter, does it?"

III

I felt sorry for Helen then. We were all bewildered, but for her alone bewilderment was defeat. And Terry hardly noticing her, smoked his pipe, as if embarrassed rather than upset by the turn that events had taken.

It was Severn who took up the cross-examination, but did it so calmly and sympathetically that even Terry's embarrassment was soon dispelled. Apparently he had had an idea that Karelsky "might have stolen" his work. He hadn't troubled much about it because what really mattered to him most of all was the revelation that his work was sound. "Sound enough to be stolen?" interposed Severn, and Terry replied smilingly: "Yes, if you like. Only really, you know, you can't steal *work*, can you? It's just *done*, and it doesn't very much matter who does it."

"It's easy enough to steal credit," said Severn.

"Credit? Yes, but who wants that? I should hate all this newspaper puffing—it would worry me. It's just as well Karelsky's saved me from it. If he'd asked me I'd have given him full permission to do all he has done.... And besides, do I deserve credit? I'd done all that work, and yet I hadn't enough confidence in it or myself to make it public. The world owes something to Karelsky."

"And you may be sure Karelsky will collect the debt in full," replied Severn.

Then June said laughingly: "Do you know, Terry, father had a wonderful idea that you should bring an action against Karelsky for theft or plagiarism, or whatever it is, and that he—father, I mean—would take up your case in court? It would have been rather fine, wouldn't it?"

"So fine," interposed Severn, "that the very ushers would have wept at my eloquence."

Perhaps it was as well to make a joke of it like that. June and her father were in some strange and mystic harmony—I had never been so certain of it as then. They laughed and chattered and made witticisms, and all the time Terry was growing younger and happier before their eyes. The Karelsky business didn't really matter; you had only to look at him to see that. "It's what's done in the world that matters, not who does it," was his way of summing it all up.

It was a happy ending—for all of us except Helen. She stayed, pale and silent, for a while, and then suddenly whispered something to Severn and went out of the room. He told us afterwards, with perhaps the faintest touch of cynicism, that she had begged to be excused owing to a bad headache.

And the conversation went on....

IV

June's eyes as she shook hands with me at the gate that evening were shining with delight. "It's marvellous," she whispered softly, for Terry wasn't far away. "It's wonderful to think that he knows everything now, and that we have nothing more to fear...."

The night had a glow of moonlight, and in it her eyes were shining—with delight, as I said, but also (I wondered) with something more than delight? I could even see her mother in her then—her mother as she had been years before.

Terry and I, having bidden our farewells, walked back down the moonlit lane to the Tube Station. He was staying with me for the night—indeed, for just as long as he wished, though the thought of his unfinished work made him eager to return to Hindhead.

He said, amidst the clatter of the Tube train, that Severn, despite the accident, was really just the same, but that Helen seemed to have changed. "I didn't understand her," he confessed.

I answered that eight years were bound to have made a difference, and that the last year had made perhaps the biggest difference of all. He nodded then, and was silent for a while. It was obvious that talking about her both attracted him and made him embarrassed.

He never mentioned now his old half-crazed idea, that he was personally responsible for all the misfortunes of the Severn family. But the idea was somewhere still in his mind, in essence the same though maybe transmuted into another semblance; and I could sense it easily enough behind the slow, baffled words with which he broke the silence eventually. "I'm more than ever sorry for her now," he told me.

That was all he said about her, but before going to bed we talked for hours about his work and prospects. He told me frankly that one of the chief causes of his earlier despondency had been the thought, which he never dared to express in words, that his work was no good. Karelsky's shabby financial dealings with him had increased that fear; he had begun to sink beneath the awful realization that he was a failure. It wasn't any spectacular success that he wanted; he had no envy of those who made their names prominent in the world's view. All he wanted was the secret inward conviction that he was doing something worth doing. And now he had it.

"All this may sound priggish," he added, "but I don't think it really *is* priggish. Because, after all. I'm only choosing the easiest path for myself. I should hate Karelsky's life of fame and sensation, just as he'd hate my life of hard work and insignificance.... We're just made differently, that's all, and we can't help ourselves."

"All the same," I said, "you ought to have what you're entitled to, if only to stop others from having more than they're entitled to. You've done the work; you ought to get the credit."

"Can't you see that it doesn't matter who gets the credit?"

"Frankly," I retorted, "I'm incapable of feeling like that about it. If there's any fame or credit to be got out of my work, I'll be glad to have it. It may be a lower attitude than yours, but it's more appropriate for earning a living in the twentieth century."

That seemed to embarrass him. He assured me that he had never reckoned my attitude as 'lower' than his in any way; it was just 'different.'

"Yours is medieval," I said, laughingly. "You ought to have been a craftsman on a fourteenth century cathedral, putting your whole life and soul into the carving of a single gargoyle."

He said that gargoyles weren't much in his line. "But, anyhow, doing that would be a nobler way of spending a lifetime than lots of the things that are done to-day—selling rubbishy patent medicines, for instance, or writing rubbishy books...."

And so we argued, half-seriously, half jocularly, far into the night. One thing rather astonished me—the extent to which he had thought about things. He disliked the modern world, on the whole, and he had his reasons for it. He said that newspapers, modern advertising, and big cities, always afflicted him with a sort of terror. He felt he couldn't 'cope with them.' It was odd, really, his being a scientist, because science was supposed to be the key-note of the new age....

"Sometimes," I said, "I think you aren't a scientist at all, but a theologian gone astray."

Oh, no. He wouldn't admit that. He had no sympathy with dogmas. But he did feel that somehow you either had to accept the modern world with an easy cynical fatalism such as Severn's, or else hate it, as he did himself, and long for something warmer and simpler....

And then he made a curious confession—perhaps the most curious he ever made. "When I thought I had failed altogether at the work I liked most, I had to try to think what I would do in the future.... And I had half made up my mind that—if they'd have me—I'd join some sort of mission affair and get sent abroad."

"And how about the dogmas then?" I asked, and he answered puzzledly: "I don't know.... I *really* don't know.... They'd have been a great nuisance, I admit—but still...."

Some sort of mission affair! I think he had been engaged on that all his life.

The next morning he left for Hindhead, full of eagerness for whatever the future might bring. And a few days later Helen visited him there.

CHAPTER ELEVEN

I

WE found out, June and I, by the sheerest accident. At the end of that week she rang me up and asked if I would care to go with her to Hindhead. Some other engagement had fallen through at the last minute, and she had an afternoon and evening unexpectedly free. "We can take the two-seater car," she said, "and we'll just stop at the hotel for tea and then come back."

We went. The sunny ride through Richmond and Guildford and over the Hog's Back (the high, windy way that June and I always preferred) was especially entrancing on that Saturday afternoon. I don't think either of us was very much surprised to find Terry out when we reached the hotel. On such a day of sunshine and cool wind there would have been something wrong with him if he'd been in. Taplow told us that he'd gone for a walk and hadn't left word when he'd return. And then, with the curious Taplow mixture of frankness and discretion, came the remark: "As a matter of fact, sir, Mrs. Severn called this morning, and they went out together."

As a matter of fact! To him, perhaps, it was only that—a fact that might possibly interest us, or possibly might not. His casualness, anyhow, helped us to curb our own astonishment. I managed to order tea, and then June and I sat together in the little window alcove of the sitting-room, each waiting for the other to express the surprise we felt. But curiously, perhaps, neither of us did. We both pretended that Helen's visit was nothing out of the ordinary; Taplow had set us the example. When he brought our tea he said: "They'll have done quite a tidy bit of walking, I daresay, sir. Lovely weather for walking—not too hot, as you might say, sir, and not too cold either."

All June said when he had gone was: "Mother hates walking."

We had tea and tried to sustain a conversation. If this manuscript were an autobiography I should devote whole pages to the thoughts and fears that invaded my mind during that meal; and yet I believe I was quite eloquent about topics that now I can't even remember. There's a sort of talk that is especially copious when one is thinking all the time about something else.

After tea I said: "Shall we wait?"—and she answered quietly: "We'll wait—for a little while." So we waited. It was already half-past six, but June was used to night-driving and there was no particular hurry. The whole year has nothing lovelier, perhaps, than those early days of May, when twilight is like the perfect curtain descending on the perfect play. And yet to me, at any rate, the passing of that afternoon seemed ominous; for we were still waiting, and each minute gave us less to talk about and more to think about. Clouds rolled up and brought the dusk suddenly, and then came heavy, beating rain. When Taplow entered to light the swinging oil-lamps the sad yellow glow peered into all the corners of the room as if to show up rather than dispel the darkness. "This ought to bring 'em back pretty quick," he said, as he closed the windows against the downpour.

Ten minutes after that they came....

II

They came like children, laughing and scampering; they had been running till they were out of breath, and both were wet to the skin. The rain gleamed on their flushed cheeks and shining eyes, and in that small lamp-lit room they looked like wild animals brought to bay. They hardly saw us at first.

Then Helen suddenly cried "Look!"—and pointed to us.

Somehow I felt that it was June or I who ought rather to have cried "Look!" I broke the awkward silence by saying that we had arrived by car not long before.

And Helen said: "Really? Did you come over the Hog's Back or through Godalming?"

"Over the Hog's Back," I answered; and she went on: "I think I prefer the other route. Godalming is such a quaint little town."

The rain was dripping off the brim of her hat and she remarked laughingly that if Mrs. Taplow could lend her some clothes she thought she had better change. She smiled at Terry as she went out of the room.

"*You're* wet through, too," I said, when she had gone, but he merely shrugged his shoulders and answered: "Oh, yes, I'll go up and change in a minute. I must talk to you first, though. I'm ever so glad you've come, but why on earth didn't you send me a card as you usually do?"

I explained the circumstances, but he still seemed inclined to protest. "If only Helen and I had known," he said, "we could have made up a party with the car and had a picnic somewhere."

"Perhaps it will do another time," I said conventionally.

He nodded with eagerness. Then he dragged a chair in front of the two of us. "D'you know," he went on, leaning forward and talking rather more to June than to me, "I've been having a great time to-day. Your mother and I have been looking all round the district for houses—or else for a good site to build a house on. We haven't quite made our choice, but we've got several ideas...." He added, with shy gentleness: "Perhaps you're surprised that I call her 'Helen?' You see, she and I are very old friends."

June spoke then for the first time since he had come in. "*That* doesn't surprise me," she said quietly. "But the house business does. Do you mean that my mother's thinking of coming to live out here?"

"Yes.... That's it.... Isn't it splendid?"

He went on to explain. Apparently, in the beginning, it had been one of my ideas, though I had no recollection of it. Briefly, the suggestion had been that since it was no longer necessary for Severn to live within easy reach of town, the Hampstead house might be exchanged for one further out. As Terry summed it up: "It's really absurd to live near a Tube station when you have the chance of being in the heart of the loveliest county in England."

"Is that Helen's opinion?" I asked.

He smiled. "She's still rather a devotee of the town, but she sees the advantages of living out here. As a matter of fact, I think to-day has converted her. It's been her first day in the country for years."

He went on to tell us, with careful and slightly boring accuracy, exactly where they had been. Then he described several houses that were more than suitable except for their initial disadvantage of being occupied by somebody else. There were one or two good sites, however, and perhaps in the long run it would be more satisfactory to plan and build a house according to taste. "It's great fun," he said, "climbing lots of hills and wondering what houses would be like on the top."

Then Helen came in attired in the rather scarecrow clothes that Mrs. Taplow had lent her. Terry laughed heartily at her appearance, and then left to change out of his own drenched clothes. We were left with Helen.

I'm setting down all this as simply and accurately as I can. I'm reporting rather than describing what happened. It's easier, especially when I come to Helen, for she was very puzzling that night. She seemed younger, happier, triumphant, even; and yet, in some odd way, terrified. She talked copiously and irrelevantly until Terry joined us, and then was suddenly silent. We had supper, and during the meal it was suggested that she should return with June in the car, and that I should stay at the hotel overnight. The plan suited me, and I was glad to agree to it.

By this time the rain had stopped and the sky become clear. Indeed, it was bright moonlight when Terry and I stood in the roadway to give a final wave to the disappearing car. Then we strolled up the cool rain-scented lane and talked.

III

It had all happened so suddenly—to him even more than to me. Crammed into a single phrase, it was Helen's return to his life, and I think he wanted to talk about it quite as much as I did.

It had astonished him, he admitted; for he had never believed it possible that they could be friends again. And especially after the trouncing she gave him about the Karelsky business....

"She apologized for that," he told me. "Not that I wanted her to—a great deal of what she said, from her point of view, was quite true.... But she did apologize, anyway. And then, of course, we had the job of house-hunting."

I asked him if he had had any idea that she was coming, and he answered: "Not the slightest. I was reading in the garden when she suddenly came in by the side gate. She was looking for Taplow—to ask him about the houses, I suppose."

"But she knew you were staying at the hotel."

"Oh, yes, but it wasn't me she came to see. But for Taplow being out, and her looking for him, we might never have met."

"Did she suggest that you should show her round the district?"

He said: "I think we both suggested it together. She said she didn't mind walking, and so naturally...."

After a pause he went on: "I tell you candidly—I didn't think either of us could do it.... Do you remember the other day we were talking about her and I told you she was different? Well, she *is* different, in one way, but in another way she's just the same—just the same as if—as if nothing had ever happened.... Do you know what I mean?"

I knew what he meant.

Then he talked enthusiastically about the time when she and Severn would live idyllically on the slopes of one of those Surrey hills. He, of course, might be working hundreds—perhaps thousands of miles away, but it would be pleasant to think of the two of them in such delightful surroundings. They were lucky to have plenty of money; they could build just where they liked and how they liked. And we—he and I—would perhaps visit them from time to time.

What could I say to him? Could I tell him the fear that was in my mind? Could I warn him that the danger that had existed eight years before was still a danger? ...

Not then.... Not, at any rate, till the danger was more evident, till I had proof as well as surmising. I said merely: "Well, I hope you showed her some good places. She ought to be able to find something or other if money isn't much of a consideration."

And he answered smiling: "Oh, yes, we shall find something. She's coming again next week...."

IV

He was so frank about it. And so was Helen. The house business (despite my first uneasy fear to the contrary) proved to be absolutely genuine. June, it was true, hadn't known about it, but Severn had, for it was he who had actually suggested the Hindhead district. So there was nothing intrinsically curious in her visits of exploration.

The ordinary work-a-day person with limited money and limited leisure has no idea of the extraordinary difficulties that confront people with unlimited quantities of both. This matter of choosing a house, for instance. When you have just so much money to spend and so much time to look round in, the chances are that you solve your housing problem quite expeditiously. Far different is the troubled lot of those whose bank balance is no curb upon the gratification of every whim. They climb to the top of high hills and wonder how a house would look from here, or from there, and whether it would be better to have it facing the sun or the prevailing winds or the river tumbling in the valley below. Then there are abstruse problems about garages and gardens and conservatories and electric light and drains and so on. Finally, there is the question of architecture. Is it to be English or classic—the Elizabethan gable or the slim Ionic pediment? ... It is all a very lengthy business, as you can well imagine.

On that second excursion to Hindhead Helen quite made up her mind that no vacant house in the district was at all suitable, and that, therefore, one would have to be built. And this, of course, meant continuing the search for a site. The site was found, if I remember rightly, on the occasion of her fourth visit, but details of aspect, location, and so on, were not settled till the ninth visit, when an architect and surveyor was in attendance.

It must have been an idyllic quest, during those long lovely days of May and June. At first the two of them walked, but walking takes up a lot of time, and besides, as June had said, Helen hated walking. So one day she came down in the big Daimler car, sent the chauffeur back by train, and taught Terry to drive. She couldn't drive herself, but she knew just enough about it to teach him, and he proved such an apt pupil that he drove her safely back to town that very night. And then the next time that the house business demanded her presence at Hindhead he called for her at the End House and there was no need of a chauffeur.

The whole thing was so frank and open and, above all, so sweetly plausible that there was no chance, even if there had been any reason, to tender warning advice. Fate, like a warm sun at noonday, was blazing down on them from a cloudless sky. Terry couldn't even wonder if her days in the country were unfair to Severn, for it was on his behalf that she was taking them. Severn, it appeared, was keen about the new house, and Helen wasn't so especially, even after Terry's strenuous efforts to make her. And how charming, how subtly reassuring was her resistance to those efforts!

He said to me one night in Taplow's garden: "The past is just a big blank—we don't mention it—it doesn't even exist for us. Forgetting isn't the right word—it's rather that we don't trouble to remember something that isn't worth remembering. We were fools, maybe, both of us—and we should be bigger fools if we discussed it now.... Besides, it's so hopelessly out-of-date. All Helen wants now is to make life happier and easier for Severn. That's why she's coming to live out here—not because she's a country-lover herself. She isn't; she's told me so quite candidly. Hyde Park, not Hindhead, is her ideal."

I asked him if he though that she and Severn were getting on better, and he answered: "I'm sure of it. She doesn't always agree with him, of course—(she didn't over that Karelsky business)—but I think she's very happy. That American fellow's coming to operate on July 19th, and she's building up great hopes about it...."

V

And June ...?

I hardly know for certain, because she said so little about her own thoughts and feelings. As a novelist, perhaps I am entitled to be omniscient, but even omniscience doesn't lead me very much further than the obvious fact that June and Helen were separated by a deep and growing antagonism. I shall never forget that night at the End House when June faced her mother with that white-hot question: "Why should you interfere?"

But after that there was never another outbreak. Maybe the antagonism sank deeper; I had the constant impression that the more June felt the less she would say; until the time came when feeling would make her almost inarticulate. Anyhow, during those long midsummer days, though I saw her frequently, Helen's name was never mentioned, and even Terry's only rarely.

We went to Hindhead quite often, and Terry was always charmingly eager to see us. Never again, after that first unexpected visit, did we meet Helen there; I think June saw to that. Usually she and Terry played tennis, or else he, with his new eagerness for motor-driving, took us out in Taplow's prehistoric Ford. With this, as with most other enthusiasms, he went vastly to extremes; one afternoon a short trip to Aldershot developed into a grand tour of three counties, ending up in a breakdown and an ignominious return by train. He was always, too, immensely keen on showing us the site of the new house and giving us full and technical details of Helen's most recent visit. Never, by a word or a gesture, did June show anything but interest, but I got so bored with climbing up the same old hill and standing in the broiling sunlight to admire the same old view, that I formed the excellent habit of staying in the car while he and June made their expeditions alone. They were usually gone about half-an-hour—just time enough for a quiet smoke and a morsel of reflection.

What sort of a game was Helen playing? I thought it over, on those and other occasions, from every possible angle, and at the end of it all I had no convictions, only suspicions as before. If, at any rate, she were playing a game at all, it was a mighty clever as well as a mighty dastardly one—the cleverest and most dastardly by far that she had ever played.... But perhaps it wasn't a game. Perhaps they were both, with blindly honest footsteps, stumbling over the old ground into the trap that time had artfully concealed.... And perhaps there wasn't even a trap. Perhaps two people who had once been lovers really *could* meet again after a space of years and be no more than friends.... Time, at any rate, would show.

Time showed, in my opinion, when Severn obtained for Terry the offer of a job and Terry asked for a few weeks to think it over. It was a junior professorship of bacteriology in an Australian university, carrying with it a commencing salary of three hundred a year, and to me it seemed so good, in the circumstances, that Terry ought to have accepted it joyously and outright. I couldn't understand what there was to think over, and his vague replies when I talked to him about it only increased my astonishment. He admitted it was a good post. He assured me he hadn't the slightest objection to going abroad; on the contrary, he thought he would prefer it, and especially a country like Australia. Quite probably he would accept—oh, quite probably; it was just that he would prefer not to give an absolutely definite answer just then.

The matter worried me, and I had the impression that it was worrying June also. Something was worrying her, anyhow; there was a quite perceptible cloud somewhere on her horizon. One afternoon I found her lying prone in a deck-chair in Taplow's garden, and sobbing—sobbing as only people can do who aren't good at putting their feelings into words. I didn't let her see me, and went back quietly into the bar-room. Terry was there, reading a letter that the postman had just brought.

As soon as he saw he me gave a triumphant cry of delight. "It's from Helen," he said, smiling eagerly, "and she's coming down again on Thursday about the house...."

VI

That settled it. I went to Hampstead the next day.

You can imagine the mood I was in, and you can imagine, perhaps, that I hadn't any very definite plans. The weather was burningly hot, and at the Tube station, to save myself the trouble of climbing the steep hill for nothing, I rang up the End House to enquire if Helen were at home. It was she herself who answered, and asked me quite politely what I wanted. The abrupt query nonplussed me for the moment, and by the time I was stammering something about a short talk, she was telling me that she was just going out, and would it do another time?

"To-morrow?" I suggested.

She was sorry, but she was afraid to-morrow was booked up.

"The next day?"

She was sorrier than ever, but she was engaged then as well. "And on Thursday I'm going down to Hindhead.... Friday might do, if you don't mind a few others being here...."

I said it didn't matter, rang off suddenly, and walked up the hill to the house. I thought then it had been a mistake to telephone, but perhaps, after all, it wasn't. For it led to that curious meeting with her on the shaded lawn beneath the elm-trees; she was lounging in a basket-chair, reading the latest novel, and had quite obviously no more intention of going out that afternoon than I had of being tricked by her most ordinary of evasions.

She showed no embarrassment. Her smile was perfect as I crossed the lawn towards her, and I could see those summer days at Hindhead written on her face in tints of pink and brown. "Hello," she exclaimed, with casual surprise. "I thought you were in town. Didn't you telephone just now?"

"Yes, but from a call-box down the road. I was on my way here."

"But why on earth didn't you tell me?"

"Would it have made any difference?"

"Of course it would ... I wouldn't have lied about going out if I'd known you were so near. Only you said you wanted a talk, and I felt so absolutely incapable of talking that I didn't think it worth while to drag you all the way from the City."

"Nevertheless, now I'm here—if you don't mind—I *do* want a talk with you."

"All right. Let's have some tea first." She rang a small silver hand-bell and then chattered languidly until the maid came. "Geoffrey's having tea in his study with that surgeon man from Chicago. I hate their scientific talk—that's why I came away."

I asked her if all the arrangements had been made for the operation, and she told me it was to take place the following Wednesday in a nursing-home.

"This afternoon is purely a social visit, I suppose?"

"Oh, purely social. They were discussing Abdominal Section when I left.... Why don't you go and join them? I'm sure you'd find their conversation much more enlivening than mine."

I said I would prefer hers, if she didn't object. Then the tea came, and we touched on other matters. She was very flippant and cynical, especially about the projected new house. "It's going to cost heaps of money, and when I've lived in it a fortnight I know I shall long for a flat in Dover Street.... I'd be bored with it already but for the excuse it gives me to see Terry."

That was how and where we began.

Looking back on it all now I find it difficult—impossible in fact—to remember the stages of the argument. Perhaps really this is because it wasn't an argument so much as a disconnected series of questions and answers. She was so overwhelmingly, so terrifyingly frank. It was disconcerting; it gave one a peculiar feeling of insecurity, like walking into an unknown house and finding all the doors closed but unlocked.

And also, she didn't care. That, I can see, makes for frankness. Having stormed her citadel, I was free to do as I chose; she offered not the slightest resistance. I asked her cautious questions at first, and she answered them; then I asked her bolder questions, and she answered them. She didn't care. I said: "I may as well tell you outright that I think you and Terry are both on very dangerous ground."

"I daresay we are," she answered. She took a cigarette from a dainty little gold case, and lit it with langorous nonchalance.

"You don't mind me giving you my opinion?"

"Not in the least."

"Will you take any notice of it?"

"Probably not."

"You just intend to do whatever you like?"

"Yes."

"As regards Terry?"

"Yes."

"But—Helen—what *is* it that you're going to do?"

"I'm not certain."

"You're not going to make a fool of him again?"

That stung her out of her somnambulist calmness. She answered, with sharp passion: "Why do you say that? Why do you insult me? I didn't ask you to come here—I even tried to stop you from coming. Why *did* you come? ... If you don't like what you're hearing, go away."

I told her quietly that I didn't like what I was hearing, but that I wasn't going away.

Then she cried out: "Stay, then. Do whatever you like—I don't care. I've made up my mind what I'm going to do, and I'll do it, right or wrong.... And if you say a word to Terry, I'll deny everything and call you a liar. *He'll* believe me."

"You'd do *that*?"

"I'd do *anything*. I'm absolutely at the limit of unscrupulousness. When *you* want anything badly enough—if you ever do—perhaps *you'll* be the same...."

VII

Here's where I'm in danger of going astray. I feel I must keep on reminding myself of the circumstances—forgetting Helen herself and thinking only of the case as it would be docketed in some psychologist's bureau.... A woman, aged thirty-eight, married to a charming, clever, and wealthy man who, owing to an accident, cannot move out of his chair. Eight years ago she had an "affair" with a man seven years her junior, upsetting his career and half-ruining his life altogether. Now, while her husband passes his dull eventless days as best he can, she meets this young man and amuses herself with him again....

It all sound pretty hopeless. And yet I can hear now her words, spoken amidst the dreaming haze of that summer afternoon.... "I'm *not* amusing myself. I'm in earnest as I've never been before. I've been in earnest ever since that night I told him the truth about Karelsky. Do you remember how wrong we all were about him? June and you thought it would do him harm to be told how he'd been swindled, and I thought it would do him good—and we were all wrong, because it just hadn't any effect on him at all! He didn't care—he was beyond things like money or fame.... There's something in him—something that makes him the sort of man he is—something that draws me to him more than love. It *is* more than love.... I could have gone without him easily but for seeing that in him.... Hilton, can't you realize? He's *straight* and he's *true*, and I've been living my life up to now with a man who laughs at straightness and truth. Can't you imagine how it is—can't you *see?*"

I remember how I was silent, and how, touching my arm eagerly, she went on: "I know what you're thinking. You're thinking I haven't been very straight and true myself.... But I *have*. I've been true to one man, and that's all you can expect any woman to be. It isn't my fault that the man I've been true to doesn't happen to be my husband.... He might have been if *you* hadn't interfered."

"If *I* hadn't interfered?"

"Yes ... that's what I said."

"You mean, I suppose, that I'm to blame for persuading Terry to go to Vienna?"

"Everything would have been different if you hadn't done so."

"You would have gone away with him?"

"Yes."

"And married him—after the divorce formalities?"

"Yes."

"And you really think that you'd have been willing to give up your life of luxury to become the wife of a man whose yearly earnings would hardly pay for your hats?"

"He would have earned more if I'd been with him."

"Perhaps a very little more. But double or treble would still have seemed poverty to you."

"I wouldn't have cared.... You think I love money and luxury, but I don't—it all means nothing to me, really. As for Geoffrey's money, it gets on my nerves—I *hate* it. Even now—in his chair all day long—he's making more of it—buying and selling shares and speculating and gambling and winning—yes, winning nine times out of ten. That's his way—he's always found winning the easiest job in the world.... Yet Terry can't even get the few paltry pounds he worked himself ill for! Oh, it's all sickening and damnable, and I wish we were all naked savages in a land where there wasn't such a thing as money.... I can't bear to think of it—it makes me want to go wild and fly at somebody's throat—anybody's—yours—Terry's—even Geoffrey's...."

I interrupted her then. I said quietly: "That's all very well, Helen, but you would have cared—years ago—even if money doesn't matter to you now. In fact, you *did* care—and that was why, in my opinion, you didn't go away with him when you had the chance. He was willing, but you weren't.... I'm not blaming you, of course. But it's rather unfair of you to suggest that it was I who stood in your way, when all the time it was you yourself."

She stumbled forward a little, as if all her body had slackened. After a pause she said slowly and not very distinctly: "If it's true—*even* if it's true—I couldn't help it...." It was as though she were pleading for some sort of mercy. She continued more sharply: "How do you know all this? Terry would never tell you anything, I know. Are you *really* clever enough to see into me, or was it only a lucky guess? ... Oh, things—*things*—as Terry used to say—what a curse they are when we want to follow our heart's desire!" After another pause she recovered a kind of cynical equanimity. "You were quite right," she said, "to smash up my heroics. I'm rather worthless, I daresay.... I married Geoffrey because he was able to give me all that a part of me craved for—charming and cultured richness—you know the sort of thing. Geoffrey always *was* rich—even before he made any money; he had rich ideas and loved rich things. Part of me married him for that, and I never knew there was any other part of me till I met Terry.... You do realize a little, don't you? I *know* you do—I somehow *feel* you do.... Not that I care very much whether you do or don't. I've made up my mind."

"For what?"

The abrupt question seemed to stir her. "I've made up my mind that—in certain circumstances—I'll take the short cut to happiness."

"Short cuts are apt to be dangerous."

"Danger? Who cares for that? There comes a time when nothing—nothing at all—counts but getting what you crave for."

"Well?"

"Would you condemn any woman to a whole life-time of wanting something that she could get any moment by having the courage?"

"I don't know. I don't know quite what it is you're proposing to do."

She said then: "Everything depends on next week—on Geoffrey's operation."

"How?"

She looked at me fearlessly. "I hope, for his sake and mine, that it's successful. For if it is—if he's going to get better—then I shall leave him."

"And if not?"

"Then—I suppose—I must just go on *wanting*...."

VIII

There wasn't in me then, and there isn't in me now when I think of it, any shred of anger with her. (That, of course is the danger, and, all the hard remorseless analysis in the world won't alter it.) I may as well confess the truth; her pleadings had stirred me to vivid sympathy with her. I felt, if it conveys anything to say so, that deep down behind all her treachery she was as true and straight as Terry himself.

And yet I wasn't on her side. I didn't agree with her. I hardly knew how much I disagreed until I began to talk about it. I remember how, as I talked, the blazing edge of the shadow crept towards us till we were in full sunlight—so hot that we had to move back. And over in another garden not far away there sounded the sharp plick-plock of crocquet-balls—delicious, enchanting accompaniment.

She might or might not leave Geoffrey, I began; that was, in a sense, her own affair. But the question of Terry was different—it was my affair, anybody's affair, as much as hers. Did she, I asked her plainly, think she was going to run straightway from Geoffrey to Terry?

She said: "Perhaps not straightway. But sooner or later—of course."

"It will just be a matter of guiding your relationship out of the Platonic paths into something more—intense?"

"Put it that way if you like."

"Of course you've been very clever. You've disguised your intentions very successfully—I'm sure he hasn't the slightest suspicion of them."

"I hope not."

I told her then the truth as I saw it. I was speaking, I urged her to believe, not as a moralist, but as a plain critic of circumstances.... She could leave Geoffrey, but—and I was quite ruthlessly frank about it—Terry would never have her. Terry, I went on, would never and *could* never be happy with the wife of another man. There was something in his make-up—conscience (if she liked the word)—which would always intervene. And when that other man was his friend and benefactor the idea became absolutely impossible and unthinkable. Then, too, there was another point. If she left Geoffrey she would destroy the idea of her that was in Terry's mind—an idea that satisfied him more, perhaps, than any other idea of her that he had ever had. "You've been a hypocrite with him," I told her. "You've made him think that you and Geoffrey are perfectly happy, that all you care about is Geoffrey's happiness with you, and that the past is just a blank. Only the other day he told me how wonderful he thought it was that you and he could be such friends again—such *friends*, mind.... It's your only real chance—to go on acting the part you've made for yourself. If you don't—if you leave Geoffrey—I think I know what Terry will do. He'll just drop you—

suddenly—without a word—as if you'd done something utterly and hopelessly caddish. It might cost him something to do it; it might shatter his faith in human nature; it might and probably would wipe out all the recovery in mind he's made so far; but he'd do it—I'm positive he'd do it. There's something in him, as you say, that makes him the sort of man he is—and that something, which you and I know but can't describe, would make him do it."

All she said was: "It wouldn't. I know him better than you. I have no fear of him."

"You think he loves you?"

"I don't know. Possibly. Probably.... But it would all come back so easily."

"And what then? Do you think he would be happy?"

"*We* should be happy." She added, with a new note in her voice: "Think of it—in all my life the happiest moments have been with Terry, and in all his life the happiest moments have been with me.... And yet you ask me such questions!"

She laid her hand gently on my arm as she went on: "Don't be angry with me for what I'm going to do. If it's wrong, then I choose to do wrong—deliberately and with my eyes open. We all have that right, haven't we?"

"It's a terrible right."

"Yes, I know. But don't preach—I'm past all that."

"I'm not preaching. It's just that I think it's such a frightful mistake from your own point of view."

"No, no...."

"Helen—don't you see?—Don't you see how *impossible* it is—how *utterly* impossible ...?"

"I know that I *can* do it ... and I *will* do it...."

༒

The sunlit lawn, and the blue sky over it, and the End House there behind the foliage of the giant elms. Someone came out of the house through the conservatories, walked briskly under the trees, and then across the broad belt of sunlight. Small of stature, rather fat, and utterly unlike an explorer to the head waters of the Amazon, he blinked owlishly as he stepped into the shadow near us.... Mr. Hermann, of Chicago.

Helen introduced us, and the man touched my hand—just touched it—with those fat clammy fingers of his—maybe the most valuable fingers in the world, anyhow. He was vurry glad to make my acquaintance.... And then, to Helen: "Can I have a few words with you, Mrs. Severn?"

"*Now?*" She had obviously assumed that he had come merely to say good-bye.

"*If* convenient."

She told him he might speak freely before me, and I wished she hadn't. Somehow I felt I wanted to get away, to walk by myself along the Spaniards Road and think over all that she and I had said; Mr. Hermann, of Chicago—(I will admit it)—jarred on me.

Then I heard him telling her that he was afraid what he had to say wasn't vurry good news.... No—she needn't alarm herself—he had just left her husband in the vurry best of health, having regard to the circumstances. It wasn't that....

"Please tell me," she said calmly.

He looked at her as if he approved and admired her directness. And he told her. I shall never forget the way her face turned ashen white as she listened; she seemed, too, in that short space of minutes, to grow years older.... He had made a careful examination of her husband, he began. It was a most complicated case, and he wouldn't use any technical language; but, to be perfectly candid, the matter was altogether different from what he had been led to expect. "You see, Mrs. Severn, how it is? Your husband's trouble is not what I thought—is not what he thought, either."

"It is more serious?" she said, still calmly.

"Oh, no. Not exactly *more* serious. Just different."

"Well?"

He coughed and cleared his throat. "The operation—if there was to have been one at all—ought to have been performed immediately after the accident. That is my opinion."

She bore it well, though she didn't—for the moment—realize all that his words implied.

"But still," she whispered, "even now...."

"Now, I am vurry sorry to say, is too late."

"Too late! *Too late?*" She was realizing a little—just a little. "You mean that you're not even going to *try?*"

"To try, Mrs. Severn, when there is no chance at all, would be plain murder."

"*No chance at all!*"

"I'm afraid not."

We stood round her chair, and though she didn't faint or do anything like that, we could see that her mind and everything personal in her had flown far away from that sunlit garden. Hermann, in his odd jarring manner, was bubbling with sympathy; he doubtless considered her emotion perfectly natural in the circumstances. "A vurry sad case," he muttered to me. "Vurry sad indeed. She's a brave woman—she'll get over it.... But at first—after having hoped so much.... By the way, I didn't tell Severn. Thought it best not to.... *Her* job, that is—or yours—do it better than an outsider...."

I nodded. "Will he always be the same?" I whispered.

"Always. Not the ghost of a chance of anything else. Never was.... Don't know how anybody calling himself a specialist could have made a mistake about it."

"He'll live, I suppose?"

"*Live?*" He put his soft flabby hand over my wrist in a way intended to be encouraging. "My dear sir, there's no need to be *too* despondent. With luck he'll live as long as you or me—maybe longer."

IX

After Hermann had gone, we went in—Helen and I—to see Severn. To *tell* him....

That which might have been the hardest thing in the world proved, after all, to be the easiest. He was reading when we entered, and as soon as he saw us he began: "I say, he's told you! I wondered if he would. I suppose he thought you'd break it gently to me...."

"You know!" I gasped.

"*Know?* I should know by your faces, anyhow. But as a matter of fact, I knew as soon as he'd finished prodding me in the back. Knew by the way he changed the subject when I questioned him. Knew by everything he said and looked.... Lawyers get used to reading faces."

He went on: "Don't look so terrible about it! ... After all, what the Law will lose, Literature will gain.... By the way, my book on Disraeli comes out next week. Give me a good review, won't you, Hilton? Something wistful and pathetic—in your own inimitable style. A sob in every line. Short paragraph about Disraeli. Column and a half about me. You know the sort of thing?"

I stammered something—Heaven knows what—and he asked me to reach a half-opened parcel that was on his table. "Advance copies," he said. "Give me one of them, will you? And my fountain-pen."

I obeyed, and he wrote my name with a great flourish on the fly-leaf. "There! My gift to you on this memorable occasion. Take it away and read it.... A gem of irony, sparkling with epigram and polished satire— that's what all the other critics will say. But you—you only—must see through it—must see the tragedy behind the mask.... Know what I mean?"

I didn't know. I don't know now. I don't know whether he was laughing at me, or whether, at this queer and desperate moment, emotion was seething in him. There were tears in his eyes, but they may have been tears of laughter.... I just don't know....

☙

Outside his room☙, with the sunlight streaming in upon us both, she took my hand in hers. All the time she hadn't spoken a word. She had sat beside him, pale and silent, gazing emptily at the shelves of books. When we left, he had smiled at her, and she had smiled back at him. That was all.

We walked into the quiet garden, where the shadows were conquering the last strip of sunlight on the lawn. The maid was clearing away the tea-cups. In that other garden not far off someone was still playing crocquet.... It was all, in a strange and curious way, reassuring.

"So now ..." I began, and stopped.

I think she knew what was in my mind, for she whispered: "I—shall keep—my word...."

CHAPTER TWELVE

I

SHE would keep her word....

All the way down in the train to Haslemere I was thinking of that. It was just such another day as its tragic predecessor—dry, windless, grey with heat that towards mid-day would become almost unbearable. If London at nine o'clock had been a tepid bath, Haslemere at eleven was a furnace. All around the grass and furze on the hills had caught fire, and the scorching, pungent smoke was drifting like a white mist over the town.

She would keep her word.... Through a night of broken perspiring sleep I had pondered over it, dreamed about it, and still there were corners of its vast ramifications that I hadn't explored. Was it for good or bad that things had happened as they had happened? Severn cooped endlessly in his chair, or Severn alive again, dazzling the world, drinking life to the full, charming, cynical, eternally young-old, with both hands ever ready to help the struggling youngster, and a paramour, might be, in every capital in Europe? Helen, living under his roof, but without love for him, without even respect, with nothing but grim and fearful rectitude; or Helen free—free to lead Terry once again into the sea of doubt and remorse? Which was the happier picture?

The night had been full of fears. They had attacked in legions from midnight till dawn, undermining everything that I had held true and axiomatic. One moment I was glad because, whatever else might happen, it was well that she should leave Terry alone. And then, the moment after, had come the fear that she might not leave him alone, even then; that she would see him, many more times, as a friend; that he would grow to love her again, without willing it, without even knowing it. Perhaps he had even begun already; perhaps that was his reason for not accepting the Australian offer. And what did it matter whether she kept her word or not, if the lure of her were already over him?

Such fears had grown by daylight, and were monstrous as I climbed that morning over the sun-scorched ridge of Hindhead. Why *hadn't* he accepted the Australian offer?

It was one o'clock when I reached the hotel, and I was in time for lunch with him. I told him, without much in the way of preamble, what Hermann had said about Severn. Naturally he was shocked and disappointed. "Poor Helen!" were his first words of comment. Not "Poor Severn!" He added then, as if sensing my thoughts: "It will be a much greater blow to her than to him, I know. She was hoping so much—*too* much—from the operation."

And June too—*she* had been hoping. She had promised to motor down that afternoon, he said, but perhaps, in the altered circumstances, she wouldn't come.

We finished our meal in rather gloomy silence, but afterwards, in the garden, I asked him about his own future. The Australian offer mightn't remain open for long, I hinted broadly.... Had he yet made up his mind about it?

"Not quite," he replied. "Very soon I'll let Severn know definitely.... But a few days can't matter, surely?"

It was all (to me) very disquieting, and I was glad to talk of something else.

June came about tea-time. She had driven from town in under the hour, and her arms, hands, and face were almost nut-brown. She seemed depressed about her father's condition, though she said very little about it. She said very little, in fact, about anything; I had never known her so taciturn. After tea, though the sun was still hot, she went with Terry to the tennis-court, while I stayed in Taplow's garden with a pipe, a bottle of beer, and Severn's *Disraeli*. I hadn't read far before I knew that it was easily the best thing (in the way of literature) that he had done, and that it would cause something of a sensation. That pleased me a great deal; it was fine to think that he had it in him to excel in a rôle to which his condition offered no impediment. Disraeli, of course suited his ironic treatment; there was much in common, I thought, between the author and his subject. Both posed strenuously all their lives, and both are still enigmas.

Yet even Severn's delightful style (more French, by the way, than English) could not keep sleep away from me for long. I closed my eyes at six o'clock or thereabouts, and when I opened them it was quite dark, though not late, because the bar was still lit up. Taplow laughed when I went in. "You was sleeping, sir," he said, "and I didn't see no reason to disturb you. The others are out—said they didn't want any supper. Yours is laid ready in the coffee-room.... Will you take beer or wine, sir?"

Beer.... The coffee-room windows were wide open, and the night air, slightly cool, drifted in with waves of flower-perfume and moths that fluttered noisily round the lamp.... Beer, cold beef, pickles, bread, and a dig out of a huge Stilton.... Idyllic meal, almost (but not quite) sufficient to dispel all the fears that ever a human mind possessed.

Afterwards I sat out in a deck-chair under the blue-black sky and smoked a cigar. It was past eleven; Terry and June would be back soon, no doubt. Perhaps they had driven somewhere in the car, and there had been a breakdown. Was the car in the garage? I was too lazy to go and look....

There was no moonlight; only the silver stars. The yellow glow from the coffee-room window died down slowly; Taplow was carrying out the lamp.... The wind breathing idly through the trees, and the scent of hollyhocks, and sleep-sleep-sleep again....

II

Voices in the garden....

It was midnight, probably; it *felt* midnight. The cigar in my hand had long ago gone out. On the lawn the heavy dew was glistening faintly; there was no light anywhere but starshine, and no sound anywhere but the voices.

Terry's voice. I heard him say: "Everybody gone to bed, of course. I've got the key, though."

And then, in answer, a whisper more to be felt than heard. "Oh, the lovely—*lovely* night! ... Terry, can't we go for another walk?"

That was June.... They had entered by the side-gate, and were standing, so far as I could judge, outside the back-door of the bar—perhaps thirty or forty yards away from me.

He said: "*Now*? Why, it's long past midnight. Hilton will be sitting up for me."

"Never mind—he won't care.... Oh, Terry—Terry—I feel so utterly miserable to-night—I don't want to go in at all."

"We *must*, June. It's *too* late to be out."

Silence for seconds—perhaps for a minute altogether.

And then: "Terry, are you going to take that job in Australia?"

I started so suddenly that my chair creaked, and I almost wondered if they would hear. But no ... the sound was drowned in a tiny murmur that swelled like a tide through the whole garden—as if the trees and the bushes and the tall hollyhocks were all stooping to listen to the answer.

It came.

"June, I've told you I must. It's a good post, June—I can't afford to let it go. It wouldn't be fair to your father."

"*He* wouldn't trouble. I'm sure he wouldn't."

"*I* should, though. I've got from Taplow a full account of all I've cost while I've been here, and when I'm earning money I shall pay back every penny of it. It's only fair."

"*Fair*? Terry, how can you *think* it's fair, when the money that's such a lot to you is so little to him? It's absurd—he'd laugh at it."

"It doesn't matter. I can't live at his expense any longer, now there's a job been offered me."

"And you want the job?"

"Yes ... I want ... my work."

Another pause, and then, out of the velvet silence: "Terry.... *Don't go....*"

"June! ... *June*! ... *What* do you mean?"

Was it an echo to him out of the past—the past that, so he had said, was just a blank that nobody remembered?

Footsteps crunched along the gravel; the latch of the side-gate was lifted up; they had gone out again into the pale, starlit lane....

III

It was past two when he came up to bed. No longer at all sleepy, I was waiting for him in the sole armchair that our room possessed; Severn's *Disraeli* was open on my knee, but it had taken me over an hour to read five of its most fascinating pages.

He said nothing at first, beyond apologizing for his lateness. I thought he looked worried and unsettled; he went to the window, lit a cigarette, and stood there for a moment with his back towards me.

"Sleepy?" he said at last.

"Not particularly," I replied.

"Neither am I."

Was it an invitation to talk? I wondered, but I knew that if it were he would soon repeat it more definitely.

He said, after a pause: "I don't think I shall sleep at all to-night."

"No?"

The less you encouraged him the more likely he was to say what was in his mind. That had always been his way.

He swung round suddenly. "By the way, Hilton, I want to take that job in Australia."

"You do?"

"Yes.... *You* think I ought to, don't you?"

I said: "From the purely personal point of view I'm just hating the thought of you taking it. But, on the other hand, you must admit it's a goodish job, as jobs go nowadays."

"Yes.... That's what I feel. And I can't go on like this...."

He dragged a small chair near to the window and sat down. "Aged thirty and beginning all over again," he went on. "No money. Heavily in debt. No position. Impossible to think of marriage—even if I wanted to.... And yet, for all that, in the things that really matter, I've succeeded. I *can* feel that, can't I?"

I nodded. "From your own point of view, undoubtedly. But there are times when the material side of life is apt to come to the front rather awkwardly."

"Yes." His voice was eager, as if he had found me interpreting his own thoughts. "Hilton, to tell you the truth, I'm in a fix.... I want to take this job, as I said—in fact, I know I *must* take it—and yet—and yet...." He hesitated, and then finished up: "There's such an odd sort of difficulty in the way."

And as always it had to be wormed out of him by degrees, though the task was easier through my fairly accurate knowledge of what was coming. June, he said, had all along been against his taking the job. She had said it was too far away, and that it wasn't good enough for him. "Of course I daresay the salary does seem ridiculous to her. She probably spends three hundred a year on her clothes."

I rather doubted that, but I made no interruption. He went on: "Anyhow, that doesn't matter.... The point is that after what she said I promised I'd think it over for a fortnight before deciding.... So now you understand why it was I couldn't give you a definite answer?"

Yes, I knew, and had guessed for over an hour, though I didn't tell him that.

"The fortnight ended to-night, and I told her I'd made up my mind to accept."

"Good."

"But then—more than ever—she seemed against the idea."

"In other words, she asked you not to go?"

"It amounted to that."

"What answer did you give?"

"I said ... I promised again ... that I'd think it over."

That, for some reason or other, made me laugh. "I'm afraid, Terry," I said, "my cross-examination of you is going to be rather stiff.... First of all, you say you *want* to take the job?"

"Yes."

"And yet you told her you'd think it over?"

"Yes."

"Are you going to think it over?"

"I—I suppose so."

"So you haven't quite made up your mind?"

"Well—not absolutely."

"So it comes to this—that a woman's persuasion stands in the way of what you want to do?"

He shook his head. "No, no. I must take the job. There's no alternative—I quite see that. But—I don't like to disappoint her."

"Or yourself?"

He said, simply: "We've been very good friends, that's all I can say."

Then he began suddenly to talk in sharp jerks of words, as if speaking the thoughts that came to him.

"Of course, in *any* case, it couldn't have gone on for long. She's young now—not twenty-one till next month.... Sooner or later, she's bound to marry somebody—somebody with wealth and position, most likely—and—naturally—it couldn't go on after that...."

"What couldn't go on?"

"Our—friendship."

I knew then, from the curious way he spoke the word "friendship", that he had begun to love her....

IV

Somehow I had never thought of that, had never even hoped for it.... And now, with all its train of dazzling possibilities, it was leaping towards me.... Not Helen—but June.... That wanted some realizing.... And with the realization, and the serenity of it, came just a faint flavour of sadness too. I think there is always a sadness in feeling that time *does* count, and that *grandes passions can* fade away.

Mother and daughter.... What sort of a battle had they been waging, silently, perhaps unconsciously, during the months that had passed? Helen, I know, had been scrupulously platonic, and maybe, after all, it was a just irony that he should come to desire no more than her friendship. But June? Was there more than friendship there?

I believe, if it comes to laying down a creed, that the love of Terry and June had grown very quietly and gradually until at last, in Taplow's garden that night, it had broken out into no more than those two words of hers—"Don't go...."

I don't know how exactly Terry and I got over the immense difficulty of his reserve. Perhaps we never did get over it; at any rate, he never admitted in so many words that he had grown to love June. But from a certain moment of that warm July night I began to talk to him as if he *had* admitted it, as if it were something obvious and perfectly understood between us. I said, for instance: "No man ought ever to think he has no chance with any woman." He didn't ask me what on earth I was talking about as I had half expected. He just leaned back in his chair, puffed restlessly at a cigarette, and pondered—until I thought he was never going to answer at all. And then, when the reply did come, it was spoken in another tone—as if the whole plane and angle of our conversation had been shifted. "It's as you said, Hilton.... Material things crop up at awkward moments. What chance would a penniless man approaching middle age have with a young girl of wealth and position?"

"It depends, of course. It depends on whether she loves him or not."

"She doesn't."

"Then obviously he would stand no chance at all."

Silence for a while after that. He looked—if the combination is even possible—triumphant and despondent—triumphant at having led his argument to an apparent victory, and despondent over the deeper issues of the discussion. Then, rather daringly after a pause, I introduced the personal element by asking him why he thought June had been so keen on his declining the Australian offer.

"I suppose she thought that—in various ways—it wasn't suitable."

"Even after you assured her it was? Do you think that in such a matter she would set her opinion against yours, unless she had some deeper reason as a motive?"

"What deeper reason?"

"Do you really mean to pretend it doesn't occur to you? To me it seems the most perfectly obvious thing that ever was. She doesn't want you to go to Australia because she doesn't like the thought of being without you when you've gone."

"Oh ... that's absurd...."

"Not a bit absurd. Do you think she's known you all this time without growing fond of you?"

"We've been good friends, of course."

"*Friends*? ... Some people would smile if you told them that. They'd say, to begin with, that she's compromised herself with you pretty hopelessly by staying here to-night.... Mrs. Taplow as a chaperon wouldn't impress them."

"*What*! Do you mean to say—"

I said, interrupting him: "Whatever I mean is not the slightest reflection on either you or her. I really needn't say that. We're broad-minded people—we don't bother about silly conventions.... But some people do—you'd be surprised how many—and my point in mentioning the matter is simply this.... Is it likely that June would risk getting herself talked about in connection with a man of whom she wasn't rather fond?"

"I don't think she cares whether people talk about her or not."

"Then depend upon it," I answered, "the crisis has been reached. When a woman doesn't care whether people talk about her or not, there's only one conclusion to be drawn. She's in love."

"Oh, that's nonsense—if you're trying to make out that she's in love with *me*...."

"Perhaps you can think of somebody else, then?"

And so it went on. It was uphill work, I can tell you, trying to convince Terry that he wasn't the meanest little worm that ever crawled on the earth.

Towards three o'clock the moment came when I judged it safe to mention the word "marriage." If, I said, he thought there was any doubt about her feeling for him, why didn't he put the matter to the obvious test? "Go to her straightforwardly and say: 'I don't want to give up your charming society, but I really must have that job. If, however, you would care to marry me and accompany me to Australia, the difficulty would be rather neatly solved.'"

Marriage? It was absurd to think of it, he said. He had never dreamed of such a thing, and he never would dream of it. He wouldn't insult her by even discussing it abstractly. What prospects had he? What sort of a life could he ask her to share with him? ... There were some things too ridiculous to be worth discussing, and that was one.

Nevertheless, I objected, he had got to discuss it, because it was the only thing left to discuss. To my mind, I said, it was only fair that he *should* give her the chance of accepting or refusing him. She had shown pretty plainly that she didn't want him to leave her; that was quite as much as she could be expected to do on her own. It was for him to take the next step.

"But—*think* of it, man! Three hundred a year for the two of us, after the sort of life she's been used to! It's *monstrous*!"

"That's for her to decide. If she thinks it is, then it is. But if she thinks it isn't—"

"Well?"

"Then it mightn't be.... You never know. Miracles have been done on three hundred a year before now."

"No man has a right to expect miracles," he said.

"Every man has a right to perform them," I answered. (Really, for three o'clock in the morning, our conversation was quite brilliant.)

But no; he wouldn't consider the matter. "Whatever you say, Hilton, you won't alter my mind. I've no right to ask for such a sacrifice— no right even to *think* of it.... If there's anything at all that I've learnt from experience, it ought to be this—that women can't bear to give up *things*—especially the sort of things that I don't much care about."

In some ways, that was the nearest we ever got to talking about the past.

"If *I've* learnt anything from experience," I countered, "it's that one woman can be absolutely and entirely different from every other."

But it was still no use; he was adamant. Whatever I said, he had some rejoinder; there was no sign of his conversion. The dawn peered over the ridge of the hills before we left off talking, and I had to admit to myself that, so far as the immediate object of the discussion was concerned, I had failed altogether. The idea of proposing marriage to June seemed to afflict him with a kind of mental explosion whenever he thought about it. It was preposterous. Rather refuse or accept a thousand jobs than commit such tempestuous folly. Incredible that I should ever have seriously suggested it.... And so on.... And so on....

And then we went to bed and to sleep.

V

All that happened last night; or, to be precise, early this morning....

It is a strange thing to have caught up with the present after so long writing of the past. Ever since I arrived here I have been at my desk; I was tired when I began, but Roebuck's iced coffee and the achievement of bringing this record up-to-date have made me feel curiously fresh and exhilarated.

It is the business lunch-hour now, and all the seats in Lincoln's Inn Fields, which is just across the road from my window, are filled with office-workers enjoying their respite. They look happy; the whole world looks happy—but that, maybe, is because I am feeling happy myself. The skies have cleared miraculously during the past twenty-four hours—have shown me Terry enslaved to June's calm and inarticulate youth, and June (I think) no less attached to Terry.

Whether it comes to anything is, of course, another matter. June is very young, and Terry's prospects are certainly none too rosy. Besides that, there is all the difference in the world between being pleasantly fond of a man and wanting to emigrate with him to the other side of the world. I'm rather afraid I lost sight of that during my argument with Terry; it all seemed just a shade easier than it is. The main and incontrovertible facts are these—that Terry will never propose to her on his own, and that if he were to take the Australian job and go away, June would be left here miserable.

I always find it so hard to know what to do—whether to interfere or not. On the whole, I lean to interference; I hate minding my own business, which is usually so much less interesting than other people's. And yet, in this case, it *may* have been a mistake to write that interfering note to June.

I wrote it in an immense hurry before leaving the hotel this morning. A sudden impulse seized me while I was having breakfast; it was 7.30; my train from Haslemere was due to leave at 8.15; and Taplow's Ford was already shaking its hoary sides in the yard. I scribbled it out in pencil and gave it to the maid to take up to June along with the morning cup of tea. But the extraordinary part of it is that I can't very well remember what I wrote. The general trend, I imagine, was to give June the tip that it wouldn't be any use her expecting *him* to do the proposing; but I hope to God I didn't put it quite so crudely as that. Probably I didn't; perhaps it was a marvel of tactful insinuation. Anyhow, it's done now, and can't be helped.

Helen is coming here to tea this afternoon; I asked her two days ago, thinking it would be a change for her if she felt too desperate. Now I rather wish I hadn't asked her. I am altogether out of the mood for skating on thin ice. It is bound to be difficult, and Heaven alone knows what we shall talk about. I shan't—I can't—tell her anything about Terry and June....

VI

11 *P.M.*

I am alone now; Roebuck has gone to bed; and there is a cool south wind blowing in amongst my papers. The day has passed most wonderfully well, and I am very happy.

Helen came, and she wasn't desperate at all. She was calm—calm as if she were ten years older than when I saw her last. Or ten years younger.... I hardly know which; I only know that a touch of her old queer fascination has come back to her, making her wonderful again. Perhaps the two days that have passed since our talk on the End House lawn have really been ten years—long enough for her soul to escape from turmoil.

There was no need for me not to mention Terry. She mentioned him herself, but in such an odd way—as if, so it seemed to me, she were very old and he a long while dead. She gossiped about him, almost; anything, everything reminded her of him. When, for instance, I talked of the new house, she said: "Oh, yes, that's in the architect's hands now. There's no more for me to do. No more scrambling up hills with Terry."

Quietly—half-mockingly—like *that*!

"Not that I ever liked hills," she went on. "I hated them. But Terry was never happy except when he was consuming vast quantities of energy. If it wasn't physical energy, then it was mental, and it wasn't mental, then it was moral.... Didn't you ever notice that?"

I had noticed it. And then she went on again: "You ought to have seen him years ago at those bacteriology lectures. He didn't *teach* bacteriology— he *preached* it. And it was the same sort of thing with the hills—he didn't *climb* them; he *conquered* them."

She talked about him effortlessly, as if she were somehow drifting in a strong and peaceful tide. When I put a question about Severn she had to fight the tide while she gave a slow and reluctant answer.... Geoffrey, she said, was very busy and perfectly the same.

But the oddest thing of all was her calm remark: "Of course it's quite easy to see what will happen. Sooner or later he'll marry June. She's quite in love with him, and he'll be with her after a while.... Do you remember years ago you asked me what I would do with Terry in the end, and I said I would hand him over when the right girl came along.... But I never thought that the right girl would be June."

"You think June is the right girl?" I asked; and she answered: "I think he will feel she is if he tries hard enough."

I forgave her for that mocking retort. I didn't tell her that already, without trying at all, Terry had grown to see in June what, perhaps, he had never seen in any other woman—a mirror of the future, calm and bright with happiness. It would have been *too* cruel to have told her that, to have smashed her dear belief that she could have had Terry for not much more than the asking. She has kept her word, and that counts none the less because it wouldn't have greatly mattered if she hadn't kept it.

We were in the midst of tea when the telegraph-boy arrived. I went out into my small lobby, and when I came back she noticed the change in my face; it was stupid not to have had more control of myself.

"Good news, I can see," she said.

And I stammered hazily something about a business affair that I had been hoping would happen.... Oh, yes, *quite* good news.

That telegram is before me now as I write ... Handed in at Oxford at 4.10 P.M. (What were they doing at Oxford? A motor excursion, presumably.) ... Received at London, W.1. at 4.50 P.M.... And then:

"Took your advice succeeded thanks June."

VII

Later.

I've been to bed, but I can't sleep, and I might as well continue this as lie awake. The clock in Lincoln's Inn has just chimed two, and the street-cleaners in Holborn are noisily busy. In a little while the Covent Garden traffic will begin; there is never a silent minute from midnight to dawn in this part of London. Not that it troubles me in the least; it is happiness—excitement if you like—that is keeping me awake to-night.

So far as I can see, I have come now to the end of this record. The future seems pretty well decided; Severn will write his books on Robert Walpole and Pontius Pilate and become as famous in literature as in everything else that he has ever touched; Terry will marry June and live happily ever after. It's an absurd phrase, in nine contexts out of ten, but I really do think it's likely to be true of those two. They're such clear-hearted people; marriage will be so tremendously simple to them. Terry will never think of any woman but June, and June will never think of any man but Terry. They'll live in a bungalow in some blazing Australian suburb, and probably they'll have lots of children—far more than Terry could possibly afford on his own income. If he gets the chance, and I daresay he will, he'll do valuable but not exactly epoch-making work as a bacteriologist. A well-known scientist told me the other day that in his opinion the importance of the Karelsky discoveries had been greatly over-rated. "They're valuable," he said, "but they're only a beginning, and the world's been treating them as if they were the end...."

Perhaps Terry will carry them further on from that beginning. But whatever he does, I'm quite certain that his name will never echo across the world. I shall never earn stray guineas by writing 'The Great Man As I Knew Him' articles in the gossipy press.

Two are still left whose future is beyond prophecy. There's Helen.... What *will* happen to her? When she hears the news about June and Terry, will she still cling to that eager, scornful belief in her own power over him? Will she keep her word for ever—will she stay with Severn as in duty bound, not to him, but to Terry? Is it even possible that in time there may grow in her some scrap of affection for the author of the best short book on Disraeli that has ever been written? Frankly, I like Severn, and I find it tremendously hard to understand how anybody else can help liking him. Yet Helen doesn't.... Perhaps, after all, they are incompatibles whom nothing, neither time nor calamity, can bring together.

And then ... Mizzi.... Strange, perhaps, that I should be thinking of her now, should see her so clearly in my mind. She writes to me from time to time, and always with some mention of Terry; her last letter came two months ago. The hotel, I gather, proceeds from strength to strength, and I shouldn't be at all surprised to hear that, having exhausted all the European languages, she's now tackling Aramaic or Siamese.... One thing I've quite decided; I shall go to Vienna this year and take this manuscript for her to read.

A quarter past by the clock in Lincoln's Inn.... Shall I write to her now and book my room? If Terry has to begin the Australian job in the autumn he'll probably be leaving England very soon, and June, I've an idea, will want to go with him. Severn and Helen are going for a sea-cruise during August, so I think, if I'm not to be left entirely alone, I'd better choose that month for Vienna. It will be very hot, but I shan't mind. I want to go to the Semmering, and up the Danube to Melk, and perhaps, in a happier mood, to Buda-Pesth again....

I'm tired now.... I'll finish the letter in the morning, and while I'm asleep it shall stay there on my desk with no more than the date on it and the words:

"DEAR MIZZI,—..."

THE END

Printed in Great Britain
by Amazon